THE PATERNITY PACT

CAT SCHIELD

HIDDEN AMBITION

JULES BENNETT

MILLS & BOON

First Published in Great Britain 2020
by Mills & Boon, an imprint of HarperCollinsPublishers,
1 London Bridge Street, London, SE1 9GF

The Paternity Pact © 2020 Harlequin Books S.A.
Hidden Ambition © 2020 Harlequin Books S.A.

Special thanks and acknowledgement are given to Cat Schield for her contribution to the *Texas Cattleman's Club: Rags to Riches* series.

Special thanks and acknowledgement are given to Jules Bennett for her contribution to the *Dynasties: Seven Sins* series.

ISBN: 978-0-263-27931-3

0820

MIX
Paper from
responsible sources
FSC™ C007454

This book is produced from independently certified FSC™ paper to ensure responsible forest management.

For more information visit: www.harpercollins.co.uk/green

Printed and bound in Spain
by CPI, Barcelona

Cat Schield is an award-winning author of contemporary romances for Mills & Boon Desire. She likes her heroines spunky and her heroes swoonworthy. While her jet-setting characters live all over the globe, Cat makes her home in Minnesota with her daughter, two opinionated Burmese cats and a goofy Doberman. When she's not writing or walking dogs, she's searching for the perfect cocktail or travelling to visit friends and family. Contact her at www.catschield.com

USA TODAY bestselling author **Jules Bennett** has published over sixty books and never tires of writing happy endings. Writing strong heroines and alpha heroes is Jules' favourite way to spend her workdays. Jules hosts weekly contests on her Facebook fan page and loves chatting with readers on Twitter, Facebook and via email through her website. Stay up-to-date by signing up for her newsletter at julesbennett.com

Also by Cat Schield

The Black Sheep's Secret Child
Little Secret, Red Hot Scandal
The Heir Affair
Upstairs Downstairs Baby
Substitute Seduction
Revenge with Benefits
Seductive Secrets

Also by Jules Bennett

Twin Secrets
Claimed by the Rancher
Taming the Texan
A Texan for Christmas
Montana Seduction
California Secrets
An Unexpected Scandal
Scandalous Engagement

Discover more at millsandboon.co.uk

THE PATERNITY PACT

CAT SCHIELD

To Nancy Holland,
my Golden Heart® sister and wonderful friend.
My world is less bright without you in it.

One

"Well, I must say," declared Rose Everett-Schuster, "I'm shocked to see you here tonight."

The evening's wine tasting, silent auction and fashion show at Spoon and Stable, a French-inspired café on Royal's main square, had been organized by Beth Wingate in support of her younger sister Harley's nonprofit organization, Zest, which operated in various overseas countries.

"I donated a case of 2014 Château Pierre de Dupré Medoc for the tasting," Grant Everett replied, knowing that offering his sister, Rose, a deliberate nonanswer would only intensify her curiosity. He maintained a bland expression even as his pulse accelerated when his peripheral vision caught his older sister's raised eyebrows and pointed gaze. "As well as a 2016 Château Margaux Bordeaux for the silent auction."

"I'm not sure that a wine donation fully explains what prompted our town's leading fertility specialist to leave his ivory tower and mingle with the masses," Rose said. "There must be something special about this particular charity that brought you out tonight."

Except for a single colossal bungle that he'd kept to himself these last five years, he wasn't a man given to secrets. Not that he was an open book. Grant didn't run around sharing his thoughts and opinions like sticks of gum, and as a medical professional, he strictly adhered to doctor/patient confidentiality.

Muttering under his breath, he cursed the impulse that compelled him to show up at a benefit for Zest when he rarely put in an appearance at any of the other charity events Rose invited him to. He had little patience for crowds or small talk and preferred to make his philanthropic contributions by way of his checkbook. But what explanation could he give that would satisfy his sister without betraying the real reason Zest had been on his radar since its inception three years earlier?

"It's a good cause," he retorted.

"They're *all* good causes," Rose drawled, displaying a dogged determination to pull some sort of admission from him. "The only thing that makes this one different is that this particular party benefits Harley Wingate's nonprofit."

"I'm not following you," Grant said, giving his sister his full attention.

Although Rose kept her eyes and ears open to glean news about Royal's wealthiest families, accumulating tidbits of gossip about everyone gathered here tonight, he suspected she was merely fishing. She couldn't possibly know how he felt about the Wingate family's youngest daughter. Hell, he wasn't sure he could define his conflicted emotions whenever she popped into his thoughts.

"A certain prodigal daughter who has recently returned home after mysteriously disappearing abroad."

"Who?" It was a weak comeback and from the way his sister's gaze drilled into him, Grant recognized that he wasn't fooling her.

"You know," Rose prompted. "The woman you disappeared with after the annual TCC ball five years earlier? And spent the weekend with."

"I have no idea what you're talking about."

Rose's lips curved into a satisfied smirk at whatever insight she gleaned from his expression. "Everyone wondered why she left Royal so suddenly a few weeks later."

"That had nothing to do with me," he countered, noting that his voice sounded a shade too abrupt. He silently cursed that he'd been provoked into explaining himself. Normally, Grant wouldn't let his sister's ribbing get under his skin, but what had happened with Harley and how he'd behaved during their last encounter filled him with regret.

"You changed after she left."

"Changed how?"

"You married Paisley," Rose went on in a more sympathetic tone. "And after realizing what a mistake that was, threw yourself even deeper into work."

At the mention of his ex-wife, he tossed back the last of his scotch and grimaced as it burned his throat. Although this was only his second drink of the night, he'd consumed both in a short span of time and could feel the alcohol buzzing in his system, awakening his emotions and unraveling his ability to use logic to stop his sister from intruding on his private pain.

Grant pivoted away from his sister and allowed his gaze to roam the restaurant. "I don't want to discuss Paisley."

Their three-year marriage had given him an all-too-clear picture of his shortcomings when it came to romantic relationships. He'd lost count of how many times she'd accused him of lacking a heart and proclaimed that he'd never loved her. Not once had he argued the opposite. In truth, he'd chosen to marry Paisley based on her attractiveness and suitability as the wife of a successful doctor and a member of one of Royal's wealthiest families. Too late, he'd discovered that she'd believed her love could change him into the adoring family man she needed. Instead, her suffocating attentiveness drove him to spend even longer hours at the hospital.

"I know that you hate to fail and what happened in your marriage is a sore spot with you," Rose said softly. "I just hope that you realize that trying again with the right woman will make all the difference."

Grant shook his head, wishing he could make his sister understand that his tendency to prioritize his work over relationships kept him from being husband and/or father material. He would just have to be satisfied with making other families' dreams come true.

"I must say, I'm quite impressed." A petite dark-haired woman had appeared on Rose's left, providing a much-welcomed interruption. Henrietta Sinclair pointed at the jewel-bright sundress created by the women of Zest and modeled by her daughter Regan, along with a dozen of the town's best-known fashionistas. "The entire collection is beautiful and so well made."

"All the fabric used is organic cotton with vegetable dyes," Rose said, highlighting the talking points from the brochure in her hands.

"What Harley Wingate has done is just marvelous," Henrietta murmured. "Her family should be so proud."

"Yes," Rose murmured. "I imagine that given the girl she was before she left town, none of them expected her to amount to much."

This last remark from Rose grated on Grant's nerves and he used his sister's distraction to excuse himself and slip away. As he wandered through the crowd, he noted that several faces reflected surprise as he strode past. Although he was well-known by this particular crowd because of his philanthropy, his expertise as a fertility specialist and his membership in the Texas Cattleman's Club, the fact that he'd attended less than a handful of social events since his divorce meant his appearance tonight had stirred up people's curiosity.

He doubted anyone besides Rose would guess he'd shown up at this particular event because of Harley Wingate. Or that she'd been the woman who'd inspired his atypical behavior at that fateful Texas Cattlemen's Club ball. The two friends he'd been standing between had no clue that his heart had given an explosive bang when he'd first spied her. Between his discretion and their thirteen-year age difference—an important detail he hadn't known at the time—no one would've imagined he'd be attracted to a girl who'd just graduated from high school. Much less that he would spend the next two days in bed with her.

Grant shuddered as he replayed how he'd felt when he'd learned the truth. He'd abruptly ended their weekend together, horrified by the image of himself as a corruptor of innocents. Not that he would use that word to describe Harley. Quite the opposite. In a slinky dress of peacock blue that skimmed her slim figure while baring her delicate shoulders and well-toned arms, Harley had moved about the ball with the confidence of a woman aware of the sensual power she wielded. In the aftermath of their weekend together, he'd realized that she'd pursued him with the same focused intent of a bounty hunter on the trail of a big score.

She'd been just the right amount of flirtatious as she'd peppered him with thoughtful questions about his work and his family's philanthropy. He'd been utterly charmed by the frank admiration in her velvet green eyes and riveted by her playful smiles that showed off the minor gap between her two front teeth. Each time her hand had grazed against him, his libido had taken a direct hit. Famished for a taste of her sweet lips, well before the last song of the night, he'd tugged her into an isolated alcove and kissed her until neither of them could breathe.

Just thinking about that night and the two that followed awakened a rush of longing within him. He shoved down the sharp hunger even as his gaze raked the crowd, automatically searching for a slim beauty with long straight brown hair. A chaotic stew of eagerness and apprehension twisted his gut and sent awareness tickling across his skin. Grant cursed beneath his breath, calling himself all sorts of a fool.

Obviously, attending tonight's party had been a mistake. The five years hadn't blunted his interest in Harley. Confronting this fact revived the question he'd dwelled on far too often since learning that she'd come home from her overseas travels.

Was their thirteen-year age difference any less remarkable now that he was thirty-six and she twenty-three?

Yes. No. Maybe.

Grant touched the traces of premature gray that had touched his temples in the last year. Men dated younger women all the time without anyone making a big deal out of it. But it hadn't just been their age gap that had set him off. It was the way being with her had awakened his emotions and made him behave in ways contrary to his normal, logical self. It continued to bother him that he'd turned a blind eye to the consequences of his actions.

Sure, the sex had been explosive, but he'd attributed their chemistry to the secrecy enveloping their tryst. Engaging in a one-night stand with a beautiful stranger was the wrong sort of behavior for a man in his position. That he'd known he was taking a risk before the hotel-room door shut behind them hadn't stopped him from spending the next two days learning every inch of her body and very little else about her.

She'd given him only her first name and he hadn't connected her to the Wingate family. Even once Grant had discovered Harley's full identity, he couldn't reconcile his vague memory of the lanky teenager he'd seen in passing at the Texas Cattleman's Club with the passionate temptress who'd rocked his world. In the aftermath of their weekend together, he'd struggled to make sense of his body's unrelenting desire for more nights with her.

In the grip of a craving that strengthened despite his dismay at lusting after a woman so much younger than himself, Grant had come to the decision that neglecting his personal life had caused his reckless behavior. Shortly after the TCC Ball where he'd met Harley, he'd begun dating a woman of suitable age and social status for Royal's premier fertility doctor. The failure of their marriage after three years reinforced his previous opinion that he wasn't cut out to be a family man.

Maybe after his weekend with Harley, he should've spent a week or a month indulging his appetite for her and purged her from his system. For a while, it might have been an ideal situation. She'd declared herself a free spirit with a whole world she was dying to explore. With neither one interested in being tied down, no doubt they both would've enjoyed the relationship for a time and then moved on.

As if his thoughts had conjured her, the crowd before him shifted and Grant realized Harley stood twenty feet away. The years abroad had created a subtle shift in her demeanor, transforming her youthful exuberance into vibrant elegance. Yet, he sensed a hint of discomfort beneath

her bright smile as if she chafed at being the focus of so
much attention.

Nevertheless, even as he sympathized, the familiar flare
of attraction surged to life. He ground his teeth against the
unwelcome rush of longing and cursed. Grant wasn't one
for brief and casual affairs. The impulsive weekend with
Harley had been completely out of character for him and
the abrupt and contentious end to their interlude had left
him with unanswered questions and unresolved emotions.

But as their gazes locked and a mixture of anger and joy
twisted his gut into knots, he was transported to another
event. From the moment he'd spied her, nothing in his life
had been the same. At the same time, Grant realized that
the same beliefs that kept him from pursuing a relationship
with a woman thirteen years his junior were still in effect.
He might desire Harley Wingate with a fiery intensity, but
acting on it was a mistake he would never make again.

The shock that went through Harley as she met Grant
Everett's eyes was different than what she'd experienced
five years earlier, but no less potent.

The night of that fateful Texas Cattleman's Club ball,
she'd been an impetuous teenager brimming with cocky
confidence, determined that the next man she slept with
would know what the hell he was doing in bed. Up until
that point, she'd only slept with her former boyfriend of
nine months and found those experiences less than memorable. From what she'd gleaned from her friends, sex
should be a lot more enjoyable than what she had been
getting from Dean.

She'd set her sights on Grant after noticing several
women watching him with intense interest. Some had even
approached and flirted outrageously to catch his attention.
His utter indifference had been the challenge Harley had

been looking for. She'd been determined to succeed where all those beautiful ladies had failed and confident that by the end of the night, she'd have him wrapped around her finger.

While the evening hadn't exactly gone according to plan, the next two days and nights had been more amazing than she could've dreamed possible. Surrendering herself to Grant's masterful tutelage, she learned just how much pleasure her body could bear and by the end of their passionate weekend, she'd been forever changed.

Harley stood frozen in place while her body lit up with longing, anxiety, hope and despair. The emotions swarmed her like a cloud of hungry mosquitos. Her ears buzzed, drowning out the conversations around her. What should she do? Cross the crowded room and say hello or send him a come-hither sign and wait for him to approach her? The last time, she'd put herself in his path after which he'd pursued her with a vengeance, giving chase in a way that set her heart to pounding and awakened something hot and primitive inside her.

Before Harley decided how to proceed, Grant turned away and walked in the opposite direction. Flooded by keen disappointment, she scolded herself. Did she seriously expect that he'd see her across a crowded room and be irresistibly drawn to her side? A man like Grant wouldn't make the same mistake twice.

"You okay?" Jaymes Owens asked, her blue eyes registering concern as she peered at Harley from beneath long, thick eyelashes.

As she blinked herself free of her memories, Harley realized that Grant was no longer in her line of sight. Had she imagined that he'd recognized her? They'd spent a single weekend together. Sure, the sex had been incredible, the sort of seismic-shifting passion that set impossible standards for every encounter since, but she'd often worried her own performance had left little impression.

"Sure," she responded after her best friend nudged her arm. "Why?"

"Because you tensed up just now. Did your mother decide to put in an appearance?"

Harley shuddered. "Hardly."

"You never know, she might show up."

"I really hope she doesn't." She shrugged at the disgusted look Jaymes shot her. "This event tonight is a big deal for Zest. I don't need her dumping truckloads of criticism and unwanted advice on me."

"She only wants what's best for you."

"More like what *she* thinks is best." Harley blinked against a sudden prickle of tears. "I don't know why I thought that I could come back after five years and things would be different. I'm not the same person who left Royal, but everyone still treats me like the entitled eighteen-year-old I was. And worse is the way I fall back into old patterns of acting like a spoiled brat who expects to be treated like an equal. Part of me wishes I'd just stayed away." Harley pushed the air out of her lungs in a dramatic sigh. "And that's exactly the sort of immature attitude I want to overcome."

The baby of the family, she'd grown up pampered and spoiled by her father and siblings. Anything she wanted, she wheedled and pouted until she got her way. Her father's stroke just after her eighteenth birthday changed everything. With Trent Wingate incapacitated, their mother became the dominant parent and Harley's world became a whole lot less fun.

Jaymes put her arm around Harley's shoulders in a comforting hug. "You've only been in town a short while. Give yourself a little time to catch your breath before you start beating yourself up."

"You're right." She straightened her spine and pushed away her melancholy.

"So, if it wasn't your mother, who showed up that you didn't expect?"

For a second, Harley considered downplaying her reaction, but she'd never kept things from her best friend. Why start now?

"I saw Grant."

"Really?" Jaymes blurted, eyes widening "Are you sure?"

"Very." The other woman's acute surprise caused Harley's heart to bang vigorously in her chest. "Is that unusual?"

"Very," echoed Jaymes, growing reflective. "You know, he doesn't show up at events like these. I bet he came because he knew you'd be here."

"I can't imagine how." Harley tried to deny her escalating excitement, but the notion that Grant might have come tonight in order to see her made her giddy. "It's not like he'd know Zest was my nonprofit."

"I'll bet he does."

The disparaging sound Harley made didn't change her friend's optimistic expression. "I'm sure he hasn't thought of me once in the last five years."

"You don't know that."

Jaymes had been there with sympathy and advice when Harley returned from her weekend with Grant, humiliated and incensed after he'd freaked out upon learning her age. Confident that Jaymes would always have her back, Harley had spilled everything to her best friend about the encounter. The two girls were very different in how they approached life. Jaymes was a rock who led with her head; Harley a swiftly moving current, mercurial and prone to impulsive actions. Like disappearing overseas when she realized she was pregnant by a man she desired and who'd made it clear he wouldn't ever consider a relationship with her.

Harley shook her head. "I'm sure I was barely a blip on his radar." Something that couldn't be said by her. Their encounter had left a lasting impression on her life. Especially in one very critical area.

"I'll admit that I don't know him all that well," Jaymes said, "but everything I've heard about him indicates that he's always been a workaholic and hasn't been romantically linked to anyone except his ex-wife. I'm quite sure that what happened between you two was an anomaly for him."

"Meaning?" Harley hated the way her heart jumped for joy at her friend's comment.

"That the weekend probably stands out in his mind."

"As something he'd never do again," she insisted, her buoyant mood dipping as she recalled how he'd started dating Paisley Barnes a few short weeks after the Texas Cattleman's Club ball.

No doubt he'd deemed the stunning blonde far more suitable in both age and experience than Harley had been at the time. He'd been so utterly appalled to learn at the end of their weekend together that she'd recently graduated from high school and railed at her in outrage that she'd intentionally misled him about everything. She'd been humiliated at being chastised like a naughty child, and refused to acknowledge the flaw in portraying herself as something she wasn't.

Harley sighed at the unpleasant memory and cringed at the way she'd stormed off like the overindulged brat she'd once been. When she'd made the decision to put Royal, Texas, in her rearview mirror, she hadn't intended to be gone for so long. However, she'd discovered that being out from beneath her siblings' shadows gave her a newfound sense of her strengths and a better understanding of her weaknesses. Worried that coming back to Royal would cause her to regress, she'd stayed away.

Eventually, however, she'd decided the best way to demonstrate that she'd matured was to face her fears. Even so, seeing Grant tonight filled her with dread. Despite how motherhood had forced her to grow up fast in the half decade since their last encounter, it hadn't changed the thirteen-year age gap between them. Was it foolish to hope that he'd give her credit for what she'd gleaned while living abroad? After all, she'd started a successful nonprofit and learned to not only take care of herself and her son, but also hundreds of women who relied on Zest to lift them out of the ravages of extreme poverty.

Pride flared, momentarily banishing her angst. When she'd originally conceived her nonprofit, she hadn't given much thought to how it might flourish and grow. She'd just recognized that people didn't want a handout. They wanted a hand *up*. Teaching a marketable skill and creating a pipeline for selling the goods created pathways that enabled these women to improve their lives. Harley's spark of an idea blew up into a giant blaze. But the issue of poverty was so enormous. The vast numbers of marginalized women in need of help so extensive. Thus, Zest was poised to grow beyond her ability to fund it. Especially now that her family's present business woes had reduced the Wingate corporate donations she used to keep Zest afloat from a wide river to a dry creek bed.

"Harley?" Jaymes had to prod Harley back to the present.

"Sorry." She grimaced at her friend's obvious concern. "I was thinking about Zest."

"We were talking about Grant."

"I know, but of all the problems I have at the moment, Zest's are the least likely to freak me out." Harley leaned into Jaymes and wrapped her arm around the other woman's waist. "You've been so remarkable all these years. I don't know what I would've done without you. If not for your emotional support and all your amazing connections for Zest, I would be lost."

"I don't think that's true," Jaymes said with a fond chuckle. "But you're welcome."

"And for letting me stay with you until I can find a place to rent for the next few months."

"Are you kidding? Sean and I love having you and Daniel around."

Jaymes had moved in with Sean Cavanaugh the year before after nearly two years of dating. The couple were devoted to each other, but seemed happy with the slow progress of their relationship.

"It's wonderful how great Sean is with Daniel."

"And vice versa," Jaymes put in. "Makes you realize that your boy needs a man in his life."

"It does," Harley agreed, guilt stabbing at her. "I know now that I was wrong to think I was all the parent he needed."

This statement encapsulated her motivation for returning to Royal, instead of a big city like Dallas, when her funding dried up for Zest. She hadn't realized the impact not having a father was having on Daniel until the mother of one of his friends shared that he had been telling wild stories about his father and all the incredible things the man was doing that kept him away. Harley's heart had broken as she'd learned how her son's imagination was working overtime to compensate for the absence of such a vital person. It was then that she'd decided to do whatever it took to fix her blunder.

"You're a great mom," Jaymes hastened to say. "I'm just glad you realize that he should get to know his father, as well."

Ever since learning she was pregnant, she'd grappled with telling Grant that he had a son. At first, she'd been freshly wounded by his rejection once he found out she was eighteen. She'd proved her immaturity by running away from her father's debilitating illness and her mother's harshness. Months later, alone in a foreign country where she didn't speak the language and weak from morning sickness, she'd decided maybe Grant had been right to chastise her for being rash and selfish. Unfortunately for her, by the time she'd dredged up the courage to tell him about Daniel, Grant had been engaged to Paisley and the last thing she wanted to do was ruin his life.

"I know I should've done it before this, but nothing about coming back here has been easy." On the endless international flight, she'd been paralyzed with anxiety over the best way to tell not just Grant that Daniel was his son but also confess the truth to her family. "And because I've kept Daniel from him all this time, explaining why I've waited so long is that much harder." Her stomach knotted. "What if Grant rejects him?" *Like he did me?*

Jaymes tightened her grip. "He won't. He's dedicated his career to building families. Why wouldn't he be thrilled to be a dad?"

Harley refrained from voicing the dozen or so answers that popped into her head.

"I'm just afraid that he's going to be angry that I waited too long to tell him." A lump lodged itself in Harley's throat while the anxious fluttering in her chest disrupted her breath. "What if he spurns Daniel because I kept the truth hidden all this time?"

"He won't."

As much as Harley trusted her friend's opinion, she couldn't shake her fears. Five years ago, Grant hadn't shown her any mercy after discovering that she'd deceived him about her age and his dismissal had been icy and ruthless. It had been one thing that Grant hadn't wanted her, but what if he didn't want his son, either? Recalling the conversation she'd had with Daniel after learning about the stories he'd made up, Harley's heart ached anew for her sweet son. He deserved a father who loved him and gave him a reason to be proud.

"I hope you're right."

Two

With the fundraiser in full swing, Grant decided it was time to slip out and head home. Putting in an appearance had been a mistake. Too many people had remarked on his attendance. Although few had asked his reason for showing up at this particular event, their curiosity hammered at him. It reminded him of those dreams people had where they found themselves naked in a public place with no idea how they'd gotten there and nowhere to run and hide.

Well, Grant knew exactly how he'd arrived at the party. The thought of seeing Harley Wingate again after five long years had been a lure he couldn't resist. That he'd seen her and continued to linger demonstrated that maybe he was hoping for something more. He grunted in dissatisfaction as the pull of unfinished business between them kept him from leaving.

Maybe if he apologized, she'd stop haunting him. As angry as he'd been with her in the moment, in the days that followed, he'd cooled off and decided he'd been more harsh than necessary. Yet, he'd stopped himself from reaching out, deciding that his attraction to her hadn't been burned out by her trickery or his irritation with it. And then one day she was gone and he'd missed the chance to take back his blunt words.

"Grant?" At the same time a low female voice spoke his name, he felt the lightest of pressure on his left sleeve. His pulse quickened to a frantic pace before he turned toward the source.

Harley Wingate stood beside him, her mesmerizing green eyes locking with his as she studied him. Her lips curved into an enigmatic smile as her hand fell away. Although he'd braced himself to run into her tonight, his brain short-circuited at the shock of her sudden nearness. His gaze swept over her. She bore his scrutiny with patience, displaying abundant poise while his nerves hissed and crackled.

"Hello, Harley."

"Wow. You do recognize me." The breathy chuckle she released betrayed that she wasn't as calm as she appeared. "I wasn't sure you would."

Was she crazy? Did she not understand how memorable their weekend together had been? For months after she'd left town, he'd replayed their time together and regretted that he'd had to push her away.

"You know perfectly well that I recognize you." The cacophony in his chest resettled into more languid rhythms as the initial surprise of their reunion faded.

"Do I?" She cocked her head. "It has been five years."

Five *long* years.

As the silence stretched between them, Grant noticed her smile growing strained and realized that she'd merely been utilizing a conversational ploy to cope with her nervousness and to jumpstart their verbal interaction. Rose had often accused him of lacking the skill to understand the emotional complexities other people were experiencing. He knew that his patients felt anxious and frustrated about their inability to grow their family without assistance and were afraid of the emotional and financial toll the fertility process might take on them. Those signals were easy to read. However, what Harley was broadcasting left him mired in confusion.

"You haven't changed that much," he murmured.

"At least you've noticed I've changed," she replied, her smile taking on a wry cast. "I'm not that silly girl of eighteen you once knew."

Maybe not, but he was still thirteen years her senior. "Of course not."

"It was really nice of you to come tonight," she said.

"I donated a case of wine for the tasting." He had no idea why he kept using this as an excuse. "And a 2016 Château Margaux Bordeaux for the silent auction."

Did she recognize the lameness of his explanation the way Rose had? Grant hated social situations that required small talk, preferring direct conversation on topics of substance. Discussing fertility options with his patients, for example, was familiar ground and not likely to raise his blood pressure. But pretending that this run-in with his ex-lover wasn't causing his heart to pound complicated his ability to keep the exchange flowing in a casual manner.

If Harley noticed his discomfort, she gave no sign. "The women of Zest appreciate your generosity," she stated with an appreciative smile.

"Was the fundraiser successful?" he asked, utilizing the safe topic to extend his time in her presence. Less than a minute in her company and he could already feel the pull of attraction wrenching him off balance.

"It's still early, but Beth thinks we have the potential of making our goal," Harley said, referring to her older sister who was well-known around Royal for her event planning and charitable activities. "Which is very exciting."

"I'm glad to hear that."

The scent clinging to her fair skin was different from the one that haunted his dreams. All those years ago, she'd worn a sophisticated perfume that when combined with her complex updo, heavy makeup and sexy gown had enabled her to appear ten years older. These days, she'd obviously stopped pretending to be more mature than her age and her light floral fragrance suited her natural, youthful charm. To Grant's surprise, her fresh face and uncomplicated hairstyle appealed to him more than her elaborate appearance during their fateful first encounter. The confidence she exuded in the simple flowered sundress that she and several others were modeling had him wanting to steal her away to somewhere private and listen to her stories surrounding her time abroad. That he was already thinking in terms of being alone with Harley warned Grant that he was heading down a dangerous path.

He glanced at his watch. "It's getting late."

"Yes," she murmured. "We wouldn't want you turning into a pumpkin."

When his gaze snagged on her wry half smile, Grant was transported back in time. That night of the TCC ball, a similar grin had produced an urgent craving to taste her soft lips. He'd never acted in such a reckless manner before or since. Yet, here he was tonight, assailed by the same eagerness to wrap his arms around her slim waist and pull her body against his. To dip his head and ravish her mouth.

"It was nice to see you again," he said, his tone made husky by the direction of his thoughts. "Best of luck with Zest."

As he turned to leave, she lightly touched his arm with the tips of her fingers. The fleeting contact seared through the layers of cloth, stopping him cold. Her hand fell away as he turned his head to regard her.

"Before you go," she began, her gaze direct and unflinching, "I wanted to ask if we could speak privately."

Despite his earlier compulsion to get her alone, Grant's impatience flared until he took stock of her expression and realized she wasn't coming on to him. Her somber demeanor left him mired in concern. Before coming here tonight, he'd prepared himself to defend against her flirtation. He'd expected an encounter with her going one of three ways. Either she'd pretend he didn't exist, act as if they'd never spent a combustible weekend together or turn on the charm in an effort to seduce him. He never imagined, however, that she'd go all serious on him.

He gazed around them at the crush of people and wondered how they could leave together without being noticed. "Now?"

She shook her head. "It's something that I should've told you long ago. But I'd prefer not to do it here. Maybe I could come by your house one day this week?"

He was struck by a strong desire to drink deep of her green eyes and plumb the real reason she'd want to speak with him after five long years of silence. Did she think to persuade him to welcome her back into his bed?

Madness.

Or was it?

Already his body tensed with anticipation while hunger raked across his nerves and sent his willpower sprawling in the dust. If she set out to seduce him, would he have the strength to turn her away? Of course, given how he'd treated her last time, he was a little surprised she'd pursue him.

With an aggrieved sigh, he shook his head. "Nothing

in the ensuing years has changed my mind," he declared. "I'm not interested in starting anything up with you."

Her eyes widened at his bluntness, but when her response came, it was delivered with cool composure. "That's a very bold assumption on your part."

Once again, Grant realized that he was not dealing with the same Harley Wingate he'd known half a decade earlier. He stared at her in confounded silence, suspecting she expected him to apologize. *Let her wait.* He'd only restated what he believed was best for both of them.

"You asked to speak with me at my home. After what happened last time, what else should I presume?"

"That maybe I wanted to catch up with you without all the eyes of Royal on us?"

"You want to catch up?" he countered, bewildered by her righteous tone. "Why now after no contact for the last five years?"

"I guess you'll just have to agree to meet with me."

Again, he was struck by her dignified manner. "Fine." It occurred to him that the sooner this conversation was over the better. "I'm free tomorrow evening. What time works for you?"

"Eight o'clock?"

"I'll see you then."

Long after Grant left the party following their brief encounter, Harley's hands trembled uncontrollably while her overstimulated nerve endings sizzled like a downed power line after a major weather event. She hadn't been prepared to see him at the fundraiser, much less get close enough to demonstrate that she was as susceptible as ever to his powerful personality and simmering masculinity.

With her senses awakened by the clean scent of the soap and shampoo he used, Harley closed her eyes and let her thoughts dwell on the imposing fertility specialist. He hadn't changed much since she'd seen him last. Although he maintained an impeccable appearance, Grant wasn't one for extra frills. His effortless elegance the night of the TCC ball had been a sharp contrast to her own heavy hand when it came to applying her makeup and the ridiculous amount of time she'd devoted to shopping for her gown and accessories. That night, she hadn't considered that the discrepancy in their approaches had demonstrated the disparity in their maturity levels. While she'd endeavored to be someone she wasn't, he'd been utterly comfortable in his own skin. Stripping off her finery had made her more vulnerable than she'd ever known. Yet, she'd found a safe haven in Grant's arms and had been changed because of it.

So many men she'd met, especially wealthy, influential ones like Grant, enjoyed bending people to their will. Despite her family's influence in town, she'd known her share of badgering and bullying by males who wanted something from her. However, Grant seemed disinterested in using either his position or his charisma to manipulate others. Which was why she'd found the way he treated her so refreshing. He basically explained what pleased him, and if she showed any sign of hesitation, he merely shrugged and let the matter drop. When she stuck to club soda at the ball, he hadn't ignored her request and pushed alcohol on her. He'd ordered the same and later whispered that she was all the intoxicant that he desired.

Besides the passion that he'd lavished on her body, Grant had spent an equal amount of consideration on her mind. Being taken seriously by someone as intelligent and renowned as the town's preeminent fertility specialist gave her a taste of what it would be like to have someone respect her thoughts and opinions.

As the youngest girl raised with three brothers and a sister who always strove to do their best, Harley had known early on that she'd never be able to compete with them. Nor did she have to because she'd always been indulged by her family. Immune to the higher standards expected of her siblings, she'd grown bold and rash.

Such reckless, impulsive behavior was what had led her to set her sights on Grant and pursue him. She'd known who he was from the start. Having seen him navigate the halls of the Texas Cattleman's clubhouse, cutting a dashing figure in his elegant suits and aloof manner, it was his untouchability that intrigued her. And made her wild to have her way with him.

But what had started out as an innocent enough idea to flirt with him escalated rapidly as they'd both succumbed to the red-hot chemistry that surged between them. Seized in passion's exhilarating embrace, the unexpected intensity of those two nights with Grant had done a number on her heart. She'd gone from teenage temptress to a woman in the throes of her first feverish love affair. With her hormones raging and her emotions churned up, she'd fallen into the trap of believing that the intense sexual connection was the beginning of the most magical relationship of her life.

Thus, on Monday morning, when he'd discovered how young she actually was, as forthright as he'd been about his desire for her, he'd been equally upfront about his irritation at her trickery. With her young psyche reeling from his rejection, she'd been nearly out of her mind with humiliation and loss. Plummeting from delirious high to devastating low, she'd tried to remind herself that she'd never meant for her encounter with Grant to be anything more than a brief, casual fling.

In the days and weeks that followed, Harley had struggled to make sense of what had gone wrong. Doubts surfaced as she replayed how he'd denied the intimate connection she thought they'd made. She'd raged against his cruel dismissal even as the truth of his words ate at her. He was a doctor with an established practice and she'd just graduated from high school. The airs she put on during the TCC ball had been to convince him she was much older than her eighteen years. She'd done a good job of fooling him. Too good. Discovering their thirteen-year age difference had slammed the door on any chance of seeing where the attraction between them might lead.

Only years later did she wonder if the annoyance he'd shown her had been anger at himself for being taken in by her playacting. Someone as straightforward as Grant wouldn't understand why she'd go to such lengths to interest him when in his mind they were unsuitable. What made matters worse was how he'd lowered his guard while they'd been together. A man like Grant would hate feeling the slightest bit vulnerable.

Still, despite all the heartache she'd caused herself, Harley couldn't regret it. If she hadn't misled him, she wouldn't have Daniel. So, even though she never got the chance to explore if she and Grant could make it as a couple, at least part of him would always be with her.

Pushing to the back of her mind all thought of her past mistakes, Harley circulated through the fundraiser, greeting people, answering questions about Zest and thanking those who made contributions for their support. Tonight, she needed to focus on the future and her plans for Zest. Plans that were in jeopardy thanks to the problems affecting her family's company.

Her gaze roved the guests, searching for some sign of support from her family. She could always count on her older sister, Beth, who'd planned the fundraiser, but Harley had yet to see any of her brothers. Since returning to town last month, her contact with Sebastian, Sutton and Miles had been limited because of the troubles afflicting the Wingate businesses. Caught up in their own drama, they had little energy to spare on their baby sister. Nor could she blame them. She hadn't come home in triumph. Zest was in trouble without the charitable funding she relied on from Wingate Enterprises.

With the company reeling from one devastating hit after another, the backlash against her family seemed to be without end. Of course, it didn't help that Wingate Enterprises was also facing one disaster after another. There were lawsuits because of the fire at WinJet, the jet plant in East Texas, that killed one man and injured three others. The family members of those men had filed lawsuits against the company, claiming that the company had falsified safety-inspection records. Harley couldn't imagine the company acting so irresponsibly, yet their names were being smeared through the press. And then while her brothers were busy trying to sort out that situation, during an inspection of the plant, drugs had been discovered. The DEA was quick to open an investigation and their first step had been to freeze all of Wingate Enterprises' assets. Once news of this got out, the double whammy caused the company stock to plummet.

And put in jeopardy Zest's future. Yet, even if the miraculous happened and Wingate's current misfortunes resolved themselves in the next few months, she realized she'd been a fool to rely on a single source for her funding. And if she planned to take the nonprofit to the next level, she'd need a lot more corporate and foundation sponsors to make that happen.

Blowing out a breath, Harley cast her gaze around the restaurant. Despite being surrounded by friends and others who applauded what she was doing with her nonprofit,

Harley felt more alone than when she'd been raising her son on her own halfway around the world. She'd invited her entire family to the event, but only her older sister had shown any interest in the project. As much as she appreciated what Beth had done, Harley wished she could rely on her family's support. But she hated to burden her brothers with her financial concerns while they were contending with so many ongoing business problems of their own.

With each new revelation of the company's wrongdoing, the entire family's reputation was also under attack. The Wingate family had long been held in high esteem by the town of Royal, but as the scandals piled up, their influence was fading fast. No one felt the sting more than Harley's mother, Ava. When she'd learned that Beth was planning the Zest fundraiser for Harley, Ava had offered up the unsolicited opinion that her youngest daughter should cut ties with Zest and let the nonprofit fail. This was the last thing Harley wanted to do, but while Beth had several solid ideas regarding fundraising, there was only so much money Harley could hope to raise given her family's downward spiral. Besides, she needed to take a more global approach with Zest and that would require a lot more staff. Staff she didn't have the means to pay unless she could convince someone known for their philanthropy to take a chance on her.

Her heart gave a little jig as she spied her aunt Piper cutting through the assembled guests in her direction. She'd always admired her mother's younger sister's ability to carry off whatever style appealed to her at the moment. Tonight, she wore her dark brown hair in a short edgy cut that showed off her elegant bone structure and highlighted her striking green eyes. A couple inches short of six feet, Piper Holloway could've strutted the catwalks of New York City, Paris and Milan with the best of them if she'd craved that sort of life. Instead, she lived in Dallas and owned a successful gallery.

"Aunt Piper!" Harley cried, touched that her aunt had made a special trip to attend the fundraiser. Throat tight, she threw open her arms, offering Piper a wholehearted welcome. "Thank you so much for coming."

Harley had always adored her aunt, who she viewed more like an older sister. Because Piper was nineteen years younger than Ava, the optimistic and enthusiastic Piper related better to her nieces and nephews than their difficult and overbearing mother. Which was why Harley had been devastated by the tension that developed between her and her aunt when Harley refused to tell Piper the identity of her baby's father.

"I wouldn't miss it," Piper said, enfolding her niece in a hug.

It wasn't the warm embrace of old, but Harley would take whatever affection her aunt was willing to give. When she first learned she was pregnant, her family had pressured her to reveal the father. Angered and humiliated by Grant's rejection, she'd been convinced that her family would badger her to deal with him. Nor had Harley wanted to put Piper's long-standing friendship with Grant in jeopardy by forcing her to keep secret that he had a son.

Now that Harley had decided to reveal the truth to Grant, she hoped that would enable her to repair her friendship with her aunt. Piper might continue to harbor some resentment toward Harley for her decision to keep her own counsel, but Harley was sure she could get Piper to understand that she'd acted in her aunt's best interest.

"Zest is doing wonderful work," Piper said. "And I know how dedicated you are to keeping it going."

Harley smiled despite the lump in her throat. "We are helping so many people and I can't let them down."

"Did your mother come?"

The question made Harley wince. "No. I'm afraid she thinks Zest is just some foolish lark of mine. She has no wish to understand how much good we've done."

Piper's dark green eyes shone with sympathy. "I'm sure that's not true. She's just preoccupied with everything that's going on with the company at the moment."

Although Harley bit down on her lower lip to keep from disagreeing, something must've shown in her expression because her aunt sighed.

"I'll talk to her," Piper promised.

"It won't do any good." Harley made no effort to fight the resentment simmering in her. "She doesn't believe in me. She never has. Why do you think I've been gone these last five years?"

Piper's eyes widened at her niece's grim tone, but nodded in understanding. "Family can be hard sometimes. Mostly they bring out our best, but as in the case with your mother, sometimes they can't help but be compelled to turn us into the worst of ourselves."

"That's sure true."

"It's good that you're home." Piper squeezed her arm. "You've been missed."

"That's nice to hear," Harley said, although she wasn't sure her absence had any impact on her family. Except maybe relief.

She offered her aunt a wobbly smile, withholding the fact that she intended to return to Thailand and the work that she'd left there as soon as possible. Too much was wrong in the world and she wanted to be a part of the solution. She didn't want to upset Piper with her future plans, but she had no intention of staying in Royal.

Three

The day after the Zest fundraiser, Grant struggled to stay focused on the simplest tasks. Fortunately, he had only two patient appointments and no procedures scheduled. Despite his staff's efficiency, he routinely oversaw all aspects of his practice and when he declared at noon that he intended to take the afternoon off, they all gaped at him. Grant pretended not to notice their confusion as he exited the clinic and headed to his car.

With eight hours to occupy himself before his meeting with Harley, Grant headed to the Texas Cattleman's Club for lunch, hoping to distract himself with conversations about rising feed prices, coping with new government regulations or the slow but steady transformation of land use from grazing cattle to hunting.

Unfortunately, the club was buzzing about the troubles besetting Wingate Enterprises and the latest scandal surrounding the discovery of drugs on WinJet's property.

As he settled at a table, he overheard a nearby group of women discussing the opening of a DEA investigation into the company's apparent drug smuggling and wondered how Harley was coping with the upheaval her family was going through.

Of course, the instant she popped into his mind, any hope of a peaceful meal vanished. Never one to speculate, Grant found himself consumed by curiosity. What was Harley so intent on saying to him after five years of silence? And why did they need to speak in private?

Frustrated at having so long to wait for answers, after Grant left the TCC, he spent a couple hours in his home gym. Usually working up a sweat enabled him to disengage his mind after a stressful day, but last night's encounter with Harley had stirred up emotions he'd thought long buried. Dismayed that he was no less agitated after a vigorous circuit of lifting and cardio, he lingered in the shower for a long time and grappled with vivid memories of his time with Harley.

The night of the TCC ball, he'd checked them into a hotel suite and spent the next two days utilizing every inch of the space, including the large shower. The sounds she'd made as she came beneath his mouth returned to him with vivid and arresting clarity. His recall was strengthened by the reawakening of his sharp hunger the previous evening when he'd spied Harley across the room. That weekend had reduced every encounter he'd had with other women to insubstantial shadows. Including his marriage to Paisley.

Guilt stabbed at him. His inability to disengage his feelings for Harley had interfered with his relationship with his wife and caused the eventual destruction of his marriage. He'd never been in love with Paisley. By marrying her, he'd elevated her position in Royal and given her access to his significant wealth, thinking that was enough to keep her happy. He'd been wrong. She'd wanted more than fondness and fidelity from him. Too late, he discovered that she'd married him believing he'd come to love her. And like with his family, he'd been unable to live up to her expectations. He couldn't help how his intellect caused him to negotiate through life and it frustrated him to be so misunderstood by those closest to him.

His doorbell chimed, announcing a visitor. Never one to let stressful situations get to him, Grant caught himself sucking in a deep breath to steady his nerves. Irritated, he marched toward the foyer and threw open the front door. Harley stood on his front porch, looking cool and composed with her long brown hair pulled back from her face in a simple high pony and floral earrings dangling from her delicate earlobes.

She wore a short-sleeved teal dress with a round neckline that showed no hint of cleavage. His heart boomed in his chest as he took in the way her modest knit garment flowed over her torso before flaring into a wide skirt with a knee-skimming hemline. This wasn't an outfit for seducing a past lover and he grew more puzzled at what had motivated her to ask for this meeting.

While he'd been surveying her, she'd taken in his white shirt and charcoal slacks. When his gaze returned to meet hers, their eyes locked for a brief second. The appreciation smoldering in her gaze sparked a matching heat inside him. Inviting her to his house was playing with fire. But dammit, he hadn't felt this alive since she left town.

Harley cleared her throat. "Hello, Grant."

"Good evening."

He plunged his hands into the front pockets of his slacks to keep from capturing her wrists and pulling her into his arms. Since they'd bumped into each other the night before, he'd become aware of a deep unfulfilled hunger gnawing at him. That neither time nor space had dimmed his appetite for her irritated him to no end.

"Thanks for agreeing to see me."

She skimmed her palms down the front of her dress, smoothing the material in a nervous gesture that drew his attention to the lines of tension around her mouth.

"Of course."

Her anxious energy hummed across the space between them, reminding him how she'd trembled as he'd undressed her that first time. He might have wondered at her jitters that night if he hadn't been equally agitated as her dress had fallen away to reveal the most perfect breasts he'd ever seen. Unbidden, his gaze slid to her chest. Her breath hitched.

As a roaring filled his ears, Grant took an involuntary step backward, thinking to escape the impact she had on him. He covered the retreat by sweeping his arm in an imperious gesture.

"Come in."

"Thank you."

She ducked her head and sent him a furtive glance as she passed. Once inside, however, she stopped dead and looked around. Seeing that she wasn't going to move beyond the wide foyer without coaxing, Grant led the way into the great room, taking the seconds to compose himself once more.

"Do you want something to drink?"

"Just some water if you have it."

"Have a seat." He gestured toward the couch before heading to the dry bar and the beverage fridge stocked with water and sodas, wishing she'd asked for something stronger. Because he certainly could use a shot of whiskey to take the edge off.

"I like your house," Harley said, ignoring his invitation to sit down.

Grant warmed to the approval shining in her eyes as she took in the neutral colors, clean lines, warm wood tones and mid-century modern architecture of his four-thousand-square-foot home. Each room boasted floor-to-ceiling windows, exposed wood beams and stark white walls adorned with large bright canvases depicting the rugged Texas landscape in full bloom.

He set two bottles of water on the coffee table and watched as Harley explored the dining room and peered into the kitchen. Although tempted to offer her a full tour—ending with the master bedroom—Grant settled for trailing after her as she slipped through the open sliding glass door and stepped onto the pool deck. Lights hidden in the surrounding landscaping gave the outdoor space a cozy feel.

"It's a house made for entertaining," she remarked as they made their way back inside. "I don't suppose you've had any parties, though."

"They're not really my thing."

Harley glanced his way. "How long have you been here?"

"Since my divorce."

Grant had never regretted letting Paisley keep their Pine Valley house as part of their divorce settlement. The location had been too far from Royal Memorial Hospital and he'd never been a fan of the French country decor his ex had preferred. His new house was less than three years old, constructed after the hurricane that had torn through Royal six years earlier, demolishing homes and businesses in several neighborhoods on the west side and collapsing a wing of the hospital.

"I'm sorry things didn't work out between you and Paisley."

Grant made an impatient gesture of dismissal. He didn't want to talk with Harley about his failed marriage.

"Why don't you just tell me why you're here," he prompted, remembering that she'd appreciated his directness that weekend they'd spent together.

He'd described how much he enjoyed her body and educated her where he'd liked her lips on him and how good she felt beneath him. She met his frankness with an openness that had made their time together the most spectacular sensual experience of his life.

"Five years ago," she began, her voice quavering, "we spent a weekend together..."

"Yes."

Her gaze shot to his and just as quickly shifted away. If she intended to seduce him, she was going about it all wrong. Last time they'd been together, she'd been brazen and sexy and so full of her own power. Tonight, she could barely summon the courage to look at him. What had compelled her to seek him out after years of silence?

From the moment he'd heard she was coming home, he had begun to debate with himself. Obviously, he wasn't immune to her charms, but how much of what he felt was because one weekend with her hadn't been enough to get her out of his system? Maybe all he needed was to see if his desire for her was honest or merely a tantalizing echo of the chemistry that had existed between them back then.

"And it ended abruptly—"

"You lied to me about who you were." The memory of her deceit tasted bitter.

"You never would've given me a chance if I told you I was eighteen. And that was the most amazing two days—" She cut off her words and blew out a harsh breath. "I'm tired of apologizing for what I did. Maybe I lied, but what harm did I do? No one knew we were together. The weekend didn't blemish your reputation."

"Do you really think I was worried about my *reputation*?"

Her eyes flared. "Then what?"

He pressed his lips together, refusing to admit the true reason why he'd been so upset. Confessing that he'd been besieged by disappointment when he learned she was so young would give her too much power. He'd spent two magical nights with his arms wrapped around the woman of his dreams. Waking up Monday morning to discover she was a mere girl had shattered something inside him. He'd opened himself up to her only to discover it had all been a lie.

"Tell me why you were so mad that morning," she prompted in soft tones.

Grant narrowed the space between them, drawn to her even as his mind issued a shrill warning to stay away. "That weekend haunts me," he rasped, cupping her head just below the silky ponytail and bending down until their lips were less than an inch apart. "It should never have happened."

He lifted his lashes and their eyes locked in a fierce staring contest. A thrill raced through him as her fingers clenched at his sleeve. Sparks danced across his skin as her breath hitched. Despite the questions dodging through her green gaze, her lips softened and parted.

Not trusting his voice, he brushed his mouth against hers, letting their breaths mingle. At the contact, her body stiffened, muscles going utterly still. Discouraged by her cool response, while his insides smoldered and sizzled, Grant was on the verge of setting her free when her nails bit into his arm.

"Grant." His name came out of her in a husky plea.

One kiss. That's all he intended to steal from her. A single taste to demonstrate that he was in control of his impulses. He could indulge his hunger and then master it. Only it didn't quite work out the way he'd hoped.

Before he could think…before she could protest, his mouth claimed hers. The first touch of their lips transported him back to a frantic embrace in a private alcove at the TCC clubhouse where he'd backed her against the wall and stolen one deep and unrestrained kiss after another. The rest of the world fell away, leaving them the only two people on the planet.

That night, she'd tasted like sweet strawberries and tart lemons. Tonight, he was treated to the sharp bite of mint as he ran his tongue over her lower lip, coaxing her to let him in. With a moan, she opened and he plunged his tongue inside her mouth, sweeping it around hers in a seductive dance.

Drowning in the pleasure of her kiss, he wrapped his arm around her waist and drew her close. Pain shot through his chest at the sheer perfection of having her in his arms once more. How had he lived without this for five years? How could he have thought any woman could give him the pleasure a single kiss from Harley brought him? His palms slid over her hips and cupped the gentle curve of her butt, lifting her into his rapidly forming erection. That she turned him on with so little effort should've alarmed him. But his body and not his mind was in control now, spurred on by the delicious noises emanating from her throat. Distantly, he recognized that he would forever worship at her feet just to keep hearing those electrifying sounds of pleasure.

Before he considered his actions, Grant bent down and swept her into his arms. His bedroom was several long strides away and he'd nearly reached the hallway before realizing that Harley was pushing her palm against his chest. He broke off the kiss and stopped.

"Stop. Please," she whispered, shaking her head. "We can't. This isn't why I came here tonight."

"Of course."

Shocked at his rashness, Grant set her back on her feet, steadying her as she swayed. At no point in the hours leading up to this meeting had he intended to kiss her much less haul her off to his bedroom. In truth, the moment he'd opened the door and found her standing on his doorstep, he'd been fighting the urge to pull her into his arms, cover her mouth with his and revisit any one of a hundred fantasies that he'd had of her over the years.

"I don't want that to happen again." He declared the lie in an icy tone that made her lips twitch into a sad half smile.

"So noted," she said somberly.

Heat pushed against his skin as desire continued to rage through him. What had happened to his self-control? He wasn't a teenager incapable of resisting reckless impulses.

"All the reasons it wouldn't have worked between us all those years ago haven't changed," he blustered on, talking more to convince himself than to establish boundaries with her.

At his curtness, her eyes flashed in a way that said her patience was running short. "I get it." She crossed her arms over her chest and frowned. "Look. I didn't come here to throw myself at you."

"Then why did you come?" he asked, his chilly manner hiding the wildfire that continued to rampage through him.

She swung away with an inpatient exhalation and strode around the room. Drowning in confusion, he tracked her agitated movements for several long seconds.

"I knew this was going to be hard," she said at long last,

coming to a halt five feet away. "But I had no idea how hard it would be."

He wasn't good at this. On a routine day, husbands and sisters and friends dealt with his patients' emotional breakdowns. Tonight, he alone must cope with whatever complex issue had created the anxiety that gripped Harley at the moment.

"Oh, for heaven's sake," he snapped, his discomfort getting the better of him. "Just spit it out."

For the briefest of seconds, she looked utterly crushed by his tone. Her stark vulnerability struck like a knife, driving between his ribs and into the unprotected flesh of his madly pumping heart.

"Fine," she said, her expression hardening with determination. "You're a father."

The second the words were out of her mouth, Harley wished she'd been less blunt as she delivered the news. One thing she hadn't learned to do in the intervening years was curb her tendency to speak her mind. Diplomacy didn't come easily, especially when her emotions ran hot like they were right now.

"You're lying."

Although she wasn't surprised by his reaction, Harley flinched at his harsh accusation. She hadn't expected that he'd believe her and couldn't really blame him for being suspicious. If someone had appeared on her doorstep and made such a declaration, she'd want the claim proved, as well.

"I'm sorry," she said. "I should've eased into that."

"You're damn right you should have."

"But I'm not lying," she continued, hoping her gravity would convince him she spoke the truth. "You have a son."

Grant showed the first chink in his armor as he rubbed his face. "It's not possible."

"That first time…" she trailed off with a shrug, letting him fill in the gap with his own memories.

He cursed. "Of course, there'll have to be a paternity test."

"Of course. I wouldn't expect anything else."

"His name is Daniel and he's four." As she spoke Grant's frown faded, his features shifting into stony lines as the impact of her words sank in. "He's an awesome kid. Smart. Funny. Too old for his years."

In fact, he reminded her so much of his dad that it was a little scary. Up until now, Grant hadn't supplied more than his genes, but in so many ways, her son was a carbon copy of the man who stood before her. Smart. Stubborn. Strong-willed. Adorable.

"Grant?"

"Yes?"

His gaze had been searching the room as if desperate for something he could grab on to, something that made sense. He looked disoriented and entirely capable of falling over. He wouldn't. Grant was a strong, powerful man. But even a big hunk could be leveled by an unexpected blow. And that's exactly what Harley had delivered.

"Are you okay?"

"As fine as a man can be whose ex-lover shows up and declares he has a son."

Guilt twisted in her chest, making it hard for Harley to breathe. As much as she longed to offer him comfort or support, she kept her distance. What existed between them was too volatile. She couldn't risk touching him again.

"It's a huge shock, I know."

He clenched his hands into fists. "If this is some twisted game…"

"It's not."

"As I said, I want a paternity test."

"We can do it whenever you want."

Instead of being satisfied with her easy agreement, his frown indicated that she'd annoyed him. What was wrong now? The test would prove she wasn't lying. Daniel was his son.

"Why now?"

"Why now what?" she asked, frustrated that he was asking all these ridiculous questions when what he should really want to know about was his son.

"It's been five years."

"Things didn't end well between us," she reminded him.

"That's a poor excuse and you know it."

She'd imagined this encounter with Grant a thousand times. No matter how often she'd envisioned his reaction, vacillating between him throwing his arms around her in joy or shouting accusations at her, she hadn't prepared herself for the moments after. Now that her emotional seesaw had stopped, Harley felt as if she'd stepped off a cliff and was plummeting thousands of feet through the air toward the earth below. The plunge was both terrifying and exhilarating.

"Fine," she groused. "I can't tell you how many times I picked up the phone to call and tell you…"

"But you didn't."

"At first, I was mad. And then afraid." She had no idea if exposing her vulnerability in this moment would get through to him or not. "And then you married Paisley and I didn't want to mess up your situation."

"Paisley and I have been divorced for a while now."

"I know, but so much time had passed and I wasn't sure…" She wasn't sure about *any* of this. "Plus I was living overseas…"

"You could've kept all of this a secret. I never would've known."

Telling him about Daniel meant he couldn't eject her from his life as he'd once done. At least she hoped he wouldn't. For a man as stuck in his head as Grant, she probably should have approached this whole thing logically. Appealing to his big beautiful brain would've given her faster results, but telling a man who'd rejected you in a big way that you gave birth to his son and kept that secret from him was too fraught with emotion for her to be rational.

"It wasn't fair to keep you apart. You deserve to know…" She paused. "Both of you."

"Because you want something from me?"

She grappled with the instinct to fling angry words at him. This wasn't how she'd wanted this encounter to go. Harley fought to subdue her unrealistic expectations. Had she really believed that after so much time had gone by, she could show up, drop this bombshell and then he would simply welcome her and Daniel into his life with open arms?

"*I* don't want anything from you." She only wished that were true.

Because while deep down she'd hoped he would be excited about being a father, rationally she knew he would process the situation with his mind before his emotions. Would he ever get to a point where he was able to embrace his boy and all the awesomeness that Daniel could bring into his life?

"Your son, however, is a whole different story." Her breath grew shallow as anxiety set in. This was the moment she'd imagined and dreaded. She straightened her spine, preparing to fight for her son's happiness with everything she had. "He wants to know his father. And I hope that his father wants to know him."

Grant wasn't the sort of man who acted or reacted with emotion. He would have to analyze the entire situation before he decided what to do. At this point, her best bet was to simply leave and let him sort through everything.

"It's late," she said, easing toward the door. "I should go."

"Come by my office tomorrow at any time and we can run the paternity test."

Harley nodded, satisfied that she'd convinced him enough to take this first step. "We'll do that."

"If the test proves I'm his father, then of course, I will do right by him. Financially and otherwise."

No hint of any emotion showed in his impassive expression as he said this and Harley's frustration sparked at his reserve. She knew he wasn't made of stone.

During their weekend together, in addition to his passion, he'd shown her tenderness and affection. His smiles had left her breathless. Yet, at the end of their time together, when confronted by something that made him uncomfortable, he'd retreated into dispassionate logic. Just like he was doing now.

"I don't need your money if that's what you're thinking," she huffed, letting her exasperation show. "I can support us. That's not what this is about."

"I realize a shakedown isn't your style." He paused for a moment. "Although given what's been going on with your family…"

"Yes. Well." She hated how he'd connected the Wingate family's recent financial difficulties with her claim that he had a son. "This is all about my conscience and doing what's right. I couldn't continue to keep him from you and not feel guilty about it."

Her son needed and deserved to know his father.

Overwhelmed by a sudden rush of emotion that sent

pain lancing through her chest, Harley scrambled to leave before she burst into tears in front of him.

"I'll see you tomorrow," she said, retreating toward the foyer, all too aware of the solid thump of his footsteps as he followed her down the long hall to his front door. He moved as if the burden of fatherhood rested heavily on his shoulders. She had her hand on the doorknob when Grant spoke again.

"Is that why you left? Because you were pregnant?"

Resentment flared as he reduced what had been a complicated time in her life down to a brief criticism of her decisions. He had no idea just how much she'd wanted to run into his arms and have him take her away from her mother's overbearing ways, her heartbreak over her father's illness and her family's disappointment. But his rejection had stung more than all her other troubles combined.

"No."

"You should've come to me."

She left his declaration unanswered and slipped through his front door. Before she reached the porch steps, she turned to glance at him over her shoulder.

"Daniel is your son," she felt driven to say. "You'll see."

And with that, she raced away into the night.

Four

Grant remained stuck in place as the taillights of Harley's car disappeared around the curve of his long driveway. The night's breath flowed around him, the insects filling the air with their incessant buzzing. His gaze swept over the front lawn as if hoping to find something in the shadows that would help him make sense of the emotion raging through him.

Wrestling with the urge to get into his car and follow her, Grant backed into his house, slammed his front door closed and sucked in several steadying breaths. When he raked his fingers through his hair, his hands shook.

This was all impossible. He couldn't be a father. They'd been careful. Mostly careful, anyway.

That first time, he'd been in such a rush to slide inside her, he'd neglected a condom, and the sensation of her bare flesh against his had been so electrifying that he'd nearly come. But despite his rash behavior, he hadn't been an inexperienced teenager. Grant had quickly recognized the danger and controlled himself to the point where he pulled out, rolled away and slid on a condom. The slip shouldn't have been enough for her to get pregnant, but as a fertility doctor, he knew that when it came to creating life, the science wasn't always predictable.

A son.

His son. Was it possible? It had to be. It would be the height of idiocy for Harley to lie to him about something so easily disproved. But what did this mean for him? For them?

The first night they met, her impulsive energy had sparked something reckless and dangerous inside him. Never before, and not one time since, had he become so obsessed with a woman that he'd been drawn to take a stranger to bed. She was his Achilles' heel. That much had become obvious as soon as he'd heard she was returning to Royal. His need to be with her hadn't faded. In fact, given the way he'd been seconds away from making another mistake, his attraction to her surged stronger than ever.

Stupid reckless lust. That's all it was. But the overwhelming power of the longing that had blasted through him when their lips collided demonstrated that underestimating such strong desire would be unwise.

Especially now that they shared a son.

Even though he'd refused to take Harley at her word and demanded a paternity test, deep down he believed Daniel was his son. Harley wouldn't make the mistake of crossing him a second time with a lie of that magnitude. She might be impulsive and emotional in her actions but she wasn't a fool.

Which meant he was a father.

The magnitude of this unexpected reality kept him up most of the night as he pondered all the ways he intended to work his new responsibilities into his life. He imagined all the firsts he would get to experience. First bedtime story. First lost tooth. First day of school.

This list drove home all the firsts he'd missed. First smile. First word. First step. Grief swelled as he pondered what Harley had stolen from him by her actions. Anger followed but was quickly pushed aside and determination stood in its place. No matter what, he would be an integral part of his son's life going forward.

His resolve strengthened throughout the night, and by the time he entered his clinic the next morning, Grant no longer cared that his staff would be wildly curious about the woman he'd instruct them to usher into an exam room as soon as she and her son arrived. They wouldn't ask why he was running a paternity test on Harley's son because they knew better than to question anything he did. But that wouldn't stop them from being curious and gossiping amongst themselves.

He caught himself jumping every time his phone rang announcing the arrival of a new patient and wished he'd pinned down a time when Harley would arrive. As the morning wound down, he began to wonder if she'd show at all. Maybe he'd been wrong to assume her claim that he was Daniel's father had been truthful.

Just before lunch, he exited an exam room after a consultation and found one of his nurses waiting for him. His gut twisted at the bright curiosity in her brown eyes, but he kept his expression bland and professional as she directed him to the room where Harley and her son waited. Thanking her, Grant headed down the hall. Hand on the doorknob, he strove for calm before entering the room.

Although he shouldn't have expected to glimpse any resemblance between himself and a four-year-old child, a trace of disappointment slipped into his awareness when he spied the child for the first time. Daniel had dark blond hair and his mother's green eyes. There was nothing of the Everett family nose or chin...no physical attributes whatsoever that could prove the boy was his son. That he'd imagined he'd feel some sort of instant connection irritated him. He was a scientist. That's not always how genetics worked. The truth was buried in the boy's DNA.

"Good morning," he declared formally, meeting Harley's gaze as he sat at the desk. "Thank you for coming in."

She looked slightly taken aback by his professional demeanor, but nodded. "Of course."

"Hello, Daniel. My name is Dr. Everett," Grant said, introducing himself. "What we're going to do today won't take but a couple seconds, and then you and your mother can get on with the rest of your day."

He pulled out one of the DNA test swabs he'd put into his pocket at the start of his day. He'd already taken a sample from his own cheek and would add it to the one he took from Daniel for the lab to process. He rolled his chair to within easy reach of where Daniel sat beside his mother.

Grant extended the swab and said, "I need to take a sample of your cells from the inside of your cheek. So you need to open your mouth."

The boy met his gaze with the stony stare that seemed far too mature for his age. Grant ground his teeth and regarded the stubborn child, unsure what to do. He was accustomed to his patients doing what he told them. For several seconds, the two stared at each other, neither relenting, and Grant noted his respect rising in grudging increments.

"Does he know why you brought him here today?" he asked, indicating the test swab.

Was the boy worried about being sick? Or did he sense Grant's tension and mistrust him because of it?

"I told him we needed to visit you because you were going to run an important test and that it wouldn't hurt."

The boy tracked the exchange between the adults with the sharp focus of someone struggling to understand the undercurrents in the room.

"You need to open your mouth," Grant repeated, wondering what he could do if the boy continued to resist. "I need to swab your cheek."

The standoff continued and Grant began to feel uncomfortable beneath the boy's unflinching regard. In frustration, he glanced toward Harley who watched the entire exchange with a thoughtful expression.

Grant raised his eyebrows at Harley, demanding that she step in. When she caught his eye, she seemed to shake herself and nod.

"Daniel, honey, can you please open your mouth so Dr. Everett can touch that little cotton swab to the inside of your cheek. It won't hurt."

At last, the boy opened his mouth, not to give Grant the opportunity to pop in the swab, but to release a string of words in a foreign language. Recalling that Harley had been in Thailand for the last few years, Grant guessed it was Thai.

"We need to run a test," his mother explained in English, demonstrating that the boy was bilingual. "Would you be happier if I did it?"

Another string of foreign words came out of the boy's mouth.

"Doesn't he speak English?" Grant asked, impatience building as the boy's defiance continued.

Grant's familiarity with children stopped shortly after conception. Once the pregnancy was deemed viable, his part was done and the mom-to-be became the responsibility of an obstetrician. If asked which part of his vocation he preferred, Grant would always choose science over the handholding his patients often required as they negotiated the deeply emotional journey from infertility to parenthood.

"Of course, he does," Harley said, "but he's unhappy with me for dragging him back to America and taking him away from his friends and all the people he knows in Thailand. This is his way of coping."

It seemed less like coping and more like punishing his mother, Grant mused as he handed the swab to Harley. "Maybe you should do it."

As if this was what Daniel had been waiting for, as soon as his mother presented the swab, he opened his mouth wide and let her gather the sample. Grant was torn between amusement and annoyance as he secured the sample. The seconds that followed were tight with awkward tension.

"The test will take forty-eight hours to run," he told Harley, getting to his feet. "I should probably take your number so I can let you know the results."

She stood as well and handed him a Zest business card. He slipped it into his pocket and turned to Daniel. What did he say to this child who was in all likelihood his son? Retreating into professionalism, Grant stuck out his hand to the boy.

"It was nice meeting you, Daniel," he said, realizing that the next time he saw the boy he'd know for certain that the child was his.

Daniel received a nudge from his mother before saying in his clear young voice, "You have gray hair, so you must be really old. Are you a grandpa?"

Harley smothered a groan as Daniel's question hung in the air. Leave it to her son to strike at the heart of what had caused Grant to reject her five years earlier. Her gaze strayed to the touch of gray in Grant's temples. In her opinion, the premature change in color added even more distinction to his already elegant appearance.

"Dr. Everett is too young to be a grandfather," Harley declared, shooting Grant an apologetic smile. While she was accustomed to her son's outspoken personality, his directness wasn't always well received. "As you can see, Daniel has inherited my tendency toward bluntness."

"He's curious," Grant replied. "Nothing wrong with asking questions."

No doubt Grant identified with his son's curious nature and could keep up with the myriad of things Daniel wanted to know about far better than Harley could. Thank goodness for the internet so she could look up fact-based questions. Others had been more difficult to answer. Her father had suffered a second stroke two years earlier and passed away. When she talked about him to Daniel, her son wanted to understand why people died. She'd struggled with an explanation he could grasp and his follow-up question of who he would live with when she died nearly broke her heart.

After saying their goodbyes, Harley herded her son from Grant's office. As they headed home, she found herself grappling with the consequences of telling him about Daniel. Her son deserved a father, but she wasn't sure that Grant had any idea what it took to be a parent, much less be the sort Daniel needed. Would Grant love him unconditionally and be willing to sacrifice anything to make Daniel happy? If he displayed any reluctance to be in his son's life, her decisions about the future would be clear.

But what if Grant embraced his new role? The man might be driven by logic, but when something penetrated the shell around his heart, he was capable of a deeply emotional response. Grant wouldn't be indifferent to his son. Pondering this new reality pained her in a way she hadn't expected.

Daniel was her whole world. Since finding out she was pregnant, he'd been her top priority, the reason she did everything. With Grant accepting that he was Daniel's father, he'd surely want to have some say in how his son was being raised. A whole new batch of anxiety besieged Harley as she realized she would have to share her son. Not only that, but the decisions she made surrounding Daniel were no longer going to impact just the two of them. Grant also had a stake in the boy's future. How had she not considered this before?

By the time Harley received the call she'd been waiting for, she'd worked herself into a complicated state of dread and hope. Seeing Grant's number light up the screen, she gripped her phone tight and barely heard his greeting above the blood pounding in her ears.

"The test confirms that I'm Daniel's father," Grant said, delivering the official results in a dispassionate tone, which was at odds with someone who had just discovered he had a son.

Harley knew better than to take his lack of reaction at face value. No doubt he'd require time to absorb the news and was determined to proceed in a reasonable manner. "We should get together and discuss how to handle the situation going forward," she said, meeting his objectivity with steady composure.

"We have a lot to talk about," he agreed. "Are you free for dinner tonight?"

The thought of spending the evening with Grant sent a thrill rocketing through her, but she shut down her strong reaction. She needed to put her son's needs ahead of her own.

"Tonight should be fine. I just need to confirm that I

have a sitter for Daniel." She'd briefed Jaymes on the situation with Grant and her friend had offered to watch Daniel any night this week. "What time would you like to meet?"

"How about I pick you up at seven?"

She agreed and gave him Jaymes's address, then spent the rest of the afternoon figuring out what to wear.

Five hours later, Grant's navy blue Mercedes came to a halt in her friend's driveway. Harley had been waiting for him and slipped out the front door before he'd extricated himself from the driver's seat.

Harley wasn't expecting any drama tonight. Grant hadn't given her any indication that he intended to be anything but civilized and logical, but her anxiety levels had still been sky high all day.

Instead of waiting for her by his car, he met her halfway up the walk. Her knees quivered as his ocean blue eyes took in her appearance. The man's imposing masculinity was attributed as much to the force of his keen intelligence and innate charisma as his daunting height and impressive physique. He positively oozed confidence.

Yet, she'd once glimpsed his wariness and knew the pain that had caused him to wall off his emotions. The weekend Daniel had been conceived, she'd been offered some insight into Grant's innermost thoughts. In the wee hours of the night, as they lay tangled together, he'd dropped his guard and given her a glimpse of his pain. He'd shared how going against his parents' wishes and becoming a doctor instead of taking the reins of the family's businesses had put him at odds with his mom and dad. Their inability to support his decisions had compelled him to take refuge behind indifference.

She'd been surprised to find they were kindred spirits in this regard and shared with him how she'd known nothing but criticism from her mother and exasperation from her siblings. Growing up, they'd often made her feel as if nothing she said or did was right. And when they'd learned she'd become pregnant, they'd chosen to scold her rather than offer their support, leaving her no choice but to distance herself from the Wingates and eventually put Royal in her rearview mirror.

In the months that followed, she'd been swallowed by bitterness and ignored all their attempts to reach out to her. Daniel had saved her from her worst instincts. Could he save Grant, as well?

"Thank you for agreeing to have dinner with me tonight," Grant said as he settled behind the wheel of the Mercedes.

"Of course," she replied, keeping her voice light. "You know I enjoy your company."

He shot her a curious look before starting the car. Harley's senses came fully alive as she inhaled his clean masculine scent and absorbed the way his proximity made her skin tingle. Fighting the impulse to lean into his space, she gripped her purse until her fingers ached and focused on calming her skyrocketing pulse. Good thing they were going out in public because Harley wasn't sure she could keep her hands to herself if left alone with him for more than the time it would take to drive to the restaurant.

As he drove, she wondered where he intended to take her. Their appearance together at one of Royal's better restaurants would be sure to spark gossip. When the town limits came and went, Harley relaxed. Obviously, neither one of them was ready to flaunt their connection in public.

Their destination turned out to be Violets, an upscale restaurant in Joplin, a good-sized town in neighboring Colonial County. As Grant escorted her to the front door, his palm grazed her back as she slipped past him and entered the cozy interior. Reeling from the heady rush of his touch, Harley filled her lungs with the delicious aromas wafting from the kitchen.

The hostess escorted them to a table set with elegant crystal goblets, flickering candles and a pot of delicate violets on white linens. Despite the elegant decor and soft lighting, the atmosphere was less romantic and more geared toward fine dining.

"I haven't been here before," Harley said. "It's very nice."

"One of my staff is the cousin of the owner and recommended it."

Harley glanced at the menu and surveyed the selections. Her mouth watered in appreciation of the cuisine. "This all looks amazing," she murmured. "I have no idea what to have."

"June recommended the beef tenderloin Oscar and the lamb loin."

"The saffron mussel soup caught my eye, as well."

The waiter appeared and went over that evening's specials and took their drink order. Harley shot surreptitious glances in Grant's direction as she continued to hem and haw over her entrée selection. With his typical decisiveness, Grant made his choice and set his menu aside. While they waited for the waiter to return, they chatted about the changes to Royal during her absence and the dramas surrounding several of the Texas Cattlemen's Club members that had occurred in the last few years. Since he wasn't one for small talk, Harley figured he hadn't yet figured out how to divulge how he was feeling. She waited until they'd received their entrées before tackling the reason they'd agreed to meet for dinner.

"Now that you've had some time to adjust," she began, savoring the butter-poached king crab that topped the beef tenderloin medallions. "How are you feeling about being a father?"

Grant frowned. "I'm getting used to the idea."

"Finding out your whole life will never be the same is a bit of a shock." Harley thought back to the moment when she'd glimpsed the positive pregnancy test. "It takes a while to get used to the idea of being a parent," she continued. "I had eight months to adjust. You've had a few days."

"Do you want me there when you tell him?"

"I don't know," she admitted. "I haven't figured out how to do that. I'm hoping it'll just become obvious one day that he's ready to hear the truth."

"One day?" Grant echoed. "That's a little vague."

Harley needed to tread carefully. She didn't want to hurt Grant, but wasn't sure how he would cope with being a father. She knew her son. Knew Daniel would throw himself heart and soul into the relationship. She wasn't sure Grant would meet him halfway.

"Harley?" Grant prompted when she didn't immediately respond.

"I think Daniel should get to know you a little before we break the news that you're his dad." Harley paid careful attention to his expression as she spoke, unsurprised that his features were carved granite.

"You do plan to tell him I'm his father."

"Of course." Harley set her fork down, her appetite departing. "It's just that I'm worried that he'll expect so much from you and it will be more than you're willing to give."

The whole time she'd been speaking, Grant had regarded her in stony silence. Now, as her insinuation hung between them, he frowned. "More than I'm willing to give? What does that mean?"

"I've created a very safe world for Daniel. A place where he's surrounded by friends who love him."

Grant's eyes widened at her frank words. "And you don't think I will love him?"

"That's not what I meant." This was going as badly as she'd imagined. "Look, the way things ended between us... I was devastated."

She regretted the confession even as she offered it. During all the conversations she'd imagined, never once did she think to blurt out that his rejection had broken her heart. What good would it do to share her emotional upheaval when he preferred to address every situation with logic? She was only going to end up frustrated and feeling that he hadn't heard her.

"We spent a weekend together," he reminded her with his typical pragmatism. "The fact that you're still bothered after all this time demonstrates that you were too young for me to have gotten involved with at all."

The ease with which he dismissed what had been a hurtful rejection after an otherwise magical weekend just reinforced that she needed to protect her son.

"You aren't wrong," she agreed. "It's just that at the time I thought you had feelings for me and the way you shut me down really stung. It makes me afraid you'll do the same thing to Daniel without realizing it. He's a sensitive kid with an enormous heart and he might not understand if you approach parenting by applying logic."

"So, you're worried that I'm not in touch with my emotions and Daniel will get hurt because of it?"

She turned her palms up. "I'm not sure yet. Which is why I'm erring on the side of caution."

"I never expected I would be a father," Grant admitted. "But I intend to be a good one."

Harley's chest ached as she acknowledged Grant's vow. "That's all I ask."

Five

Following his dinner with Harley, Grant realized if he intended to spend any extended time with his son, he'd better outfit his home with what a young boy might need.

He'd started by choosing the bedroom next to the master suite so Daniel would be close in case the tyke needed him in the middle of the night. Then he hired a painter, went shopping for furniture and purchased all the toys a four-year-old boy might desire. Normally, when it came to decorating his house, he would hire an interior designer and let the woman work her magic. But this was for his son. He wanted to be the one who personalized the space, and if Harley was impressed that he'd gone out of his way to make sure Daniel felt at home, then all the better.

Harley had mentioned that Daniel was obsessed with horses since coming to Texas, so he decided the boy would enjoy a cowboy-themed room. Imagining Daniel's reaction to each item he selected brought him a rush of pleasure.

Unfortunately, these packages were delivered after his housekeeper, Franny, had left for the day and Grant had arrived home to find an enormous pile of boxes on his porch. He'd barely finished dragging in the last of the packages when Rose paid him an impromptu visit. As she entered his home, her eyes went wide as she surveyed the massive delivery.

"Looks like you bought out the store." His sister noted the names adorning the various packages and added, "Or should I say stores."

Grant shrugged. "It's just a few things."

"What sort of things? Forgive my curiosity," she said, sounding not the least bit apologetic, "but it isn't like you to…shop. And especially not in this sort of volume. What is all this?"

Grant recognized the glint in Rose's eyes and knew that the time had come to tell her about Daniel. "They're toys and things."

"I see." Only from her frown, she obviously didn't. "Are you opening a day care?" The question was ridiculous and both of them knew it, but such was his sister's dry sense of humor. "Okay, stop scowling at me. I was just kidding but you have to admit this is odd… Even for you."

He ignored her fond mockery and expelled his breath in a gusty sigh. "The truth is, I recently found out that I have a son."

Rose regarded him blankly for several seconds as if he'd delivered the punch line of a joke and she was feverishly trying to sort out if it was funny.

"I'm sorry." She gave her head a vigorous shake as if that might put her scattered thoughts back into place. "Did you say you have a *son*?"

"Yes. His name is Daniel." Grant paused, allowing her to catch up. "He's four years old."

"You have a son? Who's four?" His sister furrowed her brow and Grant could see her trying to calculate the timing. "Who's his mother?"

Rose prided herself on being on top of all the gossip in Royal. Being presented with a massive bolt out of the blue like this was guaranteed to drive her crazy and Grant appreciated being one step ahead of her for a change. Several heartbeats passed while Grant watched his sister stew. Then, just as Rose was revving up to pummel him with more questions, Grant dropped his second bombshell.

"Harley Wingate."

If Grant thought this revelation would amaze her, he was dead wrong. Rose snapped her fingers and regarded him in satisfaction.

"I knew it! I knew something had happened between the two of you at the TCC ball five years ago."

Grant expected the next words out of her mouth to be a commentary on the difference in their ages, but once again, Rose surprised him.

"Are you sure the boy is yours?"

"Yes."

She raised one perfectly arched eyebrow at his decisive tone. "You had him tested?"

He lifted his own eyebrow in reply.

"Hmm. I'd heard that Harley was pregnant when she left town and that she refused to name the father." Rose had obviously found much in his news to muse about. "And that she came back to Royal because she's struggling to keep her nonprofit afloat."

"Whatever her reasons, I'm just glad I get the chance to know my son."

His sister barely let him finish before continuing, "Has she spoken to you about financial support?"

Despite his ongoing doubts, Grant immediately jumped

to Harley's defense. "She didn't tell me about my son in the hopes that I'd pay her off."

Rose studied him for a long moment. "Maybe not, but she put half the world between her and Royal and out of the blue she's back. That decision couldn't have been made lightly. I guess you should be glad Wingate Enterprises has been having so much trouble lately or you might never have known you had a son."

This fact wasn't lost on Grant. Had she stayed away so long to avoid him or punish him? Deep down, Grant believed it was the former. Harley wasn't vindictive. But if she assumed his feelings for her hadn't changed, her pride would've prevented her from initiating contact.

But now she was back and their recent kiss had demonstrated their sexual chemistry was as potent as ever. The way they'd both been swept up in the moment promised there would be more such lapses in the future. Pleasure sparked at the thought. Something to look forward to then.

"Did she explain why she waited so long to tell you?" Rose continued.

"Our last encounter ended rather abruptly. She was angry at me when she left town." Once again, regret twisted Grant's gut into knots. If he'd handled things better, would Harley still have fled Royal and taken his son away? "Once Daniel was born, she had a change of heart but learned that I was engaged to Paisley."

Rose nodded as if in approval. "So she took your happiness into consideration when she made her decision. But you and Paisley have been divorced for over a year. Why didn't she tell you sooner?"

"She claims it wasn't a conversation she wanted to have over the phone."

"I guess that makes sense. Besides, it wouldn't be fair to tell you and then keep you from Daniel." His sister looked thoughtful. "Of course, there's another possible reason she delayed. Perhaps she didn't know who the father was?"

"I don't know," Grant admitted. That scenario had also run through his mind, but he'd dismissed it as unimportant. "But it doesn't matter. Daniel is my son."

"I must say, I'm a little surprised that you of all people would've had something like this happen to you."

"Accidents happen."

"Not to you," Rose pointed out. "You are the last man I would've expected to sleep with a teenager, much less get her pregnant."

Five years hadn't dimmed the mix of horror and irritation he'd felt upon discovering what an enormous mistake he'd made. "You don't seriously think I would've gotten involved with an eighteen-year-old if I'd known her age."

Yet, looking back on it now, could he have resisted Harley? He'd been immediately enamored with her at the party. So much so that his brain had completely disengaged. The chemistry between them had been *that* overwhelming. Nor could he say with confidence that if she'd confessed her identity before they'd slept together, he would've walked away. In truth, he suspected that doing the right thing in that moment had been beyond his usually unflinching willpower. Only confronted with being lied to by her had enabled him to push her away.

"You didn't know? But you must've run into her at the TCC clubhouse. You had to have realized who she was before you got together."

"I don't think I did."

"You don't *think*?" she echoed skeptically. "Are you saying that you suspected, but that you ignored your instincts?"

Had he? After that weekend, he'd told himself that never in a million years would he have connected the sexy siren with the Wingate's youngest daughter. Maybe a couple times over the course of their time together he'd noticed her behaving less mature than she appeared, but his actions had run counter to normal, as well. They'd had fun. More fun than he'd let himself enjoy in a long time. Entranced by her brilliant smiles and endearing sense of humor, his serious side had taken a back seat.

"You know me," Grant said. "Have I ever willfully allowed myself to be fooled?"

"No, but maybe you wanted to believe she was closer to your age because you desired her."

"She put on a good act. And I bought it." Yet, he couldn't deny that something happened between them that weekend, something that had shaken him. "But once I found out how young she was, I put an end to it."

"I think it would do you good to date a younger woman. You could use someone fresh and vibrant in your life."

Grant snorted. "What are you saying? That I am stodgy and old?"

"I'm saying that you spend too much time in your head and you work too much. You need a partner."

"I tried that once," he reminded her. "It didn't turn out well."

Rose gave a delicate snort. "I knew from the start that Paisley wasn't the right woman for you." Oblivious to her brother's inner turmoil, she continued, "Her needy dependency drove you away."

Grant regarded his sister in surprise. While Rose hadn't applauded his choice of wife, she'd never voiced any criticism. "She wanted more from me than I could give."

"There was more to it than that. You two had nothing in common."

"We moved in the same social circles." The Everett family was invited to all the charity events held in Royal and Paisley loved attending the balls and parties. In the early months of their marriage, Grant escorted her now and then, but soon returned his energy to his demanding fertility practice.

"You need someone who can help you balance work and play." Rose shot him a sly smile. "Someone who understands how driven you are but who's passionate about her own dreams."

As his sister spoke, Harley's face popped into his mind. Was she that someone? He'd certainly been behaving differently since she'd come home. More so since learning that she'd given birth to his son. Becoming a father had given him new responsibilities and a permanent link to Harley. Suddenly, his future had a fresh, unexpected outlook.

"Someone like Harley," his sister continued as if reading his thoughts. "You are both dedicated to helping women and families. Her nonprofit helps women lift themselves out of poverty. You help women get pregnant and create new families."

"She's too young." The response came out reflexively.

Rose waved her hand. "Men date *and marry* younger women all the time."

As tempting as it was to wonder if he could put aside his bias about their age difference and see where their explosive chemistry would lead, Grant knew better. When it came to his personal life, he struggled to think outside the box and his failed marriage hadn't exactly nudged him toward a more flexible attitude.

"Dating is the last thing I should be thinking about," he said, uncomfortable with the emotions his sister's advice was stirring up. "I need to focus on being a father."

"But have you considered that Harley and her son are

a package deal? You could have both with very little effort on your part."

It was all too much to think about. Before marrying Paisley, he'd never really paid attention to his private life. He'd certainly never had good luck in relationships that would lead him to think a family was in his future. Turns out, he'd been right.

"I think my marriage to Paisley demonstrated that I should stay single."

"That's only because she wasn't right for you. If you marry the woman of your dreams, and open your heart to love, the intimacy you experience will be everything you ever imagined and more."

Rose's suggestion reminded Grant of all those times he'd resisted dropping his guard when Paisley had asked him to share how he was feeling. Tension filled him as he remembered the pain he'd caused her. He hadn't deliberately set out to close himself off from his wife, but the woman he wanted to reveal his deepest thoughts and most vivid emotions to hadn't been Paisley.

Nor was he certain he could ever let himself be vulnerable. Especially when in the past doing so had left him gripped by disappointment.

"It isn't as easy as you make it sound," Grant said, his tone indicating he was done with the conversation.

"I never said it was easy. You're more comfortable with things you can investigate and control. Love isn't like that. You need to take a leap of faith. A bit like your patients do. They trust you to take them from infertile to parents. All I'm asking for you to do is to trust someone and let them take you from loneliness to love."

"Someone?" he probed. *Or Harley Wingate?* He was letting the possibility tempt him more than it should.

"You deserve a woman who will love you despite all your flaws."

Grant took refuge in dry humor. "So now I'm flawed?"

"We all are," his sister said tartly. "The challenge is to find someone who accepts you as you are, warts and all."

Rose spoke as if simply changing everything he believed in would be the keystone to his future happiness. And maybe it was. How often had his patients struggled with fertility issues only to give up and miraculously find themselves pregnant with no help from science?

"Did it ever occur to you that she may not be interested in getting involved with me? After all, she's been doing quite well for herself in Thailand."

"You are handsome, wealthy and successful. I can name a dozen women who would be thrilled if you asked them out. If you made even a little effort, I'm sure Harley Wingate would fall at your feet."

Obviously, Rose assumed that now that Harley was back in Royal, she planned to stay. Grant didn't share his sister's confidence.

"I'll give it some thought," he replied, knowing his sister would continue to pester him until he gave in.

"Good." Rose nodded in satisfaction. "Now, when can I meet Daniel?"

"About that." Irritation flared. "He doesn't know I'm his father yet."

"Why not?"

"Harley wants to wait."

"That's unacceptable," Rose retorted. "That boy's an Everett."

Grant shook his head. "Not legally."

Although he and Harley had not discussed custody, he knew her dedication to her nonprofit's success meant she needed to stay actively involved and that meant returning to Thailand. Pain erupted at the thought of losing his son before he had the chance to get to know him. He needed a plan for keeping Harley and Daniel in Royal. Perhaps he could offer her a bargain. The funding she needed for Zest in exchange for her promise that he could spend as much time with Daniel as he wanted.

Just Daniel? The thought crept out of his subconscious and waved its arms to get his attention. Okay, so he was enjoying spending time with Harley, as well. She was beautiful, smart and injected a joyfulness into his life he hadn't even noticed was lacking.

"That's easily remedied." Rose's gaze grew steely. "Do whatever it takes to make sure you're a part of your son's life."

Harley sat on Jaymes's couch, her feet tucked beneath her while she struggled to stay focused on the dire news story she was reading on her phone. Her stomach roiled as she considered the implications of all the financial reporter had laid out. While she'd known the company's situation was bad, Harley hadn't appreciated the full scope of what was happening. She'd thought their troubles were limited to the negligence lawsuit and DEA investigation into WinJet, but the story she was reading at the moment involved the sizable number of jet contracts that were being canceled.

Maybe if the trouble had been limited to one segment of their business, they might have been able to weather the storm, but Wingate Hotels were under siege as well, as an apparent boycott of the properties had caused people to cancel their reservations. These empty resorts had then fed into the ever-cycling rumors that the hotels were mismanaged and the staff was racing for the door. In fact, Wingate Enterprises had been forced to lay off a significant number of employees based on their lower occupancy. No doubt these frustrated former staffers had been happy to bad-mouth Wingate Hotels.

Harley finished one article and queued up the next. This one proclaimed that with their stock in freefall, the company was so devalued that their assets couldn't even be sold to stop the financial hemorrhaging. As one terrible thing piled on another, the public grew greedy for more stories about the troubled Wingate holdings. Exasperated, Harley tossed her phone to the cushion beside her.

With all the turmoil the family business was in, combined with her current situation with Grant, she felt as if her world was crashing down around her. Was it any surprise that she longed to run back to Thailand and leave it all behind?

"Oh dear, more bad news?" Jaymes asked, setting two cups of tea on the coffee table before sitting beside her on the couch and bumping her shoulder against Harley's in sympathetic affection. "You really need to stop reading those stories. You're only making yourself crazy."

"I'm not sure if I'm upset or relieved that my family hasn't told me about a lot of this. There's nothing I can do to help them and reading all of this news is really upsetting. On the other hand, they always treat me like I'm a baby and that gets old."

As frustrated as Harley was feeling at the moment—and she was far removed from the problems confronting Wingate Enterprises—no doubt her brothers and her mother, who had recently taken a stronger interest in the day-to-day running of the corporation, were at their wits' end.

"They know you can handle yourself," Jaymes told her.

"I might agree with you if I hadn't come home with my tail between my legs after they cut off my financial support for Zest." Thanks to the Wingate wealth, Harley had never had to work a day in her life. "All I've done is rely on Wingate's charitable donations for Zest and my trust fund to live on."

She'd gained access to her personal trust when she turned eighteen. A mixed portfolio of stocks and index funds, it contained enough Wingate Enterprise stock that her net worth had taken a hit thanks to the financial crisis surrounding the family's corporation. Still, even if Wingate Enterprises' stock declined considerably, she would have enough money to live on for the rest of her life, providing she spent carefully.

Moving to Thailand had been spiritually transformative for Harley. She'd taken up meditation and found awakenings in the breathtaking mountain scenery, helpful villagers, even the filthy alleyways and mangy dogs scavenging to stay alive. It was all so different from her life in Texas and she'd decided that instead of living a lavish lifestyle that would certainly ensure that she blew through the trust, she'd pursue a simpler existence and put her energy into philanthropic pursuits.

"You've done a lot more than that," Jaymes said. "Zest has been so successful."

"You have to say that," Harley teased, despite her heavy heart. "You're my best friend."

"And because I love and support you," Jaymes said. "Oh, and guess what? I have good news for you."

"Yay!" Harley faced Jaymes and fastened on a hopeful expression. "I could really use some."

Her friend nodded in understanding. "A college friend of mine who lives in Fort Worth just took a position on the board of a charitable foundation that specializes in women's issues. I mentioned Zest to her, and she would be interested in talking to you about funding. She's available for lunch tomorrow if you can swing it."

"That would be incredible," Harley enthused. "Between that and Beth's charity circuit connections, I might be able to secure lasting funding for Zest."

And then what? Return to her life in Thailand and pretend that she hadn't dropped a bombshell into Grant's life? Part of her reason for coming home had been to tell him he had a son because Daniel needed to know his father. But Harley had been so focused on this drama-inducing event that she hadn't thought about what happened beyond the difficult confession. She hadn't a clue to how he'd react to her being back in his life in a big way. Never expected that he'd kiss her nor that she'd be indulging in daydreams of her and Grant together as…*what*? Lovers? Harley shuddered as longing swept through her. Parents? Of course, because of Daniel, they were bound together for the rest of their lives. But what was she to do with her feelings for him that had resurfaced with a vengeance?

Once upon a time, there had been an amazing, transformative moment for her that had ended before she got a chance to see where it might lead.

Harley thought she'd accepted that she and Grant weren't meant to be together. What if deep down she hadn't given up when he'd declared he wanted nothing more to do with her? Or when she'd left town? Or when she'd heard he'd married Paisley?

Instead, she'd pushed down the fantasy of what could've been, something that had been a lot easier when she'd been living halfway around the world. Now, once again involved with her former lover, she was confronting a dozen conflicting emotions that left her confused and uncertain.

By coming home to tell Grant about Daniel, she'd manufactured another chance to get to know him, to let him get to know her. Did she want to be with him? Harley trembled as the dueling memories of their lovemaking and his rejection played through her mind. The stakes were higher than ever now, with more hearts at risk than just hers.

Her father had been fond of the saying: the greater the risk, the greater the reward. It was at times like these that she missed him the most. He'd been the only member of her family who'd appreciated her bluntness and didn't try to control her spirited ways. His belief in her skills enabled Harley to find the confidence to make Zest happen.

"What are you thinking about?" Jaymes asked, regarding her friend over the rim of her teacup.

"My dad."

"He would've been so proud of you."

Harley cleared her throat and fought down a wave of melancholy. "I wish he'd been well enough to get to know Daniel."

"How would he have felt about Grant being his father?"

"After he got over the shock," Harley said with a half-hearted chuckle, "I think he would've approved."

"So what's next for you and Grant?"

"He's invited us to his house tomorrow to swim and have lunch." She shivered in anticipation of seeing Grant stripped down to his swim trunks. All that bronze skin and hard muscle would be an excellent test of her will-power.

"Oh, dear," Jaymes murmured, her blue eyes reflecting concern. "Are you falling for him again?"

Harley shook her head. "That would be crazy, wouldn't it?"

"Maybe. I don't know. I watched you two at the fund-raiser and he wasn't immune." Jaymes had always moved more cautiously than Harley when it came to romance. "Still, he's barely dated since his marriage ended and word is, he's not looking to get serious with anyone."

"I don't know what I'm thinking," Harley said, waving her hand dismissively. "The only reason I connected with Grant was to tell him about Daniel. As long as he and I can be friendly for the sake of our son, that's good enough for me."

Six

Following his first dinner with Harley, Grant had made dramatic changes to his work schedule to carve out as much time as possible for his son. He had four years to make up for and intended to prove to her how committed he was to being a good father to Daniel.

She'd been clear and forthright with her concerns and although he'd never admit it, not knowing the first thing about being a parent made him anxious. He could learn techniques to raise well-rounded children and read articles listing scientific tips that would enable Daniel to grow up happy and healthy, but eventually he'd have to set aside the reading material and put the advice into practice.

To that end, Grant invited Harley and Daniel over to get better acquainted. The pair arrived promptly at ten o'clock already dressed in swimsuits, eager to escape the August heat with a refreshing plunge in the pool. To Grant's shock, Daniel launched himself across the pool deck and into the water. The spray hit Grant's chest and thighs as the boy's head disappeared beneath the surface. He jumped into the water to rescue his son only to see the four-year-old pop up like a cork.

"Sorry," Harley called, amusement making her eyes twinkle even as she struggled to keep her expression contrite. "I should've warned you that he's part fish."

"So he can swim." Grant kept Daniel in his sights as he ran shaky fingers through his hair. He backed toward the edge of the pool.

"I started teaching him when he was a baby." Harley had stripped off her light cotton dress to reveal a modest two-piece before coming to sit near Grant. She dangled her feet in the water and smiled as she watched her son. "Jaymes and Sean don't have a pool so he was really excited that he could come here and swim."

Irresistibly drawn toward Harley, Grant shifted closer and rested his elbows on the sun-warmed tile that ran around the rim until his right arm was an inch from her slender thigh. The hot sun had warmed her skin, releasing the faint tang of sunscreen. Contentment suffused him as he gathered the scent into his lungs.

"You're both welcome anytime," he offered. "Even if I'm not here. I'll give you the code to the front door and let Franny know you will be using the pool."

Harley scissored her legs, stirring the water. "I wouldn't want to impose."

"Daniel belongs here," he insisted, keeping his voice low so only she heard. "And I want you to feel comfortable, as well."

"That's really nice of you," Harley murmured. "And Daniel will be thrilled to swim whenever he wants."

Grant glanced at Harley's profile, drinking in her fond expression as her gaze lingered on her son. Although Grant knew he should focus on Daniel as well, being close to her awakened strong cravings. He wanted to pull her into his arms and savor the yielding softness of her body. The urge to touch her was only partially sexual in nature. He longed to reconnect with her and physical contact was an easy way to communicate his desire for her company.

"Tell me about your life in Thailand," he said, curious to discover how she and Daniel had been living.

"Sure, what do you want to know?"

"Start with why you ended up there."

She smiled. "Aside from the fact that it's a fascinating country, it has a relatively inexpensive cost of living, which has attracted a lot of foreigners. You can't beat the tropical climate and modern conveniences are readily available, including good medical care. On top of that, the Thai people are incredibly friendly, and the scenery is absolutely gorgeous. I love how exotic it is with the brightly colored markets and the ancient temples, and yet I can go to an English-speaking movie on a whim."

"Sounds like the best of both worlds," he said. "Where did you live?"

"For the last year, I've been renting a small house in Hua Hin. It's a seaside town two and a half hours from Bangkok where Thailand's royal family built a summer palace in the twenties. It has beautiful beaches, great seafood restaurants and a jazz festival, but what I love most of all is the small-town feel and the sense of community among the expats."

Grant was surprised to discover that her description stirred his interest. He'd never considered living abroad, but she was definitely making a case for immersing himself in other cultures.

"You sound like you miss it," he declared, this realization sparking concern about her future plans. How long would he have with Daniel before she was drawn back there?

"I really do. The country's long history means there's so much to learn and explore. The slower pace and our simpler lifestyle really allowed me to tap into my spiritual side."

"I have to admit, you seem very different from the girl I met at the TCC ball."

Only the tiniest twitch of muscles at the corner of her eyes indicated that she'd been bothered by his use of the term *girl* instead of woman to describe her.

"Oh, I'm that." Self-deprecation shaded her smile. "Back then I was spoiled and selfish. Seeing for myself how happy people are who have so much less than I do has really changed my perspective. It's why I decided to live a much more minimalistic lifestyle. I don't scrimp on anything for Daniel, but why spend a hundred dollars on a meal when I can visit a street vendor and get a delicious bowl of noodles for a handful of coins?"

Daniel swam up to them and latched on to his mother's legs. "Come swimming, Mommy," the boy demanded. "I want you to throw me."

"I'm a little tired," she said, glancing Grant's way. "And I'll bet he can throw you much farther than I ever could."

"But I want you."

Mother and son locked gazes like a pair of dueling swordsmen while an unspoken argument raged between them. The intense bond between mother and son reminded Grant that Harley was raising her child by herself in a foreign country. He—who'd never felt particularly understood or supported by his parents, a fish out of water amongst his own family—envied what Harley had with Daniel.

The strength of his feelings only intensified his discomfort. He'd never expected to have a family of his own and never imagined enjoying such a tight bond with another person. Nor until this minute had he ever wondered what it would be like to know someone so intimately that you recognized what they were thinking. Fearing rejection, he'd shied away from opening himself up to such an potent connection. Yet, by cloaking himself in detachment, he'd achieved the same results. He was alone.

Raw emotion sliced through his chest in the second before Daniel nodded and turned an enticing smile on Grant.

"Can you throw me really far?"

Given Daniel's reserve toward him when they met at the clinic, Grant had anticipated a long stretch of winning over the boy. Instead, it seemed all it took to get into his son's good graces was a swimming pool and a willingness to play.

Grant gave his son an impish grin. "I sure can."

After an hour of horseplay, Daniel and Grant emerged from the pool to torment Harley by shaking their wet heads and showering her with chilly droplets. She shrieked in dismay and scrambled out of reach. Half an hour earlier, she'd retreated to one of the lounge chairs, giving Grant space to be with his son. As much as he appreciated the uninterrupted opportunity to bond with Daniel, Grant felt as if her absence had made his joy incomplete. Now, however, as her rich laughter wrapped around him like an affectionate hug, he basked in the good fortune that had brought her back into his life.

They retreated to the covered patio where his housekeeper had set up lunch. Daniel dominated the meal with chatter about his visit the prior day to the Owens family ranch where Harley's best friend Jaymes was raised.

"I'm going to be a cowboy when I grow up," Daniel announced. "Just like Sam."

"The Owens' foreman," Harley explained, catching

Grant's confused expression. "He gave Daniel his first riding lesson and claims he's a natural."

"We're going back next week," Daniel continued. "Mom said we could go on a trail ride. You should come, too."

Grant doubted his son had any idea how much he appreciated being included. "As long as it's okay with your mom," he hedged, glancing toward Harley. To his surprise, she looked agreeable.

"Do you ride?" she asked.

"It's been a while. Growing up, I used to spend my summers at my uncle's ranch just outside of Abilene."

"Come riding. Come riding," Daniel crowed.

Grant smiled at his son. "I'd like that."

"Then it's settled," Harley said. "And now, I think we should be going. Someone is due for a nap."

"No," Daniel wailed. "I wanna swim some more."

"You can stay if you want," Grant offered, reluctant for their time to end.

Harley shook her head. "He should nap before any more swimming."

"I have several guest rooms available." Grant could see protests building in Harley's expression. "I'd love it if you'd stay," he murmured, fighting the urge to reach for her hand.

During their weekend together, they'd been inseparable, finding a thousand excuses to touch and snuggle during the long hours in the hotel suite. He'd never been so obsessed with staying connected to anyone before, and after she'd fled on Monday morning, he'd ached at being parted from her.

In the intervening years, he'd used his anger at her for deceiving him to blunt his need. Until she'd reappeared in Royal, he'd believed her thoroughly purged from his system. Yet all it had taken was being in the same room with her for the cravings to start in again. Only this time the stakes were higher. He couldn't eject her from his life on a whim. They shared a son. That meant he would have to figure out what he wanted, make a plan and stick to it.

"I guess we could stay." Harley glanced away from Grant and fixed her son with a firm stare. "As long as Daniel promises to sleep."

"I will, Mommy. I promise."

After lunch, Grant led the way to one of his many guest rooms and left Harley to change her son into dry clothes and settle him for a nap. Seeing that Franny was clearing their lunch dishes, he headed into his den to check on the test results for several of his patients. To his surprise, Harley appeared in the doorway before he'd finished composing follow-up emails to his staff.

"That was fast," he remarked.

"He's really good about going to bed. He plays hard and sleeps hard," she said, waving her hands as he got to his feet. "I didn't mean to interrupt you. I just wanted to let you know that he'll probably sleep for about an hour. Please keep working. I'm going to sit by the pool."

Grant circled the desk and headed her way. "I'd rather keep you company," he replied, meaning every word. "How about we grab some sweet tea first."

"Sure."

The kitchen was both pristine and empty when they entered it. Earlier, his housekeeper had indicated she was going to spend the afternoon running errands and he suspected that he and Harley were alone. Anticipation sizzled through him.

"The glasses are there."

He pointed to a cabinet, and then selected a knife and pulled out a cutting board. As if by design, they converged on the refrigerator, Grant in search of lemons and the pitcher of sweet tea, Harley looking to fill the glasses with ice. Their bare arms grazed and that was enough to spark the wildfire chemistry between them.

"Harley."

All too aware that groaning her name betrayed his sharp need, Grant captured her narrow hips between his hands and backed her against the counter. He dipped his head and stroked his lips across hers once, twice, coaxing her to surrender. His body sang with pleasure as her bones melted and her arms went around his neck,

"We can't." She shook her head.

"You said Daniel was asleep."

"Daniel isn't the problem."

"Then what is?" He rocked his hips forward. Desire pooled in his belly as he nudged her with his erection.

She gasped, tightened her fingers on his shoulders, but leaned away from his questing lips. "We can't keep going down this road."

"Because?"

"Because…it has nowhere to go. Remember?"

Her words revived the argument they'd had half a decade earlier when he'd been the one who'd made a dramatic speech about how the difference in their ages made a relationship between them impossible. He'd been convinced that both of them would be subjected to scorn and criticism if they went public with their romantic connection.

"I do."

"Has anything changed?" she demanded. "Are you any more willing to be romantically linked to someone my age than you were five years ago?"

"You were eighteen back then. It's different now. And you're the mother of my son. That's going to get around. Plus," he continued, ignoring her reference to romance and focusing on the physical desire that sparked whenever they occupied the same room. "It's pretty obvious that the attraction between us is alive and well."

"What happened to *we aren't suited to each other in the least*?" she countered in a neutral tone, her lowered lashes hiding the expression in her green eyes.

"Back then, I spoke harshly," Grant admitted, taking responsibility for his extreme reaction. "It's not that we aren't suited to each other, it's more that I'm not any woman's ideal partner." His voice grew earnest as he continued to explain. "Women crave romance. I forget about birthdays and anniversaries. You yearn for flowery gestures and sentimentality. To be swept off your feet and adored. The best a woman can hope for from me is the occasional expensive dinner where I'm not preoccupied by work." He paused and gave a little shrug. "And great sex. Although I think you already know that."

"I get it," she muttered bitterly. "You don't want to be bothered by any romantic entanglements." She worried her lower lip as she studied him. "So, I need to decide if a sexual relationship is enough for me."

He nodded, even as he suspected that attempting a relationship of any kind with Harley—even a strictly physical one—would end in disaster. Still, seeing her disappointment, he felt compelled to draw her into his arms and comfort her with gentle hugs and slow sweeping kisses.

Of course, to do that would give her the wrong impression.

Grant shifted his hands until they gripped the counter on either side of her hips, and then pushed his arms straight. Once he was no longer touching her, some of the fog cleared from his brain.

"And if I need more?" she asked.

"Then we have a problem because I can't keep my hands

off you," he admitted gruffly. "And I think you feel the same."

She spent several seconds considering what he'd said before sighing. "No, I suppose you're right. But I'm not the same impulsive girl you once knew. I'm not going to fall into bed with you because I get swept up in the moment."

"So you'll need some convincing." He wasn't at all opposed to expending considerable effort winning her over. "That sounds like it'll be fun for both of us."

"Fun." Harley set her hands on his chest and applied firm pressure until he backed up a step. "You really are an impossible man."

In the days following the first visit at Grant's house, Daniel talked nonstop about swimming and how they were all going on a trail ride in the near future. While Harley was gratified that her son had bonded so readily with Grant, she still grappled with the uncertainty of how he would react when they broke the news that Grant was his father. Knowing the longer she waited, the more confused Daniel would be, she'd decided the time had come for revelations.

Now, however, as she stood on Grant's front porch, anxiety compressed her chest, forcing her breath into shallow gasps. In minutes, everything in her son's life would change. Tears came out of nowhere, threatening to derail her plans. Part of her wanted to snatch up Daniel and head for the nearest airport. Even as the impulse assailed her, Harley held her ground. She had no idea if keeping father and son apart so far had created any lasting damage, but to keep doing so would not make the situation better for anyone.

"Ouch, Mommy," Daniel exclaimed, tugging to free

his hand from his mother's grasp. "You're holding me too hard."

Mortified, Harley tore her gaze away from the substantial wood door in front of her and glanced down at her son. She spied his pained expression and loosened her grip immediately. Dropping to her knees before him, she cupped his dear face in her palms.

"I'm so sorry," she crooned, grazing his soft cheek with her thumbs. "I didn't realize I was hurting you."

He patted her cheek in sweet affection and smiled. "It's okay, Mommy. I love you."

Harley swallowed past the lump in her throat, wondering what she'd done right to deserve such a wonderful son. "I love you, too," she whispered, overcome with love.

Ever since becoming a mother, Harley noticed that her emotions bubbled close to the surface. Before Daniel came along, she'd been a selfish, frivolous teenager. Now, at least once a day he did something that touched her deeply.

Beside her, the front door opened and Grant's long legs appeared in her peripheral vision. Daniel glanced up at his father and Harley braced herself for Grant's impact on hers and Daniel's lives going forward.

"Is everything okay?" he asked.

Sucking in a steadying breath, Harley blinked away tears. "It's all fine," she said, pummeled by uncertainty. "Just a little mother-and-son bonding,"

Grant extended a hand to assist her to her feet. She hesitated only a second before accepting his help and caught her breath as her skin came into contact with his. She glanced up at his shuttered expression, cursing that her raw emotions doubled the impact of Grant's potent masculinity. Longing hit her like a sucker punch to the gut and she extricated herself from his grip with more speed than finesse.

Their conversation during her previous visit had rattled her more than she'd let on. Rattled. *And* tempted. But she wasn't an impulsive teenager anymore. She couldn't just jump into bed with a man because his rare smiles inspired flirtatious banter while his heated gaze sent goose bumps chasing over her skin.

Harley ground her teeth and fought to suppress the warmth pooling in her belly. Before finding out about Daniel, he'd made his position perfectly clear. He wanted nothing more to do with her. As he had five years earlier, she'd assumed that once he'd made up his mind, nothing would change it. And then he'd learned she'd given birth to his son. Apparently, he'd taken this to mean she wouldn't be so easy to dismiss. Still, he'd taken things farther than she'd ever imagined. His suggestion that they rekindle their sexual relationship had caught her off guard.

Her first reaction had been to reject it. Getting over him the first time had taken forever and they'd only been together for two days. How much deeper would she fall if she spent weeks or months with him? Yet, to deny herself more of the most amazing sex of her life didn't make sense, either.

"I thought we'd barbecue tonight," Grant said, as he and Harley followed Daniel toward the pool. "And maybe watch a movie later."

"I'm sure Daniel would love that." As her son jumped into the pool, Harley settled onto the lounge chair she'd occupied the last time. Grant sat down beside her, his long legs filling the space between them. She opened her mouth, intending to share her plan to explain over dinner that he was Daniel's dad, but Grant spoke first.

"I intend to tell Daniel that I'm his father tonight."

"Oh." Although they were both on the same page, for some reason Grant's assertive tone raised her hackles.

"The longer I wait, the more confusing it will be for him," he continued, his set expression indicating he intended to get his way. "I know you came home to find funding for Zest and I'm prepared to help you with that."

Help her how? His offer had the sound of a negotiating tactic. "And in exchange for what?"

"I want to get to know my son."

Harley crossed her arms over her chest, the muscles in her jaw bunching. "I'm not standing in the way of that."

"Not at the moment, but it seems to me that if Wingate Enterprises wasn't having financial troubles, I never would've found out about Daniel."

Grant's disapproval hit her like a sledgehammer. Driven by his criticism of her decision to keep him in the dark about Daniel and haunted by the humiliation she'd felt at his rejection, her temper spiked.

"You've rather conveniently forgotten that you made it perfectly clear that you wanted nothing more to do with me. Now you're blaming me for taking you at your word?"

"That's a terrible excuse and you know it."

"I don't know that." She strove to keep her voice low so their argument wouldn't carry over to Daniel.

If she were honest, she recognized that keeping the truth from him had been selfish. She loved her life overseas and had worried that if Grant knew, he'd force her to come home so they could share custody. She wasn't ready to give up their life in Thailand.

"You should've told me you were pregnant."

"What would you have done?" she taunted, making no effort to hide her bitterness. "Marry me?"

The question came out of nowhere, followed by a wild half laugh that used up all the air in her lungs. When she tried to inhale, Harley found her chest too tight to draw in a new breath.

Shutters slammed over Grant's expression. "Since you left town without telling me I was going to be a father, the point is moot."

Harley cursed the man's fortified walls, battlements and parapets that offered him abundant protection from where he could lob blame bombs at her. What made it worse was that she hadn't taken the high road five years ago and was stuck defending the inexcusable. She shouldn't have kept Daniel a secret from him.

"So, what are you proposing?"

"I intend to be a father to Daniel. To keep you from interfering in that, I'll give you the money you need to fund Zest."

His proposal blew her away. She'd thought maybe he'd offer to intercede on her behalf with the charitable foundation his family ran. Instead, he was promising to solve all her financial problems. She should've felt relieved, but Harley wondered if using her son as a bargaining chip would one day blow up in her face.

"How could I refuse," she bit out and instead of letting him see her turmoil, she forced a laugh. "But you could've saved yourself a whole lot of money."

Since returning to Royal, she'd had to face the reality that keeping Daniel a secret from Grant had been a mistake she could never fix. She hadn't known enough about him when they first met to know if he was interested in being a father. Although, to be fair, she wondered if Grant had any sense that having a son would change his life for the better.

He cocked his head and regarded her solemnly. "What are you saying?"

"All I needed was for you to hit me with a sentimental plea about how Daniel deserves to know you're his dad and how committed you are to being a father."

"So why have you been putting off telling him who I am?"

"When it comes right down to it, I'm selfish and a bit insecure." Noting Grant's surprise at her admission, she shrugged. "For the last four years, I've been the most important person in Daniel's life. There's a part of me that doesn't want to share him with anyone. Even when I know that he needs his father in his life. As for the money you offered, I can't accept."

"Why not?"

Harley glanced toward Daniel. "Neither my son nor I are for sale."

"I'm sorry." He reached out and took her hand in his.

The argument with Grant had chilled her, but with the hot August afternoon sun beating down, combined with the warmth of his skin against hers, Harley noticed a distinct uptick in her temperature. It took all her willpower to pull her hand free.

She smiled to cover her reluctance. "When it comes to Daniel, I only want what's best for him. That's why I told you he's your son. If I didn't want you in his life, I could've kept quiet."

"You're right." The regret on his face was a stark contrast to his earlier antagonism. "I could've handled that better."

With his apology, Harley understood that anxiety had caused him to overplay his hand. Her situation would be a lot less complicated if he'd declined to exercise his paternal rights, but she also realized that part of her was elated at the idea that Grant wanted a relationship with Daniel. After their conversation a few days earlier, she'd hoped he'd want a relationship with her, as well. He'd been clear it wouldn't be a romantic one, but sex and friendship were a tempting combination.

"But my offer to fund Zest still stands."

Harley considered this for a moment before offering him a small smile. "Thank you. I may take you up on that in the future, but right now, I have some leads I'm hoping will pan out." Her chest ached as she drew breath and called to Daniel. He raced over and she wrapped his wet body in a towel. Sitting him on the lounge beside her, facing Grant, Harley rallied her courage. "Daniel, Dr. Everett and I have something to tell you."

Pool water spiked the long black lashes framing her son's green eyes as he fixed his gaze on her. "What?"

"You remember how we went to his office so he could collect some cells from your cheek? Well, that was so he could run a test to prove that he's your father."

Daniel shifted his attention to the somber man across from him. "You're my dad?"

"I am," Grant intoned, leaning forward.

"Cool." Daniel jumped to his feet. "Can I have a snack? I'm starving."

Harley smothered a grin at Grant's surprise over his son's easy acceptance of his new role in the boy's life. *Welcome to parenthood*, she thought, *where there's a surprise around every corner.*

Seven

Snuggled on the couch in Grant's family room, Harley pondered how many hours she'd spent here over the last week, watching kids shows and movies with Daniel tucked between her and Grant. In addition to such quiet activities, the trio had gone horseback riding, visited a local petting zoo, eaten a dozen meals together and logged tons of hours escaping the August heat wave in Grant's pool.

Initially, she'd assumed that only Grant and Daniel would participate in these father-son bonding activities, but Daniel had insisted she join them and Grant hadn't appeared to mind. Being included in their outings gave her precious time with her son and allowed her to watch the connection strengthen between Grant and Daniel. Realizing that Daniel's capacity to love knew no limits, she'd stopped fussing about sharing her son with Grant and let herself enjoy the sense of belonging their little "family" brought her.

"I should probably get going," Harley said when the movie ended, reluctance shading every syllable.

Although he'd napped several times in the bedroom Grant had designed for him, this was the first time Daniel was spending the night and Harley didn't want to interfere with Grant establishing a bedtime routine.

"Don't leave, Mommy," Daniel demanded, throwing himself into her lap and wrapping his arms tight around her neck in an uncharacteristic display of neediness. "Sleep here."

"I need to sleep in my own bed, just like you do." Harley hugged him, but kept her voice firm. "Remember, you said you wanted to spend the night with your dad, and then go fishing with him in the morning."

Daniel's expression brightened as he sat back and looked up at Grant. "Can Mommy come fishing?"

"Mommy doesn't like fishing," Harley said, making a big show of wrinkling her nose so that Daniel laughed. "I'll see you after lunch and you can tell me how many fish you caught then. Now, off to bed."

She eased her son into a standing position and her heart ached as his gaze clung to her. They'd already discussed that Grant would be the one to walk him through the bedtime ritual, but Daniel wasn't completely ready to give up his reliance on his mother.

"Will you stay until I fall asleep?"

"Of course."

Harley kept a reassuring smile on her face as Grant scooped up Daniel and carried him off to bed. To keep herself busy until his return, Harley moved the empty popcorn bowl and glasses to the kitchen. She handwashed everything, returned each item to its proper place and wiped down the already pristine countertops. Half an hour later, Grant found her perched on the stool in the dimly lit kitchen, her purse over her shoulder, keys in her hand, all too aware that if she didn't make a hasty exit, she ran the risk of doing something she might regret.

"How'd it go?" she asked, slipping off the stool as Grant drew near. "Did he give you any trouble?"

"Not a bit. In fact, he was asleep when I left."

"I'm glad." Her heart began to pound at the intent look on Grant's face. "I guess I'd better get going, then."

"Or you could stay a while and keep me company."

"I'm sure you have things to do." She considered protesting as he stripped her of purse and keys, but then he ran his knuckles over her cheek and the soft caress set her hormones to humming.

"So, that convincing we talked about last week," Grant murmured. "I'm ready to get started."

She sucked in a sharp breath, determined to utter something sensible and levelheaded that would stop them both cold, but then she made the mistake of meeting his gaze. One glimpse of his ravenous need and her mind froze.

In the split-second window between one heartbeat and another, something hot and raw exploded in her. Harley snatched a handful of his shirt, ready to tear the damned thing off him if necessary.

"I really don't need any convincing," she whispered, driven by fear and wanton hunger. "I need you. Don't make me beg."

While it would've been easier for her to step into his space and press herself against him, with her blood running hot and wild, she yanked him toward her. Their bodies collided with incendiary results.

"Harley," Grant groaned, his husky voice driving her pulse to reckless speeds. He tangled one hand in her hair and searched her expression with feverish intensity. "I've been dying to do this all week."

An instant later, he slid his hand to the small of her back and pulled her hips tight against his. His mouth landed on hers in a frenzy of hard ardent kisses that set fire to her dignity. Propriety be damned. She didn't care what he thought of her in this moment or how he might spin this later. His lips were on hers and the most important thing in this moment was the rightness of his tongue sweeping around hers in a sexy dance of desire.

She wrapped her arms around his neck and tunneled her fingers into his hair, pressing her breasts against his strong, solid chest. Everywhere they touched, she burned, but she craved the mesmerizing friction of his skin against hers. The smooth and rough texture of his naked thigh as she slid her legs around him. The satiny glide of his abs against her belly as he thrust into her.

The pleasure washing through her swept away old heart-break. She snatched a fistful of his shirt again and yanked until the hem cleared the waistband of his pants. A purr rumbled in her throat as her hand slid into the gap between the fabrics and encountered his hot skin. She swept her palm over his side, fingertips riding the waves of his ribs to the hard lines of his chest. Beneath her questing caress, his nipple hardened and both of them groaned in appreciation.

Grant tugged at her hair, coaxing her to change the angle of her head. His lips skimmed along her neck, trailing fiery kisses. She quaked at the nip of his even white teeth, her hips bucking into his. He lightly palmed her breast through her thin blouse, finger tracing the top edge of her lace bra through the material. His teasing provoked a husky protest from her throat, but then her complaint turned to encouragement as he applied more pressure. Her nipples contracted as pleasure washed through her and she arched her back to drive her hips into the hard ridge below his belt. The ache thrumming between her thighs grew more impatient with each passing second. And as the primal need to meld with him dominated her, she was moments away from wrestling him to the floor and mounting him.

Harley gasped as he sucked on the place where her shoulder met her neck. Her breath caught one second, and gusted it out in the next as he rolled her nipple between his fingertips and pinched lightly. His mouth settled back on hers again as every nerve in her body screamed in ever-escalating delight.

They made their way down the hall, Grant walking backward, his fingers hooked over her hip while she made short work of his shirt buttons. By the time they reached the open door of the master bedroom, she was ready to slide the shirt off his shoulders and spread her hands over his gorgeous rock-hard abs. Determined not to be interrupted, she snagged her foot around the door and nudged it shut.

As the latch engaged, Grant stepped forward and backed her against the panel. From the fierce expression on his face, she expected his demanding, urgent kisses to begin again. Instead, he set one hand above her shoulder and grazed his knuckles across her cheek, plumbing her expression like a man desperate for answers.

No other man had ever been able to melt her with just one look. She ran the tips of her fingers down his chest, exploring the dips and ridges of solid muscle. His nostrils flared as he held himself still beneath her touch, but his breath grew more ragged as her investigation took her lower. Nevertheless, he remained immobile while she settled her lips into the hollow of his throat, flicking her tongue over his hot skin. The scent of him intoxicated her. She grazed her nail over one tight nipple and a harsh sound broke from his chest.

Knowing exactly what she wanted, Harley found the buckle of his belt and began fumbling to unfasten it. Before she finished, Grant slid his hands to the back of her thighs behind her knees and lifted her off her feet. She wrapped her legs around him, moaning as the hard swell of his erection pressed between her thighs.

She wriggled her hips in an effort to intensify the contact, craving the all-consuming bliss of being possessed by him, the delicious fullness as he slid inside her. With her clinging to him, Grant pushed away from the door and walked her to his bed. Their kiss broke as he bent and laid her down. As much as she wanted to shed their clothes, part of her was fearful of what would happen if he escaped her arms and so she maintained her tight grip. Grant lowered his weight onto her, pressing her into the mattress. Her hips rocked, frustration and pleasure building at the warm, wet skate of his mouth over her collarbone and down between her breasts.

Half a decade had passed since the two days and nights they'd spent together, but their bodies were as attuned in this moment as if they had spent the last five years in the same passionate dance.

His fingers slipped beneath the hem of her top, shifting the fabric upward, baring her lacy bra to his gaze. Eager for what was to come, Harley shimmied beneath him. Desire flared hot, and then hotter still. Her skin flushed and dampened until she was uncomfortable within the confines of her clothes.

Pinned as she was beneath his hard body, she lacked the leverage to strip away the clothing that prevented their skin from making contact. She dove questing fingers beneath his shirt to the warm silk of his skin. Powerful muscle shifted beneath her palm as she pressed him closer. She savored the crush of his hard body as he shifted her bra and released her tight nipple. He murmured something unintelligible before sucking the tender bud between his lips. The tug of his mouth on her breast sent a shot of pure lust straight to her groin. Heat pooled in her belly and she rubbed her thighs together as an insistent ache built to the point of pain.

Recognizing her sharp need, he sent his hand riding along her thigh, spreading her wide and trailing his fingers between her legs. She cursed the fabric barrier that blocked him from touching her bare flesh even as her lips parted to beg him to stop the torment. But the glide of his mouth over sensitive spots on her throat and beneath her ear left her little breath for words.

In the end, it was Grant who stripped them both bare. First her with gentle, trembling fingers that tugged and slid and, in the case of her underwear, tore everything off her before shedding his own clothes, fetching a condom out of the nightstand, and then with an obvious effort of will, stood beside the bed and let his gaze trail over her naked form.

She let him drink his fill for the span of time it took to devour his broad shoulders, sculpted chest, washboard abs, narrow hips and powerful thighs all breathtakingly defined by ropy muscle beneath bronze skin. Harley lifted her foot and trailed it up the side of his thigh. A dusting of fine black hair tickled her skin, making her smile. She held her arms out to him, coaxing him to her with a welcoming smile.

"I've waited five years for this," she said, seeing the way his eyes flared at the raw need clawing her voice. "Don't make me wait a second more."

Grant sent his gaze roaming over her naked form, his body hardening as he appreciated her lean perfection.

She was slender with small breasts, a tiny waist and narrow hips. Her dusky pink nipples caught his eye and he couldn't wait to swirl his tongue around the sweet, tight buds before devouring them. She shifted under his gaze, her breath hitching.

With a sigh of surrender, he joined her on the mattress. More often than he liked, he'd looked back on the weekend they spent together, recalling how she'd gone from sweet and shy, every inch of her skin impossibly sensitive, to a temptress who'd mastered the power at her disposal and made him lose control.

She sent her fingers tunneling into his hair as he pressed down on her and offered him a poignant smile. "Despite everything that's happened, there's no one like you."

He should've stopped to assess her statement. The deep, insightful truth of her heart awaited him within her words, but at the moment his palms were skimming over her ribs and trailing across the trembling muscles of her stomach, pausing at the edge of the perfectly manicured strip of hair that covered her mound.

"You are so damned beautiful." His voice rasped over the compliment and she smiled at him from beneath her long lashes.

"I've missed this."

"So have I," he admitted, surrendering to the flames licking through him.

Her grip tightened fiercely, nails digging into his skin, as his lips followed the path his fingers had taken moments before. Only this time, he didn't pause his downward track, but followed the seam where her legs connected to her body. His tongue tantalized her, wrenching a cry of frustration from her throat. Grinning at her impatience, he kissed his way along her inner thigh to her core, drawing her aroused scent deep into his lungs.

"I need more," she declared, rotating her hips in search of satisfaction.

Knowing what she wanted, he gave her more. Settling his shoulders between her thighs, spreading her knees far apart, opening her to him, he delicately parted the folds that kept her delicious core hidden. Bare to his sight, touch and taste, her head thrashed against the mattress as her anticipation grew. A moment later, her whole body went rigid as he flicked his tongue around her clit.

Her back arched and a hoarse moan broke from her throat as he dragged his thumb through the wetness gathering between her thighs. She flung her arms wide and grabbed handfuls of the coverlet as if only by hanging on for dear life could she survive the blissful sensations tearing at her.

Grant lost himself in the sounds, smells and tastes of her, plying her with his tongue and lips as one wrenching cry after another escaped her. Past and present collided as he drove her toward her orgasm. Time hadn't dimmed his memories of their days together. He recalled every caress, knew exactly what to do to make her wild and recognized the significance of her restless, shifting hips. The tension in her muscles rose to bowstring tautness until she thrashed against his mouth.

"You know what I love." The words poured from her lips as her body began to shake with tremors of pleasure. "Oh, yes. Like that…"

A curse slipped from her lips as her torso bucked. Determined to bring her to an acute state of rapture, Grant kept up his relentless pursuit of her pleasure, pushing her hard into her rising orgasm.

"I'm coming."

Her chest worked like a bellows as her back arched. With his eyes closed, he relished the series of quakes that wracked her. He dug his fingers into her soft flesh, holding her tight against his mouth as the sounds emanating from her grew positively frantic. Not until he heard her weak chuckle followed by a satisfied purr did he ease away.

Slowly, lazily, as if what she had just gone through left her too spent to move, she lifted her long lashes. Beneath the thick fringe, her dazed green eyes rested on his smug grin. An acknowledging smile tweaked the corner of her lips.

"You're incredibly good at that." As he dusted kisses across her abdomen, she propped herself on one elbow and reached out with her free hand to run her fingers through his mussed hair. "You were my first, you know."

Grant's head jerked up at the confession. "You weren't a virgin," he said, certain he would've known.

"No." She laughed. "But no one had ever gone down on me before." Her lashes lowered as she watched him. "And I'd never gone down on anyone before you."

"I guess you had quite an education that weekend." He smirked at her, choosing not to remark on how he'd guessed at her lack of experience given how shy and awkward she'd behaved as he'd introduced her to various pleasures.

"I certainly did." Suddenly, she twisted from beneath him and, taking advantage of his surprise, rolled him onto his back. "Let's see if I remember any of the lessons I learned."

Her long hair tickled over his shoulders and chest as she trailed her lips over his skin. She toyed with his nipples, coasting her fingertips over them until they peaked and then further stimulating them with the edge of her nails. The enticing discomfort broke open the floodgates of his need, sending what was left of his blood straight to his already painful erection.

That she knew how much he ached for her was obvious in the way she kept her hands away from where he wanted her touch. If his eyes weren't shut, no doubt he'd see a sassy smile curving her gorgeous lips. Realizing what he was missing out on, he pried his lids up. She'd shaken her hair back from her face and her gaze was roaming from his expression to his erection.

Seizing her lower lip between her teeth, she regarded his jutting hard-on with unabashed feminine appreciation. He could see the wheels spinning in her brain, anticipated her next move. Even so, his whole body quaked as her delicate fingers dipped into the damp heat between her thighs before spreading the wetness over him.

Doubly blown away by the brazenness of her actions and the searing sparks that cascaded through his body as she caught the bead of liquid on a fingertip and circled it over the pulsing head of his erection, blending his arousal with hers, the pressure in him built so rapidly that he nearly lost control.

He covered the hand that rested on him, clamping down to stop her movements. His thumping heartbeat sent blood slamming through his veins as he struggled to push down his surging need.

"Stop!" He gasped the word out.

At the desperation in his voice, her gaze flew to his and held. As if she wanted to mind meld with him in an urgent need to convey all that was in her brain without speaking it out loud. It was at that moment that he recalled how by the end of the weekend they'd come close to reading each other's thoughts. How he anticipated where on her body she craved his mouth. How she knew exactly what drove him mad.

But that had been communication between lovers who'd been intimate multiple times over the weekend. It just made sense that they figured each other out. It hadn't been a connection. That was silly. He didn't believe in fate or that couples were meant to be. Relationships took work and commitment based on shared values. Some intangible, spiritual bond that made people act like fools…that sort of thing he left to the romantics.

"Let me do this for you."

"Harley." He reached out to cup her face in his palm. "If you do this…then I can't…we can't."

"Then later," she said, and he wasn't sure if it was a threat or a promise as she reached toward the nightstand and the awaiting condom.

Snagging it with her fingers, she clamped the edge of the foil packet between her teeth and tore it open. Seconds later, she'd straddled him and was rolling the protection on. Grant trailed his fingers along her thigh, over her flat belly and circled her high small breasts, eager for the joining they both wanted so desperately.

With her gaze glued to his expression, she positioned herself above him. Anticipation licked across his nerve endings as he lifted his hands, palms facing her, fingers spread in invitation. Her lips softened into a breathtaking smile as she meshed her fingers with his, and then lowered herself onto him in a sharp deliberate move that left them both gasping.

He swore as her snug heat settled around him, hissing the curse through clenched teeth. He'd forgotten how perfect they fit. No, he hadn't forgotten. He'd blocked it out. To recall the beauty of their connection and the intense, all-consuming hunger that rose up inside him was to leave him grappling with doubt over his decision to push her away all those years earlier.

"That's more like it," she purred, her smile of breathtaking joy awakening a matching happiness inside him.

She bent down and brushed the sweetest kiss over his lips. Grant's heart clenched. He'd imagined this moment so many times over the last week and not once had he paused to give tenderness a thought. Passion. Need. Hunger. He'd planned to experience all those things. But his sudden, overwhelming need to cherish and protect left him teetering on a cliff edge with no handhold in sight.

And then she began to move and he lost himself in the incendiary friction of their joining. Lust radiated through him, incinerating his thoughts as he bucked his hips and drove deeper inside her. Lost in her own pleasure, she threw back her head and moaned.

"Deeper." Her torso flushed as the movement of her hips grew frantic and bold. "I love it when you go deeper."

So he obliged and she surrendered more of her body to him. He sank his fingers into her butt and drove into her while she matched each thrust with a twist of her hips that launched a series of signal flares through him. Each one sent his desire spiking higher and hotter until he fully expected to burst into flames.

Her breath came in shuddering pants as she neared her climax. Her movements had gone completely wild as she charged blindly toward her release. And then she was there and the sight of her shattering above him caused Grant's heart to stop as he watched it all unfold. His Harley. Sweet, beautiful and strong. Her power over him immense and unstoppable.

With his own orgasm close, Grant ground his teeth and slowed his movements. "Come for me again."

"What?" She lifted her head and regarded him in dazed shock.

"Again," he commanded, rolling her beneath him without breaking contact. "You're breathtaking when you come."

She wrapped her legs around his waist the way he loved and let her palms roam over his shoulders. He dipped his head and kissed her, driving his tongue into her eager mouth and drinking deep of her moans. She trembled at his next thrust and her arms looped about his neck as her kisses turned desperate. He rocked his hips, keeping his rhythm slow to start until the steady rhythm created a change in her breathing. She shifted the position of her knees, opening herself to his deeper thrusts and broke off their kiss to whisper in his ear.

"Make me come."

He needed no further urging and began pumping into her. They groaned in unison, lips seeking, tongues engaged in hungry, wanton kisses. He thought he could hold out and watch while another orgasm claimed her, but when she bit down on his lip, his tenuous control slipped.

"Come," he rasped, digging his fingers into her butt and driving her hard toward her climax. "For me."

He gave a triumphant cry as shudders tore through her. His body detonated a second later, claimed by an explosion of joy and lust. Incoherent words slipped from his lips. Thrusting wildly, he chased her through a maze of ecstasy, the two of them completely lost in each other.

In the aftermath, he pulled out and gathered her limp body against him. Lying cheek to cheek, he savored the soft press of her breasts and the suppleness of her smooth thighs tangled with his. The mingled scent of sweat and sex recalled the last time he'd held her like this. That night, although he'd reeled in the aftermath of their explosive lovemaking, he hadn't yet appreciated what their developing connection would mean to him.

They were good together. Better than good. They were *magic*. Grant's heart pounded and he realized it wasn't just the lingering result of their vigorous sex. He was so damned ecstatic to have Harley back in his…bed. She set her hand against his cheek, and leaned far enough away so she could gaze at him. As her smile of pure delight seared through him, Grant could no longer hide from the truth.

Harley was the dream that kept him from finding satisfaction with anyone else.

Eight

Harley arrived at the restaurant ten minutes late for dinner with her cousin Ezekiel Holloway and Regan Sinclair, his fiancée and Harley's good friend. While it wasn't the first time she'd left Daniel with Grant, it never grew any easier.

Because, in all honesty, their developing bond filled her with mixed emotions.

She'd never had to share her son with anyone and sometimes felt like a third wheel with how well the two got along. While logic told her that Grant would never replace her in Daniel's heart, when it came to motherhood and reason, sometimes the two didn't coexist.

Spying Regan and Zeke seated at a table near the window, she headed over. The two had been engaged for a few months and were planning an intimate wedding. She'd suspected for some time that her cousin Zeke found Regan attractive, but the two were such good friends that he'd hesitated to cross the line. Harley couldn't wait to hear what had caused him to change his mind. Nothing like losing herself in someone's whirlwind romance to take her mind off her own troubles.

"You two look so happy," Harley announced, enfolding her good friend in an affectionate hug before turning to Zeke. She lifted on tiptoe to wrap her arms around his broad shoulders. "It took you long enough to figure out Regan was the girl for you," she murmured in his ear, but as soon as she took her seat across from them, she noticed the couple exchanging a furtive look. Harley immediately knew something was up. She rested her forearms on the white tablecloth and leaned forward. Her gaze moved from one to the other. "Did I say something wrong?"

"It's nothing," Zeke declared.

"Nothing at all," Regan echoed, perusing the wine list.

"How are the wedding preparations going? I imagine it can be stressful planning an important event like that. Is there anything I can do to help?"

"We haven't really done much," Regan said, shooting a meaningful look in her fiancé's direction yet again.

"Okay," Harley said, "something's going on. Can you please let me in on what it is."

Zeke looked pained. "I think we should tell her."

Harley nodded at her cousin. "I think you should. After all, you know *I* can keep a secret."

Reagan's teeth flashed as she smiled. "You can, indeed."

The truth of Daniel's paternity had been something that Harley had kept to herself since learning that she was pregnant.

"In fact," Harley began, "that's part of why I wanted to have dinner with you. Both of you have been the best of friends to me and never once pressed me to divulge the identity of Daniel's father. However, I've recently decided that I can't keep quiet any longer and so I let the father know about him."

"Who is it?" Regan's eyes were wide with anticipation.

Harley braced herself for their reaction. "Grant Everett."

"*Grant*?" Zeke looked stunned. "I had no idea you two were even seeing each other."

"We weren't," Harley admitted, her cheeks heating. "It was one weekend a long time ago."

"Well, good for him," Regan declared, her eyes twinkling with good humor. "He's been the reason so many babies have been conceived in this town. It's only right that one of them should be his."

"I never thought of it that way." Zeke laughed. "How's he handling fatherhood?"

"Really well. He and Daniel are as thick as thieves already."

"So you and Grant," Regan mused. "I wouldn't have guessed. Any chance you two might make a go of it?"

Harley was shaking her head before Regan finished her question. "He's hung up on the difference in our ages." And probably a whole bunch of other things that prevented her from being a suitable partner in his opinion.

Zeke shook his head. There's what, ten or eleven years between you two?"

"Thirteen."

"So, you left town when you were eighteen." Regan's brow furrowed as she did the math. "That means he was thirty-one. I'm a little surprised… I mean, he doesn't seem the type to go for someone that young."

"I might have misrepresented my age," Harley admitted, wincing as she recalled how upset Grant had been. "He wasn't really happy with me when he found out the truth. But that was a long time ago and we're trying to be friendly for Daniel's sake."

"So, does this mean you're staying in Royal?" Regan asked.

"It depends," Harley teased, deflecting the question. "On whether or not I get to be in the wedding."

Regan shifted uncomfortably. "You know I'd love to have you as my bridesmaid."

"I was just kidding," Harley crowed. Then, seeing her friend's discomfort she threw up her hands and rushed to reassure her. "You don't have to include me. I have every intention of being here for the wedding. You are two of my favorite people, and I'm thrilled that you found each other."

"About that," Zeke began, glancing at Regan. "Since we're confessing our deepest darkest secrets tonight…"

"We're not in love," Regan declared.

"We're getting married because Regan can't get the inheritance from her grandmother until she's married or turns thirty and she doesn't want to wait four more years."

Harley was familiar with the terms of Regan's grandmother's will. She knew her friend chafed at the restriction and didn't blame her for finding a workaround. The Sinclairs were a very traditional family. But Regan was a modern, independent woman. One who was eager to strike out on her own.

"I see. I wish I could say I'm not disappointed." She eyed her cousin, searching for some sign that Zeke wished Regan felt more for him than that of a friend. But either he was good at hiding his feelings or she'd misinterpreted the way he smiled whenever Reagan was around.

While Harley hoped for Zeke's sake that the former was true, she wondered if marrying his good friend might spark romance between them. Or was she merely hoping that if love blossomed between Zeke and Regan, the same might happen between her and Grant? Although he'd been very clear that he had no intention of entering any kind of emotionally intimate relationship with her, their chemistry continued to bubble beneath the surface. What if ongoing exposure intensified their connection? Keeping her wits about her might be impossible. After all, the half of a decade she'd been away from Grant hadn't dimmed her desire for him.

But she was no longer an impulsive eighteen-year-old. And she was certain that Grant's willpower was far stronger than hers. He might let himself fall prey to the attraction between them, but he'd kicked her to the curb once. So what made her think he wouldn't cast her aside a second time? She'd just have to be happy with a friendly companionship if that's where things ended up.

"You're such a romantic," Regan said, her smile not quite reaching her eyes. "While the rest of the world is being pragmatic, you still believe in happily ever after."

"I guess I'm an optimist," Harley admitted. "I couldn't do the work I'm doing if I weren't."

"How's it going by the way?" Zeke asked. "Are you having any luck finding funding for Zest?"

"The fundraiser was successful, but didn't come close to replacing the annual contribution we received from Wingate Enterprises."

"Have you mentioned any of this to Grant?" Regan asked. "His family is one of the country's leading philanthropists."

Harley shied away from Regan's suggestion. "He's offered, but I'm not sure it's the best idea."

"Because of Daniel?" Regan asked.

"I don't want him to think that I'm using my son that way."

"But you wouldn't be," her cousin insisted. "Surely he'd know that."

"Maybe." Harley shrugged. "But if I can't be one-hundred percent sure, it's better that I find financing on my own."

Regan sighed. "I admire you. I'm not proud of the lengths I'm going to get my trust fund, but money equals independence."

"That's a fact I don't take for granted anymore," Harley agreed, comparing her comfortable childhood growing up surrounded by wealth to the desperate lives of the women who benefited from her nonprofit. "Life is a lot simpler with money than without it."

"It certainly makes the world go around," Zeke put in, shooting Regan a telling glance.

Since finding out he had a son, Grant was learning that being flexible was necessary for parenting. Thus, when Harley called at a little after ten that morning and asked if she could leave Daniel with Grant for a couple hours so she could attend a business lunch, he'd agreed.

"I'm sorry this is so last minute," Harley said, as she entered his office with Daniel. "The woman I hired to babysit had a family emergency."

"Things come up," he said, his gaze roving over her in appreciation.

Despite her harried expression, she looked very professional in an emerald-colored sheath that elongated her slim form and made her green eyes pop. Four-inch heels drew attention to her elegant calves and brought her lips within easy range of his. Grant was wondering if she'd let him mess up her soft pink lipstick as she kissed Daniel and rumpled his dark blond hair.

"You be good for your dad," she warned her son. "And no dessert unless you eat all your vegetables."

Daniel rolled a pleading gaze toward Grant who offered him a conspiratorial wink. Although he knew it drove Harley crazy, he enjoyed playing the part of the "fun" parent on occasion to get in his son's good graces.

"I really appreciate your flexibility," Harley said. "This meeting came up fast and I can't turn down any opportunities to fund Zest."

"It's no problem. My afternoon schedule has only one appointment in it. And you know how much I love spending time with my son."

"Daniel feels the same way." Harley reached out and put her hand on his arm, her touch burning through two layers of fabric and making his skin tingle. "I swear I won't make a habit of this. I've been looking for a day care that could take him a couple days a week, but everywhere I call they're full." Her eyes twinkled as she added, "Apparently, a certain fertility specialist is causing a baby boom here in Royal."

"Did you check with the Texas Cattleman's Club day care?" he asked, fighting the urge to pull her into his arms and kiss her breathless.

When around Daniel, they kept their hands off each other and their fiery chemistry buttoned down. Usually this caused a gradual heating of their simmering passion, so that by the time they put Daniel to bed, they were wild to tear each other's clothes off. Today, however, Harley was distracted and oblivious to his hunger.

"With everything going on with Wingate Enterprises…" She grimaced. "Let's just say the TCC isn't exactly the most welcoming place for my family right now."

"Why don't you let me take care of that." Grant was pulling out his phone to send a text to the woman who ran the day care when he noted Harley's hesitation. "Is something wrong?"

"The thing is," she began, frowning as she grappled with what she had to tell him. "Not all my family know about you being Daniel's father."

The little Grant knew about her strained relationship

with her family had come from Rose. From what his sister told him, Harley could barely stand to be in the same room with her mother and the woman had been overheard criticizing her daughter long before she had gotten herself pregnant and run off. Convinced he wanted nothing to do with such an emotional minefield, he hadn't asked Harley why she'd chosen to stay with her best friend rather than at her family's lavish estate where both her brothers as well as her mother lived in the massive main house and her cousins shared a spacious guesthouse.

"Don't you think it's time you did?" Grant asked. "After all, everyone in my family knows and I didn't make a point of asking them to keep the news a secret. It's only a matter of time before word gets around and it would be better if they hear about our situation from you."

"Of course." Harley gave a tight nod, her manner reflecting discomfort. "I just didn't want to have to get into a big explanation about what happened five years ago…"

As she trailed off, Grant wondered if there was more to her reluctance to reveal the truth than her tense relationship with her family. Was it possible that she didn't want their connection to come to light? Ridiculous. Yet, she hadn't exactly pushed for them to spend any time in public. If she wanted to flaunt their connection, wouldn't she suggest that they be seen dining together at the Texas Cattlemen's Club or one of the popular restaurants about town?

"But you're right," Harley said, her gaze fixed on the far wall. "I really do need to break the news that Daniel is your son." Her lips curved into a wry grin. "At least they won't be all over me for making a poor choice. When they originally found out I was pregnant, I think they believed the reason I refused to name the father was because I'd gotten knocked up by someone they deemed unworthy. And that is most definitely *not* you."

Her gaze lingered on him in a way that heated his blood. While part of him worried how susceptible he'd become to her charms, living in the moment was far less complicated than worrying about what might or might not happen in the future.

He hadn't chosen Harley. Not in any careful, deliberate way he could depend on. She'd appeared in his life like a tornado, tearing through his defenses and leaving them in pieces. Even before learning that they shared a son, his reaction to her return to Royal had been raw and visceral. She monopolized his thoughts and distracted him in ways he couldn't afford.

When they were together, he couldn't keep his hands to himself. Even the simple act of setting his palm on her back to guide her through a room gave him great pleasure. He caught himself staring at her lips and recalling the way they yielded to his kisses. He'd started saying clever things just to hear her laugh and enjoyed her fond expression every time her gaze fell upon her son.

And when they were apart, he ached to see her again. At odd times, he found himself picking up his phone to send her a text, eager to connect with her even if it was just through a few simple words.

He reached out and caught her hand in his, craving the simple contact. Her gaze grew smoky as he stroked his thumb along the underside of her wrist and a flush invaded her cheeks.

"I thought maybe you'd kept quiet because you thought they would've been shocked by the difference in our ages," he said.

"You know that never bothered me." She tried to make light of their circumstances, but he suspected her family would have a lot to say once they learned that Harley had been involved with a man more than a decade older than her. "And it's not like you're old enough to be my father." Her grin faded as she surveyed his expression. "You really can't let our age difference go, can you?"

"No."

Her exasperated sigh let him know just how weary she was of his unwillingness to stop dwelling on the thirteen-year gap between them. No doubt, it matched his frustration that she refused to consider the problems that could arise because of it.

"Does it ever bother you that your stubborn determination over a little thing like our age difference meant you lost over four years with your son?"

Grief welled at her question. Anger followed. Had she stayed away to punish him for what had been a completely reasonable decision on his part? Grant scoured her expression, seeing sadness rather than aggravation, and he had his answer. Still, her question had stung.

"You don't think that it was your youth as much as our age difference that kept me from wishing to have a relationship with you?"

"Ouch." Yet, far from being insulted by his bluntness, Harley gave a little shrug, demonstrating her willingness to consider his motivation. "I guess that's a fair question. I just wish you'd given me a chance before kicking me to the curb. We had an awesome time together that weekend. You might have been pleasantly surprised if you'd gotten to know me better. But I guess it was a situation where the timing was off. You weren't ready for a relationship and I needed to grow up."

When she lapsed into silence, he wondered if she was waiting for him to jump in and declare that he was now ready for a relationship and that she'd grown up to the point where he was considering one with her. But in truth, he was more convinced than ever that the effort involved in a committed relationship wasn't something he could sustain long-term. And he refused to give her hope.

"I'm not sure much has changed for me," Grant said, uncertain if that were completely true.

With the amount of time they'd spent together these last few weeks, he'd begun thinking of their little trio as a unit. Both his easy rapport with Daniel as well as the sizzling sexual chemistry he shared with Harley had brought him to a place he'd never gone before.

"Why are you so resistant to seeing where things could go between us?" she asked.

"It's not a relationship between us that I'm resisting," he told her, wishing she'd stop tempting him to believe in something he knew couldn't exist for him. "It's that I no longer imagine myself spending the rest of my life with anyone."

"Because of what happened between you and Paisley?" She frowned. "Don't you think it's unreasonable to assume because your marriage didn't work out that all future relationships won't, either?"

"When Paisley married me, she thought she was getting a man capable of love and heartfelt passion," he began, knowing the only way Harley would understand the depth of his flaws was to share why his marriage had failed. "But I didn't bring the sort of connection and intimacy to our relationship that she needed." And when Grant had informed her that he didn't require those things in turn, she'd left him. "I don't need the sort of connection she sought."

"Did it ever occur to you that you married Paisley for the wrong reasons?" Harley's earnest expression tugged on emotions that were different and stronger than what his ex-wife had inspired.

Doubts crowded in. What if in this particular instance he'd been wrong to rely on facts rather than feelings? His chest ached, the sensation uncomfortable and disturbing.

Logic had never let him down before. If he'd listened to his heart instead of his head, he'd have let his family pressure him into giving up on being a doctor and succeeding brilliantly at something that helped actual people he knew rather than providing aid to strangers he'd never know.

"Our marriage made perfect sense," Grant said, speaking as much to himself as to Harley.

"Not so perfect," she pointed out, "or you'd still be married."

Grant found himself glaring at her while wishing away Harley's knack for twisting his words and making him doubt his decisions. "Which is why I'm not going to make the same mistake again."

She cocked her head and considered him. "You know, it's too bad you didn't give me half a chance back then."

"Why is that?"

"Maybe the reason you weren't in love with Paisley was because…" A mischievous glint lit her eyes. "You'd already met your dream girl."

Grant saw past her flirtatious expression and self-deprecating tone to her desperate need to win him over and knew that encouraging her now would only lead to problems down the road.

"I like things as they stand right now with you and Daniel," he told her, his decisive tone causing her expression to lose its alluring sparkle.

"And nothing I could say or do will change your mind." She shook her head, forestalling his reply. "Never mind. I already know the answer." She pulled her hand free and dodged his gaze. "I'll be back in a couple hours. If anything happens, feel free to give me a call."

"We'll be fine," he assured her as he did every time she left Daniel with him.

As she departed his office, a grim shadow settled over

Grant's mood. Today's conversation had forced him out of the rosy haze he'd been floating in over the last few days. He found their current coexistence more than acceptable and thought because neither one had commented on what was transpiring between them, she felt the same way. But he could tell from Harley's reaction today that the status quo wasn't sustainable.

Clearly, because he was Daniel's father, he would forever be a part of Harley's life, as well. It was problematic that she wanted him to consider taking their relationship beyond being lovers and Daniel's co-parents and have them dive headfirst into a complicated tangle of romantic emotions. All the unrealistic expectations that would follow, involving them becoming a true couple and staying together forever, would only lead to disappointment for all of them.

He needed her to understand that while they were clearly having fun in the moment, he had no intention of marrying again. Yet, the tricky part would be to find a balance between rejecting her fondest wishes and easing her into his way of thinking without hurting her irrevocably.

Her dedication to Zest demonstrated that she would eventually return to Thailand. If he angered her, she could leave tomorrow and who knew how long before he saw her or his son again. The thought of losing either one of them made his gut churn. Grant quickly tamped down his anxiety.

He would have to figure out a way to convince her to stay in Royal without promising what he couldn't deliver. Daniel needed the stability of both his parents in his life and for both of them to get along. Because only that would make things better for all concerned.

Nine

Not long after her dinner with Regan and Zeke, Harley realized she'd better break the news to the rest of her family before the rumor mill got ahold of the story. To that end, she asked Beth to organize a dinner party for the family. Her sister had recently become engaged to Camden Guthrie and was living with him at his Circle K ranch.

Her brother Miles and his fiancée, Chloe, as well as Aunt Piper had arrived a little early and as the clock ticked toward seven o'clock, Harley wondered, with everything going on with Wingate Enterprises, if her brothers would be too busy to come. However, to her delight, both Sebastian and Sutton arrived and as Cam ushered the twins into the living room, Harley realized it was the first time all her siblings had been in the same room since she'd returned from Royal.

"Where's Mom?" Harley asked. Since her brothers were living at the Wingate estate with Ava, she'd assumed they'd all come together.

"She'll be along," Sebastian promised, his evasive answer intensifying Harley's anxiety. "But probably not for dinner."

As much as she'd dreaded her mother's reaction to finding out Grant was Daniel's father, now that Ava might not be here for the announcement, Harley felt even worse. She'd hoped to confront her mother's displeasure as soon as possible. Now, she'd just have more time to worry.

When Harley had asked Beth to host the dinner party, she'd explained that the time had come to reveal the identity of Daniel's father. She had wanted to share the news with her whole family at the same time, but since Ava hadn't put in an appearance, Harley decided to go forward. Not wanting to draw the moment out longer than absolutely necessary, as soon as they were all seated and the first course had been served, Harley cleared her throat.

"The reason I've gathered you all here tonight," she intoned with a half smile, hoping to lighten the mood before she dropped her bomb.

"Let me guess, you need money." Leave it to Sutton to ramp up the awkwardness by pointing out their dire financial situation.

Although her brothers were identical twins, with towering six-foot-two-inch frames and athletic builds, stylishly cut short dark blond hair and the family's signature green eyes, their personalities made them easy to tell apart. Growing up, Harley had nicknamed her oldest brother Serious Sebastian, and he certainly hadn't lightened up since he'd taken over as CEO of Wingate Enterprises.

Sutton had a more carefree manner, always the first one to suggest a prank or tell a funny story. But Harley could tell the company problems had taken their toll on him, as well. As CFO of Wingate Enterprises, Sutton had been the one who proposed that they not just reduce their charitable contributions but cut them off entirely when the business started having problems.

"That's not what this is about," Harley said, baring her teeth in an edgy smile that warned them all that she might be the baby of the family, but she was no longer a little girl. "Although if you could figure out who at Wingate Enterprises might be smuggling drugs into the country, so the company can be cleared of the accusations and restart their charitable contributions, that would be great."

"No one at the company is smuggling drugs," Sebastian grumbled, shooting a glance at his younger brother.

"We've been looking into things," Miles said, an edge to his manner that always seemed more pronounced when he was around his family. "Based on the quantity of drugs found, we don't think there's any indication that one of our employees is engaged in an actual drug operation."

Like Harley, Miles had turned his back on the Wingate's money and power and started Steel Security, a company that catered to high-powered clientele, offering both physical and online protection.

"But something *is* happening," Harley put in. "I mean, the DEA is investigating the company."

"They won't find anything," Sebastian said definitively, his gaze touching on each of them. "The company is clean."

"Why is all this happening?" Beth shuddered. "It feels like the family is under attack."

Seeing the twins exchange a look, Cam put a protective arm around Beth's shoulders. "Yeah, what's really going on here? Is someone out to get the family?"

Miles sighed heavily. "We don't know."

When a heavy silence fell over her family, Harley cleared her throat a second time, eager to redirect the conversation back to where she wanted it.

"The reason I asked Beth to organize tonight's dinner was to tell you something about Daniel." Seeing that she had everyone's rapt attention, Harley gathered her courage and began. "When we returned from Thailand, I decided that Daniel needed to meet his biological father. So I reached out to him and we've been talking." She felt her cheeks heat as she considered all the other things that they'd been doing, as well.

"Who is he?" Miles asked. "Or is it still a secret?"

"No. It doesn't make sense to keep it under wraps anymore." Harley pressed her damp palms together in an attempt to tamp down her anxiety and announced, "Daniel's father is Grant Everett."

Piper was the first to react. She looked aghast. "Grant?"

"The fertility specialist?" Beth made no attempt to hide her shock. "I didn't even realize you knew him."

"We met at the TCC ball five years ago," Harley said simply, reluctant to volunteer more than she had to.

Sebastian crossed his arms and frowned. "How long were you two dating?"

The warmth in her cheeks rushed over all her skin, but she maintained an air of dignity as she answered, "We didn't actually date. It was more like we spent a weekend together."

A silent twin communication passed between her brothers. They were a year older than Grant, so obviously they would've known him—or *of* him—in school.

"Did Everett know how young you were?" Sutton shook his head as if struggling to understand and Harley wondered if Grant would be receiving a phone call or two later.

She heaved a sigh, wishing everyone would just get over their age difference. "He didn't actually know how old I was until later. So don't go blaming him for taking advantage of me or something equally ridiculous. If anyone took advantage," she declared smugly, "it was me."

"Is he planning on stepping up now?" Sebastian asked.

"He already has." Harley immediately rushed to Grant's defense, leaving no room for doubt. "He loves Daniel. And Daniel adores him."

"So does that mean you're going to share custody?" Beth asked.

Leave it to her practical big sister to spear straight into the heart of her dilemma.

"We haven't discussed it," she admitted, acting as if none of this was any big deal. "At this point, the two of them are getting to know each other."

"But you said you're going back to Thailand," Piper said. "Or have you changed your mind?"

"My plan was to come back to Royal and find funding for Zest so I can continue the work I've been doing. And that work is in Thailand." Harley spoke this last part slowly for emphasis. "So, eventually Daniel and I will be heading back there."

"And Grant is okay with that?" Miles exchanged a profound glance with Chloe before returning his attention to his sister. "If I had a son, there's no way I'd let his mother take him halfway around the world."

This was the exact sort of brotherly highhandedness that had driven Harley to leave Royal. Yet, she was no longer an impulsive eighteen-year-old with a short fuse and kept her voice calm as she responded. "Grant understands our life is in Thailand. And he has been very clear about never wanting a family."

Miles snorted. "You don't think he'll change his mind after spending time with Daniel?"

"I don't know," Harley admitted, gripped by the now

familiar tightness in her chest as she considered how complicated her life had become since returning home.

On one hand, she was enjoying the time she and her son spent with Grant and she adored how Daniel was responding to his father. She also loved seeing him blossoming amongst his friends at the TCC day care, but when he talked about how much he missed those they'd left behind, Harley was torn. She should be glad that her son had such a big heart, but it meant that being parted from those he loved hit him hard.

"Well you better figure it out," Sebastian said, amplifying her irritation with his condescending big-brother routine.

Instead of shooting back with a sarcastic quip, Harley lifted her chin and calmly declared, "Trust me when I tell you that I will do what's best for Daniel."

And if that meant staying put in Royal so he could have his father in his life? Harley would cross that bridge when she came to it.

To her relief the conversation soon shifted away from her news and returned to the company's troubles. She learned more details about the circumstances surrounding the fire at the WinJet plant in East Texas and the subsequent lawsuit that claimed her family had directed the falsification of the inspection records.

By the time they moved from the dining room back to the living room, Harley's head was spinning. Given everything she'd learned tonight, she recognized that Wingate Enterprises was not going to be the future source for Zest's funding. Which meant she'd have to figure out where to turn next because she couldn't keep the nonprofit going with nickel and dime fundraisers.

Lost in thought, she didn't notice the arrival of a new visitor until her mother's fragrance filled her nostrils. Instinctively, she recoiled from the scent, turned around and regarded Ava's tight mouth and hard gray-green gaze. As usual, she wore her dark blond hair in a classic chignon and the touch of elegant gray at her temples added gravitas to her timeless beauty.

"Well," Ava huffed. "It seems as if you and I need to have a little chat."

Bristling at both her mother's authoritarian tone and her tardiness, Harley was momentarily caught off guard by the sight of Keith Cooper—Uncle Keith, as he wanted her and her siblings to call him. As if being their father's best friend—and after his death, their mother's "special" friend—gave him some deeper connection to them. Harley shuddered. *What was Ava thinking to bring him here?*

"About what?" she asked breezily, wondering which of her siblings had ratted her out.

"Daniel's father is Grant Everett?" Ava declared, making it sounding as if Grant was some lowlife criminal instead of a wealthy, accomplished doctor, as well as a member of one of the town's most philanthropic families. "What were you thinking?"

"What was I *thinking*?"

She'd been thinking that Grant was the most brilliant, fascinating, sexiest man she'd ever met. She'd been thinking that being with him made her happy. She'd been thinking that she was the luckiest girl on earth to have caught his eye.

"He's nearly twice your age."

Harley ground her teeth. "You can keep your opinions to yourself about Grant and me. I'm really not interested in hearing them."

"I'm your mother. I have a right to say whatever I want to about the mistakes you've made."

Growing up in the shadow of her talented and ambitious

siblings, she'd often relied on reckless behavior to make her presence known. Being good had never gotten her any attention, so she'd been bad. And then they'd noticed her.

"My mistakes?" Harley's gaze flicked to where Keith stood talking to her brothers. "What about yours?"

"What are you talking about?"

"Was this thing between you and Keith going on before my father died?"

Ava's eyes went wide at her daughter's insinuation, but Harley couldn't tell if her surprise was genuine or merely great acting. "How dare you ask me such a question!"

"That's not an answer."

"You are being completely ridiculous."

"Am I?" Harley ground out. "Because it seems like your devotion to my father all these years has been nothing but an act. It wouldn't do for you to get a divorce. That would affect your standing in this town. Especially when everyone found out you were having an affair with his best friend."

"I wasn't," Ava sputtered, shocked at her daughter's attack. "We never—this is outrageous."

"I might've been young, but I noticed the way he looked at you. And Dad told me how it was between the three of you when you were in college."

"What do you mean *how it was between us*?" Ava asked, her unruffled manner belying the hard light in her eye, put there by her daughter's accusation. "We were all friends. It wasn't until after I graduated that your father swept me off my feet."

Carried away by the emotional upheaval of her homecoming and the tumultuous last few weeks with Grant, Harley craved an outlet to vent her distress. Her mother was the perfect choice.

"Yet, you barely waited until he was in the ground before you ran off to Europe with Keith. That's not exactly the picture of a loving wife."

"What are you accusing me of?"

"I think it's pretty obvious. You and Keith have been carrying on for a long time." Harley frowned. "The only question is how long."

Diamonds flashed as Ava waved away her daughter's accusation. "Don't be a child."

"I'm not a child. I see what's been going on."

"Keith feels nothing but friendship for me," her mother declared in dismissive tones. "He's been married three times."

"And you didn't notice how similar each of his wives was to you?"

"You are being completely ridiculous."

When her mother rolled her eyes, Harley realized there was no way Ava would come clean and admit any wrong-doing. Not a surprise for a woman who routinely criticized those around her and spent no time at all in self-reflection.

"I'm not being ridiculous," Harley argued, even as she wondered why she was wasting her breath. For years, she'd felt guilty about leaving Royal just when her father needed her, but if he'd been able to speak, he never would've asked her to stick around. Especially given the toxic atmosphere between mother and daughter. "Even before Father had his stroke, you neglected him."

"I didn't come here today to be attacked by you."

"Well you certainly didn't come to have dinner with your family," Harley countered. "So why *did* you come?"

"To warn you that this family cannot take any more scandals. If Grant Everett is Daniel's father, give him whatever he wants when it comes to the boy. I won't have the Wingate name dragged through the mud because of you."

Harley felt as if she'd been slapped. "That's not Grant's style."

"Don't be so sure." Ava arched her elegant eyebrows. "Men can play dirty when it comes to getting what they want."

Harley's entire body flushed with panic at the thought of losing her son, but she turned her mother's warning back on her. "Maybe the men you know."

How far would a man like Keith Cooper go to get what he wanted? Before Harley could give the matter any thought, her mother delivered one final punch.

"Don't imagine for one minute that Grant won't do whatever it takes to keep hold of his son. All I ask is you don't do something stupid and stir up more trouble for the family."

"I assure you that Grant and I are on the same page when it comes to Daniel." But the minute she said it, she couldn't help but wonder if it were true.

When Harley appeared on his doorstep after having dinner with her family, Grant took one look at her stormy expression and put his romantic inclinations on hold.

"How'd it go tonight?" he asked, taking both her hands in his and walking backward toward the living room.

Harley grimaced. "It went great until my mother showed up late and accompanied by Keith." She'd spoken at length about the man and her suspicions about his relationship with her mother. "She knew it was supposed to be a family dinner. Why did she have to bring him?"

Keith had been her father's best friend and since Trent Wingate's first stroke had been advising her mother on the company, as well as more personal issues. Far from seeing the relationship as simple friendship, Harley had speculated that they'd been carrying on for years, possibly even before her father's illness. Especially after Ava had spent a year in Europe with him not long after her husband's death.

"He and her husband had been friends since college," Grant pointed out. "Maybe he considers him family."

"Ugh! Don't even go there." Harley was so preoccupied with her own thoughts that she didn't seem to notice that he'd coaxed her down the hall to the master bedroom. "I don't like him. And I'll certainly never think of him as part of the family."

She stripped off her earrings and the simple gold bracelet that she'd donned as her only accessories to the floral dress crafted by the women of Zest. Sweeping her long brown hair aside, she presented her back to Grant so he could unfasten the zipper. Both of them took for granted the easy familiarity that had grown between them in recent days.

"Is it just Keith's appearance tonight that has you all worked up?" he asked. Dispensing with the zipper, he cupped his hands over her shoulders and nuzzled her temple, hoping to redirect all that passion into something that would leave them both deliciously satiated. "Or is there something else?"

Harley slipped from beneath his touch and let the dress fall to her feet. Clad only in a lacy pink bra and matching panties, she stepped out of the dress before scooping it off the floor.

"It's just my mother being my mother. She's always on a mission to tear me down. Nothing I do is ever right." Harley crushed the garment in her hands. "I wish I'd never come back here."

Although he recognized that Harley was more upset over her encounter with her mother than Grant had ever seen her, he recoiled as her words lanced through him. Anxiety spiked. Despite how well they'd been getting along these last couple of weeks, in the back of his mind lurked the certainty that Harley intended to take Daniel back to Thailand. He hated the thought that arguing with her mother might cause Harley to leave sooner than planned.

"I swear nothing I do is ever good enough for her." Harley continued to rant as she marched into his closet to hang up the dress. "She's never once given me any credit for the job I'm doing raising Daniel by myself, or acknowledged the number of people I've helped through Zest."

Reemerging from the closet, she stormed across the room to the dresser where she placed her jewelry, opened the drawer and pulled out a nightgown. After turning to face him and without a hint of invitation in her eyes, she stripped off her bra and underwear, bestowing on him a provocative glimpse of her glorious, naked body, before sliding the silky cobalt blue gown over her head.

"I'll bet if I won the Nobel peace prize, instead of congratulating me, she'd point out every single thing my siblings have accomplished since kindergarten."

With her delicates gripped in her hand, she headed back to the closet where the hamper awaited their dirty clothes. When she reappeared once more, she was twisting her hair into a loose messy bun on top of her head. She secured it with a clip and sighed.

"I know I'm not alone in how I feel," she began, her voice heavy with compassion.

The weekend that they spent together, she'd asked him why he was single. He'd explained how isolated he felt growing up because his interests diverged from what his parents wanted for him and that they'd struggled to understand him. His family was dedicated to their charitable foundation work and maintained an active social life. While Rose had taken after their parents, Grant had been more interested in intellectual pursuits, and they struggled to relate to their introverted, bookish family member. When it became obvious that he intended to have a career in medicine rather than join the company business, his parents gave up on him. He was the oddity in the family. The one who'd disappointed his parents by going into "service."

Although he'd relayed this narrative without any emotional display, the way Harley had acknowledged how much this must have bothered him, he'd been overwhelmed with relief. Until that moment, he hadn't realized the depth of the grief he'd bottled up, or the damage he'd done to his psyche by closing himself off to further hurt.

Looking back now, he realized he'd come to trust her in those unguarded moments. She'd been right when she'd said that something had sparked between them that weekend. So much so that the powerful connection had disturbed him. He'd shied away from the attachment, rejected its importance. Thoroughly rattled by the burst of unruly sentimentality, when he'd discovered that she'd deceived him, he'd grabbed at this excuse and slammed the door shut on his emotions, setting a bar in place to keep them permanently locked away.

Harley came to stand before him, her fingers going to work on the buttons of his shirt. She tugged the hem free of his pants and finished unfastening the front. In the middle of stroking it off his shoulders, she paused and gazed up at him.

"Why are some parents driven to find fault with everything their children do? It's as if…" She trailed off, swallowing bitter words. "You know what I'm talking about."

Grant stripped off his shirt and cast it aside. Wrapping one arm around Harley's waist, he drew her into a comforting embrace. She leaned into him, setting her cheek against his shoulder and wrapping her arms around his neck. Although her mood was somber, just holding her in his arms stirred his blood. Yet, despite that, he was happy to offer her sympathy if that's what she needed right now.

"The sooner I get back to Thailand the better," Harley continued in dark tones, unable to stop fuming over her encounter with her mother.

Grant's heart twisted at the thought of losing his son. "When you say sooner…?"

"I thought after being gone for five years that I could come back and things with my family would be better. But they treat me like I'm a child. Nobody gives me any credit. I started an amazing nonprofit that helps women, but all they see is their baby sister who made the mistake of getting pregnant when she was eighteen."

"Daniel and I have barely had the chance to get to know each other," Grant said, realizing she wasn't paying attention to him. "I need more time with my son."

"I'm sorry for dumping all this on you." Her arms encircled his waist as all the fight drained out of her. "It's just that my mother drives me crazy. She couldn't be bothered to arrive in time for dinner and only showed up to warn me not to drag the Wingate name through the mud."

"How did she think you'd do that?"

"She has this idea in her head that you and I are going to go to battle over Daniel. As if we would."

Grant opened his mouth to voice the concerns that had been growing each time she mentioned taking Daniel back to Thailand before thinking better of it. Harley's mother had hurt her so, of course, her reaction would be to want to put as much distance between them as possible. That she wasn't thinking about him or her son at the moment was obvious. And with her in this mood, Grant understood that the last thing he should do was alienate Harley.

She'd already demonstrated her eagerness to get back to her regular life. Once she cooled down, he hoped she'd become more reasonable.

But even if she didn't hop on a plane in the near future, her outburst had solidified one critical factor. At the moment, he had no legal right to Daniel. If she so desired, she could prevent him from spending any time with his son and there wasn't a damn thing he could do about it. At least until he resolved his paternity claim.

"What am I doing?" she moaned. "Why do I let her get to me?" Harley rolled her head and gazed up at him. Her eyes softened as she asked, "How was your night?"

"Great. Daniel and I went to dinner at the Royal Diner."

She lifted her hand and rested it on his bare chest above his heart. As if she noticed the sudden uptick in speed, she grinned. "You don't say. Let me guess what you had. Hamburgers and milkshakes?"

"You know us well."

He dipped his head and grazed her lips with his, determined to push their earlier conversation aside so he could concentrate on the here and now. A lusty groan poured from her lips as he cupped her breast and flicked his thumb over her tight nipple.

"Take me to bed, you handsome hunk," she purred, sliding her hand up his thigh and brushing her fingertips over the growing bulge behind his zipper. "I wanna get naked with you."

"That's the best offer I've had all day," he murmured against her neck as her fingers went to work on his belt.

He growled as her fingers slid down his zipper before reaching into the opening. Lust assailed him and blood pooled in his groin at her hot probing touch. Snagging two handfuls of the silky nightgown in his fist, he tugged at the material.

"Remove this," he commanded in a guttural rasp. "I can take care of the rest."

Seconds later, they were both naked and facing each other across the narrow gap, breathing hard as their excitement rose.

"Bed," he ordered, pointing toward the king-sized bed they'd been sharing these past few nights. "Now."

Her eyes twinkled mischievously before she squeaked at his glower and rushed off to strip back the covers, throw herself onto the mattress and await his pleasure.

He followed her after a beat, determined to squash all thoughts of her mother from her mind. His lips and hands came at her in a rush, but she was already rising up to meet him, her fingers tangling in his hair to draw his mouth to hers. As their lips fused together, her tongue darted out to lure him to the exotic pleasure of her mouth.

She spread her legs and drew him into the cradle of her thighs, playing a treacherous game as his unprotected erection slid along her core. The glide of his bare flesh against hers once again demonstrated just how dangerous she was to him.

Shifting away from temptation, he eased down her body. His lips trailed over her neck and into the hollow of her throat before drifting down into her cleavage and up the gentle swell of her breast. He teased her nipple with the edge of his teeth, drawing a moan from her throat. Closing his hand around her other breast, he applied the perfect pressure to make her moan. Her hips lifted off the mattress, encouraging him to slide his hand between her legs.

"Grant," she whispered, her voice a breathy plea.

He lifted his head so he could observe the flush cascading over her skin, put there by the heat his hands and mouth had stirred in her body.

"I need to feel you inside me." Her voice broke until it was nearly a whimper. "Don't make me wait any longer."

"Not yet," he growled, arousal making his voice harsh. "Come for me first like this."

Her breath spiraled out in a rush and her eyes closed. She threw her head back as every muscle in her body tightened. Watching her surrender to erotic oblivion was the sexiest damn thing he'd ever seen and he locked his full attention on her, his hands guiding her through every wave of her shattering climax, filing away this moment to relive again and again.

To think he could've had five years of this. Five years of pleasure and happiness. Of connecting with the one person who understood and accepted him. He'd been a fool. An arrogant idiot, too afraid of letting his guard down to appreciate how wondrous the surrender could be.

And then he remembered their earlier conversation and a chill swept over him. It was all just temporary. Over and over, Harley spoke of her life in Thailand. Of her intention to return once she'd funded Zest. She hadn't come home to be with him. Nor had she returned to Royal so he could meet his son.

Just as she had her life planned out, so did he. That their goals were in opposition to each other—hers to return to Thailand, his to remain active in his son's life—meant he had to keep his purpose unclouded by emotion. For the moment, she was his only link to Daniel and that meant she held all the cards. Until the balance of power evened out, he would be wise to keep his wits about him.

Ten

Harley lay facedown in Grant's big empty bed, her arms and legs splayed across the mattress, and let the tranquil white noise of his shower sweep over her. Right now, he'd be running soapy hands all over his hard, muscular body, washing away all signs of their lovemaking. An ache bloomed between her thighs at the thought of joining him, but she was uncertain about facing him until she sorted out what she was feeling. Instead, she replayed the moments since she'd been awakened by his lips coasting down her neck.

Morning sex with Grant had a different vibe than noon, evening or nighttime sex. Slower. Softer. His kisses reached deep into her soul, soothing her like the first touch of dawn on her face. She'd buzzed with contentment as his hands skimmed her curves and coaxed her body awake. By the time he'd slid into her, she was floating on a cloud of bliss and poised to climax.

That deep extended orgasm had left her breathless and her heart wide open. Caught up in his own pleasure, he'd buried his face in her neck, her name a sweet moan wrenched from his throat, and hadn't noticed her bite her lower lip as tears sprang to her eyes. The urge to cry had come out of nowhere and she had no defense against the sneak attack.

A week ago, she'd stopped returning to her empty room at Jaymes's house in the wee hours of the morning. She wasn't sure who'd suggested that it would be easier if she just spent the night. As tempting as it was to read something into their unofficial living arrangements, she couldn't help but think great sex and convenience comprised Grant's list of reasons why he let her stick around.

A chime erupted from the dresser where their phones sat side by side, the tone alerting her to an upcoming appointment. With urging from the ever-organized Grant Everett, she'd started using her calendar to keep track of everything she had going on. Today, she was attending another lunch with the foundation board member Jaymes had introduced her to. They were meeting at eleven o'clock and she had to run Daniel to day care before making the drive to Fort Worth.

Having no idea of the time, she slipped out of bed and donned her discarded nightgown as she crossed to the dresser. As she reached out to touch the screen and wake up her phone, the shower ceased to run. Momentarily distracted, she didn't realize she'd chosen the wrong phone until the screen displayed the photo of her and Daniel that Grant had chosen for his wallpaper. The sight made her smile. A second later, her good mood faded as she read what the appointment banner showed.

Grant had made an appointment with an attorney.

Harley's stomach twisted as she took in the implications. In the seconds before the screen faded to black, she memorized the name of the attorney and law firm and quickly searched the internet while she revisited every conversation they'd had about her eventual return to Thailand. As she'd feared, the lawyer Grant was meeting with specialized in family law.

Bile rose to her throat. Was he planning on taking Daniel away from her? There was no question that he had the money and power to do it. Especially with her family's current troubles calling into question her financial stability. Harley took a couple deep breaths to steady herself, unclear how a man who'd just rocked her world in the most loving way possible could be out to hurt her.

On the other end of the spectrum, however, maybe he was simply meeting with an attorney to legally establish himself as Daniel's father and had no interest in seeking custody of any kind or preventing her from leaving the country with his son.

Needing some space to think before she confronted him and said something foolish, Harley headed toward the kitchen, lured by the scent of coffee. Grant's housekeeper was mixing up Daniel's favorite chocolate-chip pancakes. Harley snagged a cup of coffee, added a splash of milk and headed for her son's room to get his morning started. To her delight, he was already up and dressed in the clean clothes Grant suggested they put out for him each night. After smothering him in kisses, she shepherded Daniel into the bathroom to brush his teeth and comb his hair, fighting back melancholy at the way her baby grew more independent with each day that passed.

What would happen if she were forced to split custody with his dad? Yet, how could she be so selfish as to deny Grant the joy Daniel brought into his life?

"Mommy, are you okay?"

Harley met Daniel's gaze in the mirror and saw that a tear had escaped and was running down her cheek. She dashed away the moisture and summoned a brave smile.

"I'm fine. It's just that I'm so proud of you." She wrapped her arms around his slim form and crushed him to her. "You're my little man."

He wiggled in her snug embrace, protesting half-heartedly until she released him.

"Go get breakfast," she told him. "Franny made your favorite pancakes."

"Yay!"

He raced from the room and Harley took a few seconds to collect herself before heading back to the master bedroom. Grant was sliding into a navy sports coat as she entered. Her heart turned over at the sizzling look he sent her way. She took a sip of her coffee, before sauntering over to tweak his pale blue tie and smooth her hand down the front of his coat.

"You look very handsome," she said, peering up at him from beneath her lashes.

"And you look gorgeous as always." He cupped her cheek and dipped his head for a lingering kiss that left her weak-kneed and breathless. "Good luck with your meeting today. I'll see you for dinner."

The glow from Grant's kiss lingered as she showered, dressed and drove to the Texas Cattleman's Club. It wasn't until Daniel scampered away to join the other kids that her earlier worries came back to haunt her. Seeing the way Daniel was settling into life here in Royal with his father and all his new friends, Harley wasn't sure if she should move them back to Thailand, after all. But staying would make it harder to ignore family obligations. She couldn't avoid dealing with her mother or pretend that a couple dinner parties would ease the tension between her and her siblings. Plus, she was used to doing as she liked without a dozen people shoving their opinions down her throat.

And then she had to consider that Grant had met with an attorney. That was a threat she couldn't ignore. Suddenly, taking what funding she'd secured and running seemed like a smart option. The longer she lingered in Royal, the more attached Daniel would get to living here. And the more time Grant would have to stake his legal claim to his son.

As she made her way back to the front door, she spied her sister, Beth, striding in her direction with purposeful steps and altered her course to intercept her. At Harley's greeting, Beth looked up from the tablet in her hands, but her dour mood didn't change.

"Is everything okay?" Harley's stomach twisted in concern. Did Beth's peevish expression mean there was more trouble brewing for their family? "Please tell me nothing else happened with the company."

Beth noted her sister's worry and set a hand on Harley's arm in reassurance. "It's nothing like that."

The whole family was jumpy these days with disaster looming at every turn for Wingate Enterprises. Harley had known challenges with her nonprofit, but the size and scope of Zest was nothing compared to the vast holdings of Wingate Enterprises. She certainly didn't envy all her brothers had to manage on an average day, much less with the series of woes recently befalling the corporation.

"I'm working on the annual TCC ball," Beth continued. "Even though it's a few months away, there's a million things to do and every day I swear something else gets added to my plate."

Goose bumps rushed over Harley's skin as her sister mentioned the annual TCC event. At that same ball five years ago, her life had been forever changed. She hadn't yet decided if she'd still be in Royal, much less whether she'd attend this year's ball. As much as she needed to return to Thailand and start putting her funding to good use, the idea of leaving town and taking Daniel away from Grant dragged at her. Torn in two different directions, weighing the pros and cons of each left her completely stuck.

"I'm sure you have everything completely under control," Harley said.

Beth had organizational strengths in abundance. Harley wished she possessed more than a sliver of her sister's capabilities, but she was more of an idea person rather than an implementer. Except where Zest was concerned. Although, she hadn't done it alone. Jaymes had been a huge help.

"You're sweet to say so," Beth said. "And actually, the event is coming together better than I expected. In fact, I just found out that one of the local radio stations is offering a complimentary makeover and a ticket to the event for one lucky listener."

"At a thousand dollars a plate, that's an awesome prize." Harley pondered whether that listener would have his or her life changed at the ball the way she had and hoped that was the case.

"There've been a lot of big donations this year," Beth said. "People are feeling unusually generous. I'm not exactly sure why."

Harley wondered if any of her family was amongst those who were making big donations. With all the trouble that Wingate Enterprises was having, it would be a public relations boon to show their support of the local community. Especially now when so many of Royal's most influential residents had turned a cold shoulder to the Wingate family.

"What's this year's theme?"

"We're doing a masked ball."

Harley oohed in appreciation. She could see the potential in donning a sexy dress and mask for a little anonymous flirting with Grant. A thrill spread through her as she imagined the pleasure she would get from stalking and seducing Grant Everett at a second TCC function. Unless, of course, someone else caught his eye this year. And that's when it hit her. She didn't believe that Grant wouldn't change his mind about falling in love and getting married again. What truly worried her was that he wouldn't choose *her*. She was running back to Thailand to avoid watching the man she wanted fall for someone else.

"That sounds like a lot of fun," Harley said, more subdued that she'd been a second earlier. "Maybe I'll have to stick around long enough to attend."

Beth looked surprised. "You're leaving?"

"My life is in Thailand," she reminded her sister, bracing against Beth's frown. "I can't just abandon Zest and stay here."

"What about taking Daniel away from Grant?"

Grant might not be interested in a relationship with her, but Harley knew exactly how much he wanted his son. Guilt flooded her, but she refused to let it decide her actions. She couldn't put her personal life on hold forever. And that's exactly what would happen if she stuck around. Grant had asked to get to know his son, but he hadn't given her any hope for the future. Nor had Harley asked.

"He knows our lives exist on two different continents. His practice is here. Zest is in Thailand."

"I don't envy your decision," Beth said heavily. "I have no idea what I would do in your shoes."

Harley's chest tightened. She hated being in a no-win situation. "Whatever I do, someone is going to get hurt."

"I know you've been spending a lot of time together. Is

there a chance things will work out between you? I mean, you share a son. Grant will always be in your life. Could you see yourself with him?"

"It's confusing," Harley admitted, giving voice to what had been bothering her these last few days. "He claims he's not interested in any kind of permanent relationship."

Beth hugged her tablet to her chest and frowned at Harley. "Have you asked him how he feels about you?"

"How does one go about asking the father of your child if he could ever love you?" Harley quizzed in dry tones, hiding her anxiety behind dark humor.

"Are you in love with Grant?"

"I don't know," Harley admitted, but that was far from the truth. Given the way he'd rejected her then and his determination to avoid any emotional attachment to her now, the notion filled her with alternating flashes of fear and longing. "To be honest, I'm terrified to go there."

Yet, all she needed was the tiniest bit of encouragement from him, some sign that he wouldn't reject her love and the cork would be out of the bottle. Even thinking about it now made her want to cry. She had years of pent-up longing and desire rumbling through her like an active volcano. And these last weeks with him, getting a taste of how amazing her life could be if he would just let her in…

"I'm in love with him," Harley admitted. "But it's hopeless."

"Maybe not. You'll never know unless you decide what you want with Grant is worth fighting for. And then go for it."

Harley wished it were that easy. "Just because you got lucky in the romance department doesn't mean everyone does."

"But look at Miles," Beth countered. "Did you ever imagine he'd fall as hard as he has for Chloe?"

"No." Harley thought back to the family dinner and the way her brother had doted on his fiancée. Seeing that whole different side of Miles had given her pause. What she wouldn't give for Grant to look at her that way. As if he'd given her his heart and soul.

"True love really does conquer all." Beth's radiant smile made her sister wince.

"If you say so."

Harley's heart became a stone lump in her chest. As much as she wished her feelings for Grant were only an echo of her long-ago crush, coupled with great sex and their connection through Daniel, she'd grown more and more convinced that she was truly in love with him.

"I do." Beth's eyes glowed with fervor. "In fact, I bet Grant already realizes that you are the woman he can't bear to live without and he's just waiting for the perfect moment to tell you."

"Well, that would be something," Harley remarked, wishing she had a speck of her sister's optimism. "In the meantime, I'm just going to take it one day at a time."

Two days after Grant met with the family law attorney about establishing his paternity claim to Daniel, he came home to an empty house. It was Franny's day off and the plan had been for him to take Harley and Daniel out for dinner. Usually Harley picked their son up from day care and brought him over to swim in the late afternoon before he got home. Grant had grown accustomed to the vibrant energy and unrelenting noise of the four-year-old and the silence that greeted him had a weighty, oppressive feel to it.

Grant searched his cell phone, but found no message about a change of plans. If something had come up, surely she would've notified him. They were supposed to be celebrating. The night before, in the wake of his meeting with the lawyer, he'd repeated his offer to fully fund her nonprofit. This time when she demurred, he hadn't taken no for an answer and had written a sizable check with the promise of more to follow.

Despite having grown up in one of the town's wealthiest families, Harley had learned to live simply in Thailand and selflessly shared her time and energy, harnessing the power of Wingate Enterprises' charitable contributions to help those who had little. The more time he'd spent with her, the more he accepted how much good Zest was doing. He no longer believed that his fertility practice was more important than Harley's transformative crusade to lift women out of poverty by empowering them to help themselves.

Which was why he'd been so surprised that her thanks the previous night had such a hollow ring to it. He'd thought she'd be relieved that he'd agreed to provide the much-needed funds to keep it going. Yet, it seemed like no matter what he said or did, the state of things between them deteriorated with each passing day. The level to which this bothered him only fueled his uneasiness.

Exhaling harshly, Grant dialed Harley's number and when she didn't answer, followed up with a text.

Are we still on tonight? Shall I swing by and pick you up?

He'd no sooner sent the text than Harley was walking through his front door. Grant was swept by an overwhelming sense of relief. What had he been thinking? That she'd run off again and taken Daniel with her? Given his abrupt lightheadedness, no doubt that's exactly what he'd presumed.

"Where's Daniel?" he asked a little too sharply, seeing his son was not with her.

She shot him an odd look. "I dropped him off at your parents' ranch so they could spend some one-on-one time with their grandson."

He should've felt relief, but a trace of coolness in her manner caused his stomach muscles to clench. "So are we picking him up there?"

"Actually, they've invited us for dinner. I hope that's okay."

"Of course." He stood staring at her, wondering at her unhappy expression. "Is something else going on?"

"Were you ever planning to tell me that you'd met with an attorney this week?"

He cursed silently. "How did you know?"

"I saw the appointment pop up on your phone." Although she was obviously trying to keep it together, her voice quavered. "Are you planning on seeking partial custody of Daniel?"

Remorse flooded him as he realized he should've had a conversation with her before contacting an attorney. He was accustomed to taking action without discussing the ramifications with anyone. And concern about his paternal rights made him more inconsiderate than usual.

"I met with Lloyd because I want to legally establish that Daniel is my son." Grant was well aware that he hadn't answered her question. When her gaze continued to bore into him, he added, "I haven't taken any steps in that direction."

"But you're thinking about it?"

They could no longer exist in a bubble, insulated from reality.

"I'd be a fool not to."

Harley reached into her pocket and pulled out the check he'd given her. "I told you my son isn't for sale," she said, extending it to him.

Treating her like Paisley had been a mistake. Harley wasn't going to be pacified with tokens that had no meaning. "That's not why I wanted to help you."

Her skeptical look said it all. "What did you think would happen if I took the money?"

"That you'd stay in Royal."

"And if I didn't stay?"

Suddenly, her strong reaction and the disquiet he'd been feeling all day began to make sense. He saw now that his gesture had been both a bribe and a threat. He'd been warning her that he possessed the resources to help or fight her. The choice was hers.

"I can't lose my son," he answered quietly, his tone deadly serious. "I really hope we can come to an understanding."

"Maybe I would be more open to that if things were different." Harley gazed at him with hope and frustration fighting for dominance in her green eyes.

"What sort of things?" he asked, determined to find a way to make them both happy.

When they had been together five years earlier, he'd gone into the weekend recognizing that she'd been too young for him. Not as young as she turned out to be. But someone who had a lot of life to live before she'd be happy settling down.

Since she'd come home, he'd started to see her in a whole new light. Harley was no longer the pampered daughter of a wealthy family. She'd lived on her own halfway around the world and was raising a child as a single mom. And it impressed him to no end that she'd been so touched by the desperate plight of others that instead of turning away, she'd started a nonprofit to help women lift their families out of desperate poverty. Her level of experiences had surpassed that of an average twenty-three-year-old.

So why was he so reluctant to give her the credit she deserved? Because he'd have to treat her as an equal and acknowledge that they shared a lot in common from Daniel to their passion for helping people to a deep, unquenchable sexual chemistry. And couples with a lot less going for them made permanent relationships work.

"You've been clear about what you want," he said, aware that he'd been existing in a vacuum, avoiding tough questions about the future and unwilling to imagine his life without her in it. "You've made it clear your reasons for returning to Royal were to find funding for Zest."

"That's true, but since coming home, a lot has changed. I love being with you and Daniel. But I want more. A lot more." Harley turned imploring eyes on him, begging him to meet her halfway. "I want us to be together like a real couple."

"You know how I am. What I can and can't give you."

She nodded. "I know what you believe you're capable of, but I want to be the woman you can't live without." Harley drew in a shaky breath, revealing just how scary this conversation was for her. "And now I need to know what you want."

Since she'd returned to town, he barely recognized himself. When it came to her, instead of taking in information and making thoughtful decisions, he was far more likely to act out. He yearned to be with her, longed to wrap her in his arms and sink into the harmony they'd discovered these past few weeks, yet the need left him feeling exposed and unsteady. And if giving her what she wanted meant he would be like this all the time, that was more than he could handle.

"For now, I just want more time with my son." And with

her. Yet, he couldn't bring himself to confess a feeling that he didn't understand and risk building up her hopes only to disappoint her later.

A shutter fell over her features. "How much more time?" Her sharp tone made her sound unreasonable, but Grant knew he was to blame for her disappointment.

"As much as I can get." He grabbed her hand and squeezed. "Don't go back to Thailand."

"How long do you expect us to stay?" she demanded. "A week? A month? A year? How long do you want me to put my life on hold with no promises from you?"

He didn't have a number. There was something between them. He just wasn't sure where it would lead or the sort of form it would take. And not being a man who made snap decisions, all he could do was hope she'd stick around while he made up his mind.

"I don't want you to put your life on hold," he said, yet that's exactly what he was asking her to do. "But there has to be some way you can run the nonprofit from here."

"Maybe I could, but I don't want to."

Harley pulled her hand from his grasp and closed her eyes, making a visible effort to calm down. When her lashes lifted once more, she appeared to have found a new center of gravity. She regarded him with such purpose that he backed up half a step. In a flash of insight, he recognized that she was asking him to voice how he felt about her. To bare his soul and commit to the hungry emotions that burned brighter each time they came together. He wasn't prepared for that. He didn't believe he'd ever be.

"I need a reason to stay, Grant."

Sudden panic consumed him, flushing adrenaline through his veins. Even so, part of him longed to throw caution to the wind, confess that he'd grown accustomed to having her around and trust that she'd stay in Royal because she'd see it was the right thing to do for both her and Daniel.

"There are plenty of reasons."

"I need one from you," she clarified, her manner calm, but determined. "Something that matters."

"Royal is your home," he said. "You and Daniel have family here."

Harley shook her head. "I no longer consider Royal my home and I've lived for years without my family. They never supported me the way my friends have. Both here and in Thailand." She paused and her eyes narrowed. "But your response didn't give me what I asked for. So let me be clearer. What about us?"

Buffeted by doubts and his fear of rejection, Grant wished he could let go of the past and be the lover, friend and partner she needed him to be. With his head and his heart vying for dominance, he maintained a neutral expression to conceal how badly this conversation was shaking him. This was why he'd avoided romantic entanglements, preferring to keep his existence plodding forward at an organized, consistent pace.

"Us?" he echoed. "You and Daniel?"

"You and I." Her sharp gaze drilled into his. "I'm giving you the chance to tell me if that's something you want."

"You're asking if I want you," he reiterated, buying time while his frenzied thoughts whirled, refusing to give him clear answers that would satisfy her. "Of course I do."

"But not in the way I want you," she guessed. "Five years ago I fell in love with you."

Her confession stopped him cold for several thundering heartbeats.

"That's ridiculous," he retorted, all too aware that she was awaiting his response. "We were together one single weekend. No one falls that fast."

"Even you've heard of love at first sight. Well, that's what happened to me." She looked so damned sure of herself as she spoke that Grant was filled with envy. "I really believed by the end of that weekend that we were meant to be together. And then you found out how old I was and you were so mean about it." Harley let that sink in before continuing. "I've spent a long time thinking about what happened. What I did wrong. And what I decided is that we were awesome together. So what if I was thirteen years younger? You claim you weren't worried about your reputation and if that's true, then you sent me away for some other reason. What was it?"

"Going into the weekend, I never planned to see you afterward and by the end of our time together, it became clear to me that you weren't going to just walk away."

Harley scowled and shook her head. "Maybe I was a one-weekend stand for you at the start, but something happened. The longer we spent together, something wonderful sparked between us. We talked about driving to the Gulf Coast so you could take me to your favorite beach and about a new restaurant you wanted us to try. Why would you say those things if you didn't plan on ever seeing me again?"

Why? Because until he'd found out her true age, he'd been absolutely smitten with the passionate creature who'd been sharing his bed. Being with Harley had made him feel like he was standing on the edge of a cliff. But where he'd formerly assumed a new beginning with other women would end in disappointment, being with Harley had convinced him he could fly.

"You were so enthusiastic about the things you enjoyed," he explained. "I merely let you believe I wanted them, too."

Her breath rushed out in an impatient hiss. "That's not the way it happened. Why are you acting like this?"

"Like what?"

"Like you're blind to how good we are together. Or maybe it's your opinion that what's between us isn't enough for you." She sunk her teeth into her lower lip and her lashes fell, obscuring the hurt in her eyes. "That I'm not enough for you."

"The fault doesn't lie with you," he assured her, taking her fingers in his and squeezing gently. "My track record with relationships isn't great and I can't promise to make you happy."

"You don't know that. You have no idea what I need to be happy."

Grant's throat tightened at the misery in her tone. "Maybe not, but I know Paisley was not happy because I couldn't give her everything she needed."

And if Paisley had been disappointed in his inability to give her the intimacy she craved, how much more harm would befall someone who led with her heart like Harley?

"I'm not Paisley," Harley fumed, "and I wish you'd stop painting us both with the same brush."

"Okay, forget my ex-wife. Let's talk about how I disappointed my parents when I chose to become a doctor rather than join the family business." Grant found his tone darkening with grief as he tried to make her understand. "It wasn't easy on me knowing that I let them down, but I could never be happy unless I followed my own path."

She stared at him in grim silence as she processed what he'd said. "And the path you're on doesn't have room for me." Blinking rapidly, she dashed the back of her fingers over her damp cheeks. "If that's your final word, then I guess I have to do what's best for me."

"Meaning?" Too late Grant saw that he'd done too good a job of pushing her away.

"Obviously, if there's no future for us, there's no reason for me to stay in Royal."

Even though he'd known that his words would shatter the rapport between them, Grant believed he was doing the right thing. Until now.

"Then you've left me without a choice," Grant said, angry with himself and with her. "I'm not going to just let you take Daniel halfway around the world."

She must've been expecting that because nothing in her manner reflected surprise. "Have you thought about what this will do to Daniel?"

"Have *you*?" he snapped, furious with her for forcing his hand. Why couldn't she just be reasonable? There was no reason why she couldn't run Zest from Royal. Instead, she was taking Daniel away to punish Grant because he couldn't be a lovesick fool. Damn the woman for demanding more than he could give!

"I guess we are at a stalemate." Harley tossed her head like an unruly filly.

Grant growled in pain as every fiber of his being screamed at him to give her whatever she needed to be happy again. "I guess we are."

Eleven

In the days that followed the revelations that Grant would never consider taking their relationship any further, Harley channeled all her energy into Zest. To her chagrin, now that she wasn't spending any time in Grant's distracting company, her productivity had increased tenfold. How much more could she have accomplished if she hadn't wasted so much energy on something that could never be?

"I've been thinking that it might be time to shift my focus to Dallas and pursue donors there full-time," Harley said, eyeing her best friend to see how Jaymes would react to her plan.

"Are you sure you don't want to take Grant up on his offer of the funding and give him the partial custody of Daniel that he wants?" Jaymes asked the question patiently, despite having already discussed the sore subject with Harley several times in the last week.

She'd come back to Royal to shore up Zest's finances

and she'd been foolish enough to think she'd succeeded when Grant had offered to back her nonprofit. That he'd done it to guilt her into staying in Royal felt like a huge betrayal. Add to that his decision to pursue a legal claim to Daniel and Harley was regretting that she'd ever come back to Royal.

"You know how much I hate being bullied."

Harley dug her nails into her palms to stop the tears that threatened. She knew it would be easier for Grant if she and Daniel remained in Texas, but at the moment, she wasn't feeling particularly open to making things easier for him.

"I know you think that the best thing for Daniel is for him to spend as much time with Grant as possible," Harley continued. "But the work I'm doing in Thailand is very important as well and I can't bear the thought of leaving Daniel behind while I'm halfway around the world."

"And the fact that Grant isn't interested in having a relationship with you doesn't affect your decision at all?"

The burn of his rejection continued to smart. "Do you blame me for being hurt because he won't give us a chance?"

"It's not just you," Jaymes reminded her. "He said he's never going to marry again."

"So where does that leave me?" she demanded, her heart constricting painfully.

Denying that she wanted Grant in her life as both the father of her son and her lover had become impossible. The mere touch of his gaze made her entire body leap with joy. She only needed to be in the same room with him for her core to be mobbed by urgent impulses until she wanted nothing more than to throw herself into Grant's arms and revisit his passionate lovemaking.

"Am I just supposed to be okay that Grant is perfectly

content to have me in his bed whenever he feels like it and for us to act like a family when it's convenient for him?" Harley grumbled. "All my life I've been either ignored or underestimated by my family. Is it so wrong to want the man I love to love me back?"

Seeing the shock on Jaymes's face, Harley wished she'd reined in her bitterness. She'd bared her heart and confessed that she'd fallen in love with him five years ago. His response had been to dismiss her feelings, declaring the emotional attachment impossible simply because they'd barely known each other.

"No, of course not," Jaymes said, "but you can't expect him to love you back just because you think he should."

"I know. If he would just stop putting up walls," she complained, "but he won't." If he'd been willing to offer her the slightest encouragement, she would've compromised her plans and figured out how to run Zest without being in Thailand full-time. Instead, he'd insisted that he'd never feel the same way and her stubborn pride was all that saved her from making an even bigger fool of herself.

"I'm in love with him and he refuses to even consider giving us a chance," Harley continued. "How do I just accept that?"

"I don't know." Jaymes reached out a comforting hand and squeezed her friend's arm. "But if you run back to Thailand, aren't you just giving up?"

While Harley knew she was no longer the immature eighteen-year-old who'd run off when life got too complicated, if she repeated her mistake of five years earlier and behaved like one, she wouldn't be the only one to suffer.

"I'm afraid that if I don't give up, I'll be the one giving in and settling for less." Harley released a quavering breath. "Maybe it's all a moot point. The fact that he's unwilling to budge from his current position leads me to think that he's right. I would be forever unhappy with what he's willing to offer."

"Sounds like you've made up your mind about returning to Thailand. Do you have any idea when you're going to go?"

"I told Beth that I would stick around and attend the TCC ball. It seems like a fitting bookend to my relationship with Grant since it was at that same ball five years ago when he and I met. This year's gala will mark the moment when I abandon all hope that we have a future."

"So, you haven't abandoned all hope yet?" Jaymes asked, her expression suddenly optimistic.

Struck by a sudden bout of indecision, Harley considered how she should answer her friend. Hadn't she accepted that Grant would never give their relationship a fighting chance? Why then was she questioning what might happen if she stuck around for one more week? Gave more of herself to him? Maybe she could wear him down like wind and water carved rock.

Harley sighed as her vacillating mood shifted once more. "Maybe not all hope."

With everything blowing up in his personal life, Grant was relieved to get back to his practice where stability and discipline reigned. But in order to give his patients the quality of care they came to him for, he had to force down his frustration over Harley's stubborn insistence on returning to Thailand and taking his son away from him. It went against his beliefs to meet with patients and not give them his full and complete attention. This particular characteristic had driven Paisley crazy because she'd expected to receive the same focused attention he lavished on his patients. No matter how much she complained about his distance, Grant never seemed to be able to give her what she needed.

How strange that everything about his relationship with Harley was the exact opposite. Since she'd returned to Royal, he found himself constantly distracted. When he wasn't dwelling on her soft skin and lush mouth, he cataloged her various smiles and how each one messed with his emotions. His ability to focus on matters at hand suffered, thoughts tangling with emotions until he couldn't separate them.

After how he'd behaved around her five years earlier, he should've done a better job keeping his distance from her. They could've co-parented their son in a civil, cordial way and not fallen prey to the chemistry that set fire to his blood. If he'd remained in control, he wouldn't be plagued by uncertainty. If he hadn't kept tumbling into bed with her, could he have handled things better? Making love to her had stirred up his emotions, making him reactionary rather than rational.

His desk phone buzzed, letting him know that his next appointment was waiting. Grant got to his feet with an impatient huff, wishing he could fling his worries aside as easily as a dog shed water. Unfortunately, the anxiety that clung to him was more like spiderwebs and proved difficult to escape.

"Here's Gracie Diaz's chart with her labs," his nurse declared, handing him a file. "She's in exam room three."

"Thank you." Grateful for something concrete to focus his attention on, Grant opened the file and began scanning the results as he strode down the hall.

Yet, despite his best efforts, his emotions continued to churn as he opened the exam room door and strolled inside. Gracie Diaz sat with her hands clasped in her lap, white knuckles betraying her nerves. Seeing the stress in her beautiful dark brown eyes, Grant reined in his own disquiet. Although he rarely knew much about his patients beyond the medical information written in their files, Miss Diaz had become quite a household name in recent months after a lottery win took her from an anonymous personal assistant to a celebrated multimillionaire.

"Hello, Gracie," Grant said, softening his expression in the hopes that he would put her at ease. "How are you doing today?"

During her last visit, she'd been quite loquacious as she'd shared how much her life had changed in the past few weeks and spoken of her dream to be a mother. As was the case with several of his patients who were single, she'd decided to become pregnant through in vitro fertilization. In preparation for that procedure, Grant had initiated a standard barrage of tests to ensure that everything would go smoothly. The results had been less than ideal, but nothing he couldn't remedy.

"I'll be doing better after you tell me the results of my tests. Your nurse said you wanted to see me again before we started the procedure. Does that mean you found something wrong?"

"It's nothing serious," Grant said. "Just a minor hormone imbalance that could affect your chances of getting pregnant if we don't treat it."

This news relaxed her somewhat. Her lips softened into a big smile. "Well, that's a relief," she said with an unsteady chuckle. "I was convinced you were going to tell me I wasn't a good candidate for in vitro."

"No. Nothing like that."

"Good. I've wanted to have a baby for so long now and before the money came along, I didn't have the resources to make it happen."

Never once with all the couples or single women who'd

come to him wanting a child had he ever pondered their strong determination to create a family. However, after spending time with Harley and Daniel, he understood the drive. His fierce attachment to the boy wasn't a decision he'd made. It was a gut-deep response to a primitive yearning. He couldn't will it away any more than he could change the color of his eyes. It was part of him that he accepted without conscious thought.

Thinking about his son stirred Grant's concern and frustration that Harley intended to take Daniel back to Thailand. Why couldn't she see that their son was thriving in Royal where he had immediate access to both his parents?

"You have no worries about raising a child by yourself?" he asked, stepping past the boundaries of his standard professionalism.

"Not at all," she said eagerly, showing no signs of discomfort at his inquisitiveness. "Especially now that I have the financial resources to give my child everything they could ever possibly want or need."

Grant cleared his throat. "You don't think your child needs a father?"

"I think as long as I have a strong male influence in his or her life, it will be just fine." Obviously, it was something she'd come to terms with already. Perhaps she'd already had this conversation with more than one individual and had her rationale all sorted out. "And someday if I marry, then obviously I would hope that my husband would want to adopt my child."

"So you're not opposed to having a man in your life?"

Gracie blinked in surprise, but didn't appear at all upset by the inappropriateness of his question.

"I can't control my love life." She shrugged her shoulders and sighed wistfully. "However, this I can control.

Making a family on my timetable. Maybe that's selfish on my part, but I will give a child all the love and devotion they could ever need."

Grant considered all the men who hadn't stepped up when they fathered a child and all the women who had no choice but to raise children on their own. There were pros and cons to both sides of the story. He had no doubt that Gracie's child would be as well-adjusted as Daniel. Harley was an outstanding mother and Daniel lacked for nothing. The boy knew he was loved. But that didn't mean that Grant intended to back off and let Harley take his child away.

A bond had formed between father and son. He deserved to have partial custody of his son. But at what cost? He couldn't help but feel he was in a lose-lose situation. With Grant living in Texas and Harley living in Thailand, Daniel would be the one who truly suffered.

Yet, the boy wouldn't be the only one. Each time Grant thought about living without Harley, the ache in his chest grew. He'd ignored her unhappiness, believing that she'd eventually be as content with their little family as he was. Realizing just how eager she was to escape Texas left him feeling empty and raw.

Five years earlier, he'd rejected her and she'd vanished from his life, taking his son with her. Since learning about Daniel, Grant told himself if he'd known what he'd risked, he would've reasoned with Harley instead of letting his emotions get the better of him. Because now, he recognized that the way he'd rejected her had been born of anger at her deceit and shame that he'd been overwhelmed by desire for someone he realized was not just too young for him but too young to be treated like a casual sexual encounter.

Yet, here he was on the verge of losing his son a second time. Not because he hadn't used logic to persuade

Harley, but because he was still afraid of the emotions she aroused and the discomfort that always seemed to follow when he gave in to them.

In the wake of telling her family that Grant was Daniel's father, the only person besides her mother who continued to keep her at arm's length was Piper. Given how close she'd been to her aunt growing up, Piper acting as a combination of big sister and surrogate mother, their estrangement had hit Harley hard. And because they hadn't had a chance to talk since her aunt found out that Grant was the secret Harley had been keeping, Piper's disapproval remained an obstacle between them.

Now, as the situation with Grant had grown even more emotionally fraught, Harley knew she couldn't go on another week without making peace with Piper. To that end, she called her aunt and invited her to dinner. Since Jaymes and Sean were in Houston for the weekend, celebrating his father's sixtieth birthday, Harley decided to borrow their kitchen to prepare a few traditional Thai dishes. Daniel was spending the night with Grant so the two women would have the privacy to speak their minds.

Unfortunately, things did not go as smoothly as Harley had hoped. Daniel had been feeling off all day, complaining that his stomach hurt. Although he wasn't running a fever or showing any symptoms, he demanded her full attention. The food preparations she'd intended to make didn't happen as she snuggled beside her son and read stories to him. Then Grant called and told her he was running late and wouldn't be able to pick Daniel up until nearly seven o'clock. Given her son's possible illness, she'd been half tempted to keep Daniel with her, but Grant was a fully licensed medical professional, capable of dealing with a little boy's stomachache and she didn't want Grant to think that she was keeping his son away from him.

By the time Piper arrived at six o'clock, Daniel had rallied enough to watch cartoons in the living room. Harley was mortified that she was in the midst of chopping vegetables and nowhere near ready to serve her guest the delicious meals she'd had planned. But far from being put out, Piper poured herself a glass of wine, rolled up her sleeves and pitched in. Half an hour later, the divine smells emanating from the kitchen filled the entire house.

For the last few weeks, Harley's emotions had been bubbling dangerously close to the surface. Now, as she and Piper worked in harmony, without any of the charged atmosphere that had highlighted their relationship lately, Harley found herself close to tears.

"I'm so sorry I didn't tell you that Grant was Daniel's father," she blurted out in a shaky voice, grabbing the kitchen counter to steady herself. "I was just so hurt and mad at him and worried that because you were good friends, you'd tell him I was pregnant."

"I'm sorry you didn't feel like you could trust me," Piper said, her expression regretful. "And even sorrier that you were right. I probably would've been so angry with him that I would've marched right over to his house and berated him for acting so recklessly." Piper shook her head. "Even now I can't get over that he…"

"Slept with an eighteen-year-old?" Harley supplied helpfully when her aunt couldn't bring herself to state the obvious. "And got her pregnant?"

"What the hell was he thinking?"

"To be honest," she began, her lips twisting into a rueful smirk. "I didn't give his brain much of a chance to function."

Piper threw up her hands. "I don't want to know." She

paused for a second and then asked, "I hear you and Daniel are spending a lot of time with Grant."

"We were," Harley said. "But it's only Daniel now. Grant and I—"

"Stinky beans! Stinky beans!" Daniel bounded into the kitchen, lured away from the television by the familiar scents of where he'd grown up. "I love stinky beans."

"I know you do," Harley said. Stink beans, or *petai*, were strong-flavored beans from a twisted pod that she stir-fried with yellow curry paste and shrimp. "Do you think your tummy is feeling up to trying some when it's ready?"

"You bet."

In addition to the stink bean dish Daniel loved, Harley was making *pad kra pao*, a street food made of chicken stir-fried with lots of chilies, garlic and a big handful of basil all served over rice, as well as a shredded green papaya salad dressed in lime juice, palm sugar and fish sauce.

The doorbell rang as they were shifting the completed recipes to the dining room table. Leaving Piper and Daniel to finish without her, Harley went to answer the door. Grant had finished his business and arrived ahead of schedule to pick Daniel up.

"Hi," she said, overwhelmed by a rush of longing as his gaze swept over her, noting her bare feet, stained apron and flushed cheeks. "You're early."

"I hope that's okay," he said, looking beyond her as if hoping for an invitation. "Wow. Something smells amazing,"

"Daddy!" Hearing his father's voice, Daniel raced toward them, displaying none of the sluggishness he'd exhibited earlier in the day. He threw himself at his father and Grant swept him up. "Mommy made stinky beans. Do you want some?"

Grant raised an eyebrow and glanced at Harley. Unsure if he was questioning the name of the dish or asking if he was welcome, Harley gave a shrug and gestured for him to come in. What else could she do when her son so obviously wanted his father to join them?

"Are you sure this is okay?" Grant asked after setting Daniel back on his feet so he could lead the way to the dining room.

"Of course," she lied. "The more the merrier."

For her son's sake, she would duct tape her broken heart and soldier on.

Before heading into the dining room, Harley detoured into the kitchen and brought out another place setting.

"Oh, good, you're staying for dinner," Piper murmured. "Harley made enough for six."

"It smells delicious," Grant said as he settled into his place.

"Dig in," Harley instructed, pouring him a glass of wine.

Throughout dinner, her determination to remain civil when they were around Daniel was tested every time Grant attempted to snag her gaze. She refused to give him access to her pain. Grant was not a concerned friend. He was her former lover and as such, he'd lost the right to inquire after her emotional state. He'd torn her heart out and didn't get to ask her if she was okay about it.

"We should probably get going," Grant said to his son, as Daniel scraped every last bit of mango sorbet out of his bowl.

"Can't we spend the night here?"

Harley felt the curious press of Piper's gaze on her as she raised eyebrows and waited for Grant to extricate himself from the sticky situation. She had no problem relinquishing her parental duties for the moment.

"That's not possible," he said, his attention studiously avoiding Harley.

"Mommy and I always stay at your house," Daniel pointed out, something he'd been mentioning on and off to Harley in the week since she and Grant had called it quits. "Why can't you stay here?"

"Yes, Grant," Piper purred, contributing to the chaos. "Why can't you stay here? I'm sure Harley would be happy to put you up on the couch."

Harley was torn between laughing at Grant's discomfort and kicking her aunt under the table. She knew it was wrong to use her son's innocent request to torment Grant, but he deserved a taste of what she'd been dealing with since their estrangement.

"Neither one of you can stay," she told her son. "Tonight is supposed to be a girls' night only for Aunt Piper and Mommy. Now go get your backpack so Grant can take you to his house."

Daniel surveyed all three adults before nodding. "Okay, Mommy."

"Why don't I give him a hand," Piper said, springing from the table to follow after her great nephew, leaving Grant and Harley alone.

She immediately got to her feet and began to clear the table. From the look on Grant's face, he had something on his mind and she refused to sit around and let him voice it. Nor did she want to unload any of the turbulent thoughts spinning through her head. They'd both said everything pertinent and she might not be fine with it, but she knew a dead end when she saw it.

"It was really nice of you to let me have dinner with you," Grant said, pursuing her into the kitchen with a stack of dishes.

"Daniel invited you," she pointed out.

"You could've said no."

She leveled an exasperated look at him.

"The food was incredible," he said. "I had no idea you could cook like that. And, of course, the company was great, too. I've missed—"

"Don't."

She'd offered him this. She'd opened her heart and presented him with a ready-made family who loved him and he'd made it clear he had no intention of moving their romantic relationship forward. He wanted everything the way he wanted it and she wasn't okay with that.

"Harley..."

Panic enveloped her at his melancholy tone. She shook her head to stop him, afraid he might say something that would sway her treacherous heart. She had to hold herself apart from him and maintain a clear head if she intended to navigate what could become a tricky custody situation.

"We're fine. I'm fine. Everything's fine."

Desperate to flee, she started to go past him, but he caught her arm, long fingers encircling her bare skin. Longing shot from the point of contact to her aching heart. She was poised halfway between throwing her arms around his neck and yanking free of his grip when he spoke again.

"I missed this." His husky murmur battered at the wall she'd raised to hold back her misery. "I miss us."

So do I.

"I think it's pretty obvious that Daniel does, too," she said and nearly swooned with gratitude as his hand fell away.

She hardened her heart against his dazed expression. He looked nearly as shell-shocked as when she declared her intention to return to Thailand. She kept telling herself that there had to be some way to make all of them happy.

But at the moment, she couldn't figure out how. Either she stayed in Texas and gave up her dream of expanding Zest's good works to other countries. Or she gave up partial custody of her son. She no longer feared that Grant would demand full custody, but even half of Daniel was too much of a sacrifice. It wasn't fair.

After Grant escorted Daniel out the front door, Harley and Piper cleaned up the dishes and put the kitchen back to its former pristine condition. As the dishwasher began to hum, Piper turned to her niece with bright eyes.

"You two are—"

"Oh, please don't tell me we're acting like idiots."

Piper snorted. "Well, that, too, but what I was going to say is that you two are crazy in love with each other."

Harley put her hand on her chest as her heart gave a sickening lurch. Anguish stopped her breath for a beat. "I'm in love with Grant, but the feeling is not mutual."

"Don't be so sure. That man's in pain."

"Because he's afraid I'm going to take Daniel back to Thailand before he can sue me for partial custody." The tightness in her throat eased. "I've decided I won't."

"Won't go back to Thailand or not before you give Grant partial custody?"

"I love them both too much to separate them. Although it's not going to be easy to keep Zest going from halfway around the world, I've decided to stay in Texas. But not in Royal. I don't think I could face running into him all the time. And I want to avoid as much Wingate family drama as possible. Maybe Dallas."

"I know how much your nonprofit means to you," Piper said. "That's quite a sacrifice you're making."

"It's only fair since I was responsible for Grant missing out on the first four years of Daniel's life."

Piper studied her niece for several seconds before enveloping her in a warm hug. "You have developed into an outstanding woman. I'm so proud of you."

Harley put her arms around Piper and hugged back. "You have no idea how much that means to me. I've been so miserable without you."

"We both let our stubbornness get in the way." Piper pushed Harley to arm's length and gave her a little shake. "Use that same bullheaded determination when it comes to Grant. That man loves you, but he'll never admit it if you give up on him."

Harley sagged in defeat. "I've said and done all I can. Grant is going to have to figure out what he wants on his own."

Twelve

When Piper called and invited Grant to her gallery for an opening, he almost begged off, but decided a weekend in Dallas to clear his head might be just what he needed. Even though he wasn't scheduled to see Daniel until Monday, he shot Harley a text to let her know he'd be out of town for the next few days. She responded with a neutral, Have a fun weekend, and he left Royal early Saturday morning, feeling like his entire world was falling apart.

With nearly the whole day to kill before the opening, he met a friend from medical school for lunch. He hadn't seen Josh since the birth of his third child and found he had a whole new appreciation for the pride with which his friend showed off pictures of his beautiful family. Grant whipped out his own smartphone and flashed all the photos he'd taken of Daniel and Harley. His heart ached at how happy they all looked.

"I can't believe you have a son," Josh said, eyeing a

particularly charming picture of Harley and Daniel nose to nose, grinning at each other. "Where has he been all this time?"

"Thailand." Grant noticed the acute pang in his chest at the thought of his son being halfway around the world. "He was born there."

Josh looked sympathetic. "You didn't know?"

"Things didn't end well between the two of us before she moved, and then I got married and Harley didn't want to interfere in my life."

"But now she's back."

"She is," Grant said. But a gulf existed between them as wide as if she and Daniel still lived halfway around the world.

"Kids are great, aren't they?" Josh continued. "I mean there are days when mine drive me crazy, but my life would be so much less without them."

"I never thought about being a father until Daniel came along," Grant admitted, his mood thoughtful. "Now it's all I want."

His buddy glanced at Grant's phone screen once more. "You guys look really happy."

Grant turned the phone and regarded the image of himself with Harley and Daniel. Just staring at the picture lightened Grant's whole being. The three of them were laughing. Their connection so clear. That day had been great. Amazing. Spending time with Harley and Daniel had brought him more joy than he'd ever known.

But it hadn't lasted, just like he knew it wouldn't. He and Harley wanted different things and like with his marriage, it had been only a matter of time before their varying expectations drove them apart. Still, comparing his relationships with Harley and Paisley wasn't fair. His entire marriage hadn't stirred the sort of emotional squall that a single weekend with Harley had done. At the time, he'd considered that a good thing. But since his marriage hadn't worked out, Grant wondered if he had a clue what was truly best for him.

The question remained unanswered when Grant entered Piper's gallery later that night. He assumed she'd invited him as a patron of the arts. To his surprise, Harley's aunt made no attempt to convince him to buy anything. Instead, she herded him into a corner and fixed her dark green eyes on him.

"What's going on with you and my niece?" she began without preliminaries.

"What do you mean?" he asked, not intending to dodge her question, but hoping she would clarify whatever point she was trying to make.

"For weeks now, Harley has been Grant this and Grant that. And Grant and Daniel this and Grant and Daniel that. But now she tells me she's not going to stay in Royal. I thought you two were trying to make it work."

"Yes, well." Grant crossed his arms over his chest. "It's not working."

Piper gave an impatient snort. "So, what are you doing about that?"

"To start, my intention is to be legally recognized as Daniel's biological father."

"That's smart."

"Damn right it is," Grant snapped. "He's my son. I have rights."

"Of course you do. But isn't there a better way to go about getting what you want?"

Grant stared at Piper, noted her intent regard, but couldn't quite fathom what she was trying to get at. "Such as?"

"What about you, Harley and Daniel being together?"

When he continued to regard her blankly, she added, "As a family."

The suggestion went through him like a lightning strike. "Too many things have gone wrong between us. I don't think she'll have me."

"Have you asked her?" Piper asked, looking unimpressed by his grumbling.

"I have." Hadn't he?

Grant had tried bribing her with funding for Zest and when that had failed, he'd blustered about her decision to take Daniel away.

"I've made it perfectly clear that I want more time with Daniel."

Piper rolled her eyes. "You took the easy way out by making all of this about Daniel."

Because fixing his custody situation was something tangible and within his control. "It is all about Daniel."

"Is it?" Piper countered slyly. "I don't think so. Why don't you try telling her you love her and see what happens?"

Grant opened his mouth but no words came out. Long ago, he'd learned a hard lesson. It hurt too much to let his heart lead the way. And yet, could he honestly say that logic had guided his decision to become a doctor against his parents' wishes? Wasn't his crusade to help create families a deeply personal, emotional mission for him? Every successful procedure brought him satisfaction because he had enabled another's joy. If all that was true, why did he use professionalism to isolate himself instead of celebrating with his patients?

Because if he allowed his emotion to flow, he might not be able to rein himself back in.

"Harley loves you," Piper declared. "You love her. What are you so damned afraid of?"

Before he could answer, Piper's gaze shifted past him and something in her expression sent an electric shock of fear through Grant. He knew Harley stood behind him and the ache in his chest made it nearly impossible to catch his breath.

"This is the moment to declare how you really feel about her," Piper said, squeezing his arm in encouragement.

"I don't know if I can," he admitted, the admission born of fear and an instinctive need to avoid pain. It was like being asked to perform surgery on himself without anesthetic. The hurt would be intense, but it was something he needed to go through to heal.

"You can." Piper hit him with a stern look before she moved past him. "Don't hold anything back."

Grant tracked Piper's retreat for a couple seconds before shifting his full attention to Harley. As soon as their eyes locked, she began to turn away. No! In that instant of abject panic, he recognized the truth. He loved her—deeply, passionately, without reason or sanity. Confronting this reality was as terrifying and perilous as he'd expected and something he'd been running from since the moment she arrived back in Royal.

"Harley, wait." Grant crossed the space between them in three gigantic strides and caught her hand. "I need to talk to you."

Her chest rose and fell on a huge sigh. "Look, you win," she said, her shoulders slumping in defeat. "It wasn't fair of me to keep you away from Daniel for the last four years and it wouldn't be right for us to go back to Thailand now. So, I've decided that we're staying in Texas."

Her decision should've thrilled him. Instead, his confidence cracked beneath the impact of her sacrifice. "I'm glad."

"I figured you would be." A cynical smile twisted her

lips. "And Daniel's happy here. He's made new friends and all his family is here."

Nowhere in any of her rationale had she mentioned anything that benefited her. Grant knew how hard she'd worked to make Zest a success and that running the non-profit from Texas wasn't ideal. Yet, she was willing to dial down her dreams so her son would benefit from having his father in his life and Grant couldn't even confess how important she was to him.

"It's great that you're staying," he said, "because…"

His entire world would change with the next sentence he declared. Did he confess the unvarnished truth of his heart and work damned hard to make her happy? Or should he continue to play it safe and slowly but surely fail to live up to her expectations? Harley wouldn't be satisfied with half measures and excuses. She was the sort who went all in and would expect him to do the same.

"I think you and Daniel should move in with me."

Harley gasped. *Move in with him?*

"Have you thought this through at all?" The question flew from her lips before she had a chance to weigh the best way to respond.

"No," he admitted, looking more than a little stunned by his impulsiveness. "But it's exactly what I want."

It would be the height of foolishness to assume he meant anything other than what was utterly practical. Of course, Grant needed her. He needed her to stay in Texas so he'd have access to his son. If she returned to Thailand, Daniel would go with her. Grant intended to take her to court, but those things took time. She could be gone before the custody battle happened and he'd be forced to wait until she returned to the states once more to assert his rights.

"Why?"

"I need both you and Daniel in my life."

"You need us," Harley echoed, schooling herself not to read anything into such an unsatisfying answer. "And you think living with me is the price you have to pay in order to be a full-time father."

Her heart broke as she recognized the folly of her dream to become a family with him. Why hadn't she listened when he told her that he wasn't marriage material? She'd deceived herself into believing that he hadn't truly loved Paisley. Or that they hadn't suited each other. He'd claimed Paisley had expected too much from him. That she'd demanded more than he could give her.

Harley had convinced herself that he would stop relying on his logic and trust his emotions when it came to her. She knew he loved Daniel, even if he couched the affection in a word like *need*. And she was starting to think he held some sort of fondness for her. But friendship wasn't enough. She couldn't be satisfied with whatever portion of himself Grant was willing to give. She wanted everything he was and to give him all of her in return. The best and worst of each other. The passion and the reason. To be friends, lovers and soul mates.

"Don't be ridiculous," he said, scowling at her. "The only reason I asked you to move in with me is because I can't bear to live without you."

Weeks earlier, his words would've been music to her ears. Now, she worried that he was only telling her what she wanted to hear so he could arrange everything to suit him. But what if he was truly ready to give their relationship a chance?

"Why the change?" Before she gave in, she needed to hear his motivation. "What do you really want?"

"I want you." He took her hands in his and squeezed gently. "I have since we first met."

Harley's throat locked up. "Why are you telling me this now? Do you think that I will fall so madly in love with you that I won't reconsider returning to Thailand? Or is this your way of keeping me happy until we settle our custody arrangements?"

Grant shook his head. "Have you ever thought of me as manipulative?"

"No." She surveyed his expression while her heart pounded. "But a week ago you told me we had no future. Now you're asking me to move in with you. Forgive me for thinking you're desperate enough to keep Daniel around that you're willing to do anything."

"A week ago I was convinced that the only way I would be happy is if I had everything the way I wanted it." Grant freed one of her hands so he could cup her cheek.

Harley latched on to his wrist for support as her knees wobbled. "A week ago, you wanted me to stay in Texas. Today, I told you I would." She drew in an unsteady breath. "Isn't that everything you want?"

"Not everything." Grant dipped his head and grazed his lips over hers, before murmuring, "I need you."

Harley's heart softened beneath his fervent tone, but she was too afraid of being disappointed to give hope a chance. "Because I'm Daniel's mother…"

"Because I love you."

To her dismay, the words she'd longed to hear him utter awakened skepticism, not joy. "Grant…"

He set his fingertip against her lips, silencing her. "What can I do to convince you?"

Immediately, her mind latched on to the one crazy, outrageous thing she wanted more than anything else, knowing it was something he'd never in a million years do. But as she stared at the man she loved, the words trembling on her lips, Harley knew she could never bring herself to ask him to make such a sacrifice.

"You don't have to do anything," she heard herself saying and recognized that it was true. How could she expect him to trust his feelings for her if she didn't have confidence in them?

"What if I go with you and Daniel to Thailand?"

Harley's chest spasmed at his earnest expression and for a moment she couldn't breathe. "You can't."

He shook his head. "I can. It'll just take me a little time to make arrangements. Many of my clients are undergoing treatment and I can't abandon them when they are on the verge of creating families of their own. But if I don't take on any new patients, I should be able to go with you in a couple months."

She laughed uneasily, surprised and unsure how to respond to such an incredible offer. "Are you sure?"

"I've never been more serious about anything in my entire life."

Believing that he was indeed committed to following through, Harley immediately backpedaled. "I can't ask you to do that."

"You didn't ask," he pointed out with a wry smile. "I offered to go with you. I was serious when I said I needed you. And Daniel. Yes, you're a package deal. And I wouldn't have it any other way. I want us to be a family. Whatever that involves. Wherever you are—whether it's in Royal or in Thailand—I want to be with you. You have my heart. And where it goes, I go."

It was everything she'd ever wanted to hear from him and so much more. Harley squeezed her eyes shut, her entire body buzzing with energy. This was the moment to embrace what he was offering her and spend the rest of her life as the happiest woman on earth. To take that leap of faith. To believe in him. In them.

"I love you," she whispered, all fight rushing out of her. "And because I do, I can't take you away from what you love."

"What I love is you and Daniel and the family we make when we're together. Everything else is mere distraction that keeps me from noticing how incredibly lonely I was before you came back into my life."

The throb of profound emotion in his voice was the sweetest music Harley had ever heard. Grant's entire life was driven by logic. For him to recognize and relish his love for her and acknowledge his longing for them to become a true family was all she'd ever wanted.

"I belong with you and Daniel," he continued, his fingers tightening as he pledged his heart. "You're my home. So you see, it doesn't matter if it's here or halfway around the world. I can be a doctor anywhere. What I can't bear is being without you and Daniel."

Harley could barely see his features dissolve into a breathtaking smile as tears filled her eyes. She blinked, trying to clear her vision and felt a hot trickle make its way down her cheek. Grant's thumb whisked away the moisture as his lips met hers in a reverent kiss that left her senses soaring and the blood rushing fast and hot through her veins.

Surrendering to unbridled joy, Harley wrapped her arms around his neck and kissed him back, leaving nothing to his imagination. She surrendered her whole heart and gloried as he gave her his heart in return. Passion simmered as the romantic embrace went on and on. His fingers tunneled into her hair and caressed her cheek, making her feel safe and adored.

Leaving all their misunderstandings behind, Harley

promised she would no longer hide from him how she felt. Good or bad, she was determined that she would share her deepest thoughts with Grant. They might disagree. They might even fight. But she would trust him to listen.

"You and Daniel are my everything," she confessed, beaming up at him. How was it possible that she'd gotten so lucky? The icy chill of loneliness she'd suffered these last five years vanished as happiness blazed inside her like the sun.

"I'm sorry it took me so long to understand how important you are to me. If I hadn't been such an obstinate fool five years ago, we wouldn't have lost so much time."

"You weren't wrong back then," she said. "I had a lot of growing up to do. Becoming Daniel's mother and the years abroad with no one to rely on but myself enabled me to figure out who I am."

"I lusted after the woman you were," he declared with a wicked grin. "but I adore the woman you are."

Harley's heart melted at the mixture of fondness and passion in his gaze. All she'd ever wanted was for someone to love and appreciate her.

"You know that we don't need to leave Royal for me to be happy," she said. "I understand how important your work is to you."

"And that's exactly why I'm able to leave it behind." Eyes glowing with affection, he cupped her face in his palm. "My family never made an effort to understand me. You see what motivates me and appreciate why I am the way I am."

"I love your big beautiful brain and your selfless dedication to helping women conceive. You don't help people for the accolades or the money. You create families because that brings people joy. Anyone who doesn't understand that is a fool."

Harley barely finished speaking before Grant crushed her body to his and pressed ardent kisses to her lips. She wrapped her arms around his neck and gave herself over to the bliss that flooded her. As she lost herself in his thrilling embrace, she thought about the journey she'd been on since the troubles began plaguing the Wingate fortune. The financial downturn she'd suffered had forced her to come home, but it was her heart that had been impoverished. Only when she'd set aside her pride and believed in love had she been gifted with all the riches that were Grant's devotion.

"We're going to make this work," she murmured in wonder when at last he lifted his lips from hers. She framed his face with her palms and smiled.

"We're going to do more than that," he assured her, his eyes glowing with tender passion. "We're going to make people's lives better and we're going to be very *very* happy doing it."

* * * * *

HIDDEN
AMBITION

JULES BENNETT

To my girls, Grace and Madelyn. Thanks for keeping things running while I was pressed for time with this deadline. You two are my world.

One

Haley Shaw bent over the gift boxes, searching around the obscene bouquets of flowers and cupcake boxes, just trying to find her damn yellow highlighter.

"That's quite a display."

The low, throaty voice was all too familiar…and all too arousing.

Haley straightened and turned to face a smirking, sexy Chase Hargrove. The persistent man was vying for the coveted position of CEO of Black Crescent Hedge Fund. The successful investment firm had been through hell and back, and Haley had stuck through it all—which made her the target of all the résumés and all of the bribes. Hence the gifts cluttering her normally pristine work space.

"I assume you were referring to the flowers and boxes and not the fact I was bent over with my backside facing you while looking for my highlighter," she stated, smoothing down her conservative dove-gray pencil dress.

His deep brown eyes held hers. "Of course."

Sure. That naughty grin gave him away and she had a feeling a powerful man like Chase always held his emotions and cards close to his chest. He wanted her unnerved, thrown off track. Well, it would take a hell of a lot more than charm and a little flirting to really get her attention.

Haley prided herself on her professionalism. She'd worked too hard, overcome too much, to land where she was. True, she was an executive assistant, but she had power here at Black Crescent and she never let her emotions, or a man, get in the way of her duties.

Not even this sexy man who was very qualified to take over the coveted CEO position and potentially become her boss.

"Do you have an appointment?" she asked, knowing full well he didn't.

Chase had been popping in and out over the past several weeks, ever since Josh Lowell had announced he was stepping down and the CEO position would be available. Chase had turned in a rather impressive résumé and had even landed an interview a few weeks ago. The position had been offered to Ryan Hathaway, but ultimately, Ryan turned down the coveted title. So the search continued as Chase moved closer to the top of the list. Hence Chase pursuing the job…and her.

Not that she minded a sexy distraction, but she really did need to get her work done and there was no chance of that as long as Chase stood at her desk with that panty-dropping stare.

Maybe he really was here for the job, but he spent an exorbitant amount of time charming her.

Haley was Josh's right-hand woman and everyone thought she was the gatekeeper in regards to the top position. Haley had to admit, she didn't hate all of this attention. Who could be mad when cupcakes, flowers and chocolates were delivered on the daily?

"I do have an appointment," he amended with a naughty, crooked grin. "With you."

Confused, she crossed her arms over her chest. "Me?"

"For lunch."

Oh, he was a smooth one. He thought he could waltz in here, pour on the charisma and she'd just take him up on a day date? Clearly he knew nothing about women…or at least this woman. She didn't let anything interrupt her work. Or at least, she never did before him.

"I'm not free for lunch." She lifted one vase, then another, on her desk, glancing for all the things she'd lost in this chaos. "But you go have a nice time."

"What are you looking for?" he asked, obviously in no hurry to go.

"My highlighter," she informed him. "I keep get-ting all of these gifts and I've run out of room for things I actually need. I normally have everything in a designated spot, but now…"

She tossed her hands up, frustrated with how quickly her space had become unorganized.

"When we go to lunch, we can stop and get you as many new highlighters as you need," he suggested. "My treat."

Haley glanced up and really wished her belly would stop doing those schoolgirl flops over a hot guy and his offer to buy her dollar markers.

So what if his shoulders perfectly filled out that black suit jacket? So what if his messy hair looked like he'd just rolled out of his lover's bed? He wouldn't be rolling out of her bed, so she really had no place fantasizing about such things.

She had important issues to tend to and getting distracted by a man who likely wasn't interested in her, but in how far she could get him in this field, was not one of them.

The phone on her desk rang and she sighed. "If you'll excuse me, I need to get back to work."

She took the call and moments later when she hung up, she was surprised to see he had actually left. But there wasn't a doubt in her mind that Chase Hargrove would be back. A man like that never gave up.

Chase clutched the surprise in his hand and headed into Black Crescent Hedge Fund for the second time that morning. Determination and revenge were a combination that no rejection could penetrate.

No matter how many times he had to show his face, flirt a little or buy silly bribes, he'd sure as hell do it. A little humility was nothing in comparison with what his family had gone through at the hands of Vernon Lowell.

The sneaky bastard had squandered millions and disappeared fifteen years ago, but Chase would never forget the struggle his family went through after his father was framed by Vernon to take some of the fall.

Chase's father had landed in prison for a few years, paying for his actions after Vernon had left a neat and tidy paper trail leading right to their door.

Now Chase had the opportunity to seek his own justice, since Vernon was never caught. His son Josh was now at the helm, and Chase didn't find him exempt from the damage.

He hadn't counted on the perks of the revenge plot, though. Getting an eyeful of Haley Shaw was certainly an added bonus. There was something about her unruffled attitude that made him want to just get his digs in where he could…which was why he didn't mind one bit that she'd caught him staring at her ass.

He wasn't a jerk or a guy who took advantage of women. He respected women, but if a male held the position that Haley did, Chase would certainly be going about this via a much different route.

As he stepped through the double glass doors, he nodded to the receptionist and headed toward the elevators. One day soon, this would all be his. Chase had the credentials and was more than qualified to settle perfectly into the CEO position. But if not, then he'd at least get the scoop he needed to help bring Black Crescent down for good. They deserved nothing less and Haley was inadvertently going to help him.

As for the top slot here, Chase didn't need it. He sure as hell wasn't hurting for money, but he wouldn't mind adding another investment firm to his portfolio.

Chase stepped out of the elevator and walked toward Haley's large circular desk, and once again the overwhelming scent of flowers assaulted him. He shouldn't be surprised at all the candidates vying for her attention, though they were being too predictable. Boxes of gourmet chocolates? Oversize floral arrangements? Cupcakes from the local bakery? Please. Those candidates were amateurs and utterly boring.

Haley had her back to him and was holding a stack of papers, muttering beneath her breath. A woman getting caught up in her work was damn sexy, but he wasn't here for seduction. Shame that. Having Haley under different circumstances wasn't something he'd turn down. Classy, smart, powerful... She was the entire package of sex appeal.

Chase pushed lustful thoughts from his head and tapped his knuckles on the edge of the desk. She startled and glanced over her shoulder, her wavy blond hair framing her face.

"Back so soon?" she asked, quirking a brow.

Damn if her sarcasm didn't up his attraction to her. He had to admit, this challenge wasn't proving to be boring. He actually looked forward to his interactions with Haley.

Chase held up the present. "I brought you something."

Her eyes darted to his hand and she turned fully to face him. "Seriously?" She laughed as she circled her desk. "Is that a bouquet of highlighters?"

He extended the gift. "You couldn't find yours and you had enough flowers and gourmet-cupcake boxes."

She stared at the bundle for a second before she took the variety of colors. The wide smile on her face was like a punch of lust to his gut. Not exactly what he'd come looking for, but something about her simple style and natural beauty appealed to a side he didn't want to be appealed to.

Lust and desire didn't follow guidelines, though. He couldn't help this attraction and he couldn't help but wonder if she was getting that kick of arousal, as well.

"Well done," she told him with a wide grin. "I admire someone who thinks outside the box."

Chase shoved his hands in his pockets. "Admire enough to go to lunch? You do get a lunch break, right?"

"I do," she confirmed. "But I'm not going to lunch with you. I have other plans."

"Cancel them."

She cocked her head. "Are you always demanding?"

"When I see something I want."

And there it was. A glimpse of desire he hadn't quite been sure about flashed through her eyes. Well, well, well. Maybe he could keep working this angle and come out with the job and a side fling. Win-win.

"Fine," she conceded. "We'll go to lunch, but we will not talk business."

Not talk business? No problem. He could gather information from her without her even realizing he was doing so. He hadn't gotten this far making billions by not being able to read people.

Besides, he'd already worn her down—by a bouquet of highlighters, no less. Chase was confident he would get damaging intel from her and she wouldn't have a clue she'd even let him in.

"Lead the way," he said, gesturing to her door.

Chase followed those swaying hips and reminded himself he was here for a purpose, a vendetta, not to see how quickly he could slide that zipper down and have her out of that body-hugging dress.

Only time would tell which one of them came out on top... But Chase didn't intend to lose.

Two

Haley nodded her thanks to the concierge as he opened the door for her and Chase. The posh, up-scale restaurant was a bit over-the-top for a lunch between virtual strangers, but this was where he'd chosen and she actually did love their Mediterranean salad.

"Welcome back, Mr. Hargrove," the hostess promptly greeted them with all smiles. "I have your usual table all set up."

Haley bit the inside of her cheek to keep quiet as she followed the hostess back to the corner of the restaurant. The intimate table for two offered a spectacular view of New York City, one she appreciated when she ate here at night.

Once they were seated and alone, Haley glanced

across the table. "So, how many women do you bring here, Mr. Hargrove?"

"Chase," he corrected with a crooked grin. "And not many."

"Yet you have a usual table and I can't imagine a man like you eating alone." She pulled in a breath and leveled her gaze. "Chase."

His eyes dropped to her lips the second she said his name and she seriously wished she would've kept the *Mr. Hargrove* in the conversation. It wasn't like her to get all tingly at the sight of a man, but no man had looked at her like he wanted to devour her…at least not in a long time.

Maybe she needed to date. Perhaps she'd been working too much. Once this new CEO position was filled, she would work on her social life. But not with a man like Chase Hargrove.

Chase was a man who no doubt liked nice things, always had a sexy woman on his arm and demanded people to bow to him. She'd seen enough of his type over the years in this business to know exactly what he required. She was most definitely not his type.

No, Chase flirted and was no doubt going to all this trouble to get into that top slot at Black Crescent. She wasn't stupid, but she'd let him play his little game if that made him feel better about himself.

And, hey, she got new highlighters and a lunch out of it, so this wasn't a total loss. Besides, the view across the table was rather appetizing.

"I'm confident enough to eat alone," he replied. "I

often meet acquaintances here or friends and, yes, I have brought a date here a time or two."

"And what category are you sliding me into?" she asked, smoothing the cloth napkin onto her lap.

Those dark eyes shielded by heavy lids could make a woman forget whom she was dealing with. But Haley wasn't a ditz, despite how she'd been treated for years by her family.

She'd fought damn hard to get where she was today, with no help from her parents. Being an executive assistant wasn't easy work and oftentimes could be overlooked considering the amount of behind-the-scenes tasks that were involved. That wasn't the case with working with Josh. They clashed every now and then, but they also had a mutual respect for each other.

And now they were working closely together to find the perfect replacement to take Black Crescent into a successful, prosperous future.

Haley prided herself on how loyal and dedicated she had been to a company that had floundered amid the biggest scandal this town had ever seen and had climbed back up out of the ashes.

True, she may have gone only to a community college, but that didn't make her degree any less important or inferior to her brother's Ivy League status.

"Which category do you want to be in?" he retorted.

Pulling herself back into the moment, Haley pursed her lips and weighed her answer, but thankfully the waiter came by. Of course Chase knew the man by name, asked about his work, made a joke and laughed. This must be a favorite hot spot for Chase... or the man owned the place.

Josh trusted her to see things he didn't. Allison Randall, the executive recruiter Black Crescent hired, did the professional vetting on his résumé. Everything was perfect.

Too perfect? Haley made a mental note to dig into Chase's past and find out just what he was up to. Of course, he'd had a remarkable résumé and all of his references had checked out, but she wanted to know more. She wanted to dive into that personal side of him that he hadn't revealed.

Haley didn't believe he'd go to all this trouble just to be the CEO of Black Crescent. And she certainly didn't believe he was trying to sway her into dating him—maybe bed her.

Haley and Chase both placed their drink orders and sent the waiter away. Before they could circle back to the conversation, her cell chimed and she slid the phone from her purse. One glance to the screen and she sent Chase an apologetic smile.

"I need to take this," she told him.

Chase nodded. "I understand. Business first."

But it wasn't the business he was thinking and she didn't necessarily need privacy, so she eased back in her seat and answered.

"Marcus," she greeted. "I was going to call you this afternoon."

"I just wanted to touch base with you regarding

the latest funding," her right-hand man told her. "The latest investor doubled their original donation."

Haley gasped. "You're serious?"

She didn't miss the way Chase stared at her, hanging on every word. This call had nothing to do with Black Crescent and everything to do with Haley's charity that was like her baby.

"Very," Marcus replied. "That means we can take on seven more high school seniors."

Haley closed her eyes and pulled in a deep breath, relieved they could take on more teens in need. This was the best news. She'd been struggling to get to the stack of applicants from area high schools.

Her nonprofit, Tomorrow's Leaders, aided teens who wouldn't be able to go to college without the funding of an outside source. Not every kid wanted a student loan they'd have to pay back before some even found a job. These underprivileged kids deserved the best opportunity for a solid foundation to jump-start their futures and Haley was all too happy to make it happen.

She had been that underprivileged kid. Her parents had put her older brother through Harvard, but that had sucked up their entire savings. They'd believed he would become some master surgeon or celebrity attorney… Hell, she didn't know what their plans had been. All Haley knew was they had low expectations for her and no money to expand her education beyond high school. So Haley had worked her ass off to pay for the community schooling and graduated top of her class without any outside help.

"I will take this evening and look through the files again," she told Marcus. "I can't tell you what a blessing this is to know we can take on more kids."

"I knew you'd be thrilled. That's why I wanted to call and not text. I hope I didn't interrupt anything."

Her eyes met Chase's again and he didn't even bother to hide the fact he was staring.

"Your timing was just fine," she stated. "I'll get back with you late tonight or early tomorrow about the applicants."

Haley disconnected the call and slid the phone back into her purse.

"Kids?" he asked, raising his brows.

She smiled. "Well, teenagers, but considering I'm thirty-four, they're kids to me."

"You work with teens?" he asked, clearly shocked, and if she was reading him right, maybe a little impressed.

"For several years now," she confirmed, proud of the work she'd done all on her own. "I run Tomorrow's Leaders. It's a nonprofit organization that assists college-aged students who wouldn't otherwise be able to go. Not everyone wants the black cloud of student loans looming over them when they graduate, and many kids can't afford to further their education and they aren't all eligible for scholarships."

Chase listened, his eyes never wavering from hers. Not everyone knew what she did in her spare time. Not that she wasn't extremely proud of the work she'd done, but she wasn't one to brag and she didn't really have the time to socialize between finding a new CEO and running her charity.

"Impressive," he stated as he leaned back in his chair. "You're one busy woman."

"Which is why I often eat lunch at my desk," she informed him.

"Then I'm doubly glad I got you out of there."

Chase smiled, which really shouldn't make her belly do flops, but the man was a little more potent than she'd first given him credit for. She had to remain on her toes where this one was concerned.

"How long have you been doing this nonprofit?" he asked.

Haley never tired of talking about her cause. She didn't talk to many outside of her office or those directly involved with Tomorrow's Leaders. Her family didn't even know what she did, but then again, she rarely saw or spoke to them.

But who knew, maybe Chase would want to become a donor.

"Twelve years," she informed him. "As soon as I finished school, I started campaigning for donors and working to get something up and running. The first year, I was only able to help one guy, but that was better than nothing. Even if I could only help one person a year, I would still fight just as hard for funding."

Chase stared across the table, then leaned forward, resting his forearms on the white cloth. "What makes you so vigilant about this subject? You went to college, right?"

"I did," she confirmed. "But my backstory is not up for discussion."

Discussing her whys for the whole nonprofit organization wasn't her favorite topic, and the last thing she ever wanted was for someone to believe she felt sorry for herself. She didn't pity her childhood or how she managed to make it through college. If she didn't have those hardships, she wouldn't be the strong career woman she was today and she wouldn't have founded Tomorrow's Leaders. Maybe her parents hadn't done her a disservice after all.

Added to all of that, Chase was still out for his own gains and she didn't want to give him any insight to her personal life. This was nothing more than a lunch between strangers. If he was trying to seduce her, well, that was a whole other level of consideration for her to think about.

"Maybe on our second date," he stated with a grin.

Haley laughed. "This isn't a date."

"No? Well, then we'll have to fix that." He curled his hand around his water glass and tipped his head. "Friday at eight. I'll send a car to pick you up."

Haley stared at him for a moment before she busted out laughing. "Does that usually work for you? Just to demand like that?"

He shrugged. "Do you have other plans?"

"My personal life really isn't your concern," she replied.

"And yet you shared your nonprofit with me and had such compassion in your tone," he retorted. "I'd say that's pretty personal."

"Maybe I was hoping you'd want to donate."

His lips twitched and she knew he was biting back a smile. Good. He needed to keep those sexy smiles to a minimum for her sanity.

"One hundred thousand dollars."

"Excuse me?" she asked.

"I'll give Tomorrow's Leaders one hundred thousand dollars if you go out with me on Friday."

Haley narrowed her eyes, disappointed he'd resorted to buying her. "I can't be bought, not even for my foundation."

Obviously he wasn't used to taking no for an answer, but he might as well get used to it because she was not giving in. Okay, the highlighters had won him a lunch, but no more.

They placed their orders and Haley really wished she would've stayed in her office for lunch like always. She had too much to do, too many things to oversee, and she honestly hated leaving in the middle of a workday.

Being so valuable within Black Crescent made her feel a sense of worth, one she hadn't found with anything else in her life. She'd come there as an intern straight out of college and had only grown with each passing year. There were secrets she knew that she would never reveal, and that was why Josh Lowell entrusted her with the daunting task of helping him find his replacement.

Because she was the longest-standing employee, résumés were sent to her and not to Josh, or even to Allison Randall, the executive recruiter.

Haley and Josh had both laughed about the fact people were wanting to deal with her, because she wasn't the final decision maker. Although, she rather enjoyed knowing how powerful some people thought she was.

Her cell chimed again and she didn't even apologize for taking this next call. After Chase had offered a ridiculous amount to take her on a real date, she didn't care what he thought or if her manners were lacking.

Josh's name lit up her screen and she slid her finger across to answer.

"Hey, Josh."

"Haley, sorry to interrupt your lunch. I just had a quick question."

"No problem at all."

The waiter came with their food and Chase made work of cutting up his chicken, but she knew he was hanging on every word.

"I can't find Matt's résumé," he began. "I had it before his first interview and I wanted to look at it again."

The names slid through her mind, but Matteo Velez stood out. Matt's résumé was impeccable and he'd aced the first interview.

"I still have it on my computer," she told her boss. "I'll get it to you as soon as I get back."

"I ran into him the other evening when I was out with Sophie," Josh told her. "He bought my dinner, actually."

Josh chuckled, but Haley rolled her eyes. Everyone thought they could get ahead by buying their way, but that didn't fly with her. She'd rather have actions, not money being tossed around.

A lesson Chase would do well to learn.

"Please remember, I'm going to need someone personable I can get along with once you're gone and I don't know Matt too well."

"I promise not to leave you with a bastard," Josh stated. "Get me his résumé when you can. With Ryan out of the running, I just want to look closer at Matt. He did seem like a nice guy, and that was before I found out he bought my dinner."

"I'll be back in thirty minutes and I'll get it right to you."

"I knew I could count on you," he stated before hanging up.

Haley really did dread the day when Josh would leave. He'd been an upstanding boss and she'd come to think of him as a friend. But he wanted to start a new chapter in his life and she really couldn't blame him.

After the scandal with his father disappearing and pilfering millions from clients, Josh had rebuilt Black Crescent Hedge Fund. His twin, Jake, had wanted nothing to do with the family business and had taken off for Europe. And their youngest brother, Oliver, had his own issues, namely being a recovering addict and professional partier. He had his own mess of a reputation to overcome, and stepping into the top role of a tarnished hedge-fund company was not a position he was ready for.

So, Josh stepped up and Haley had been right there by his side, helping him rebuild. People who went through hell together shared a special bond. It would take one very exceptional man or woman to replace someone as strong and resilient as Josh Lowell.

"Sounds like the hunt is still on," Chase casually mentioned as he pierced a baby potato with his fork. "I imagine you and Josh are having a difficult time narrowing down a potential replacement."

"No work talk," she reminded him with a smile. "But if you want to talk business, you can tell me what exactly you do. I want to know what's not on your résumé."

"Eager to learn more about me?" he asked with a mischievous grin. "I deal with investments, but I also travel and help other companies across the globe work on strengthening their own firms."

Which sounded like the perfect replacement for Josh. But Chase would have to have more than the perfect answer to get the position, and this certainly wasn't an interview.

"Are you from here?" she asked.

"Born and raised about twenty minutes away," he told her. "My father was also an investor and my mother was a stay-at-home mom. I'm an only child. Nothing much to tell, really. I went to college on a full-ride football scholarship. My parents struggled a bit, so I'm not sure we could've afforded it other-wise."

That would explain that broad frame and she

could easily see him in the role of a star athlete. She also wouldn't mind seeing him in those tight pants.

Focus, Haley. You don't even like football.

Haley was surprised at how similar they were in fighting for what they wanted and being so head-strong, but she wasn't going to admit any such thing. Chase was clearly looking for that edge up and she certainly wasn't going to just hand him the ammunition.

All of her attraction aside, Josh had the final say over the new CEO, and Haley wasn't so sure being sexually drawn to your new boss was the best position to be in.

"I have updated my résumé since my first interview," he went on. "You have a new copy in your inbox."

Shocked, she set her fork down and dabbed her mouth with her napkin. "And when did you resend?"

"Right before I came back with your gift," he explained. "I rebuilt a multibillion-dollar firm in Europe and I included those stats and references. They'll all give me a glowing recommendation, by the way."

Damn it. He was getting more qualified by the moment.

Haley instantly had a vision of working with him day in and day out. She'd been side by side with Josh for years now and never once had she been attracted to him, not in the intimate way. He was certainly a handsome man, but she'd never gotten those giddy feelings…nothing like with Chase, and she'd only been with him for an hour.

Giddy? No. Almost arousing, which was even more dangerous.

Yeah, working with Chase Hargrove for hours on end would be a mistake. No doubt he would continue to try to wear her down.

Good thing she was on to him.

Three

Chase felt confident about his lunch date with Haley. Flirting came easy and he'd actually found himself caught up in her beauty, and suddenly charming her didn't seem to be a chore.

He'd been stunned to learn of her charity work. That someone with a demanding career spent her spare time helping those less fortunate was a hell of a turn-on…and quite a juxtaposition to how the Lowells were.

Sure Joshua gave money here and there, probably guilt money, but the Lowells still held themselves up on another pedestal, towering above everybody else.

Chase stood in his living room and stared out the wall of one-way windows overlooking the river. The lights from Falling Brook sparkled against the darkened sky and calmed him. Though his mind continued to race, he at least felt peace about where he was heading.

Plotting and planning had gotten him to where he was today. Being a prominent international investor gave him an obvious edge up to slide into the CEO position at Black Crescent Hedge Fund. Not that he cared about that position. He wanted information to bring the company and the Lowell family down once and for all.

He'd seen his parents struggle after all of their savings were lost. His father had gone to prison for fraud thanks to Vernon's antics, and those attorney's fees hadn't come cheap. His mother had ultimately suffered a nervous breakdown and had needed medical attention. Nothing motivated Chase more than someone harming those he loved. His parents were doing so much better now, but that heaviness still hovered over them. They certainly weren't the same, but they were still a strong family and still pushing through each day to be their best.

Chase needed to continue to get closer to Haley. She'd thrown him off his game for a moment when she'd started discussing her charity. How did she find time to run such a thing when she was always at Black Crescent? Her job as executive assistant was demanding and he knew she put her entire heart and soul into that position. If the woman never even took a lunch break, that was loyalty and dedication on another level.

Did Josh demand that type of work or was that all Haley wanting to go above and beyond?

Clearly she didn't have much of a social life between the two full-time jobs vying for her attention. He made a mental note to check into Tomorrow's Leaders and find out all he could about what sounded like a brilliant charity. Whether she agreed to a date or not, he would make a sizable contribution because he loved the concept. He would do so anonymously so she didn't think he was literally trying to buy her affection. He wasn't that much of a bastard. That's something the Lowell family would do to get attention and make gains.

But Haley would agree to a date with him, with or without the monetary help. He wouldn't mention the donation again, because that had been a little shady. The words had slipped out before he could think better of it and he'd immediately regretted putting her in that position or making her feel like she was nothing more than a bribe.

Just because he'd charmed her into lunch didn't mean he would be able to go that route again. No. Someone like Haley needed to be kept on her toes and surprised. He didn't miss the way she smiled and was actually impressed with the ridiculous highlighter bouquet.

Chase pulled his cell from his pocket and sent off a quick text to his assistant, putting his next plan into motion. An immediate reply confirmed why Dave was the perfect right-hand man. He would get right on it and now Chase just had to do a little more charming with Miss Shaw. The highlighters were a nice touch, but that gesture had barely scratched the surface of his next tactic.

Chase smiled as he headed toward his in-home gym. He needed to hit the weights, maybe the punching bag, and burn off some energy. He had big plans to carry out and a woman to mentally seduce… though if she wound up in his bed, well, he wouldn't exactly turn her away.

Haley hadn't had time to do much digging on Chase. A whole new flood of résumés came through her inbox, not to mention more flowers she'd had to find room for.

The bouquets were getting ridiculous so she'd started passing them out to coworkers. Now every office in the building had an obscene display and she could at least see her desk again.

Those cupcakes, doughnuts and chocolates had made their way to the break room, too. If she ate everything that had come her way, she'd need a new, bigger wardrobe, and that wasn't something she had time for.

Haley settled back in at her desk and scooted closer to her computer. The bundle of highlighters on her desk caught her attention and she couldn't help but smile. She didn't want to smile at Chase's gift. That's what he wanted her to do. He wanted her to think about him…which was basically all she'd done since their impromptu lunch date.

No, it wasn't a date. It had been a meeting of sorts.

She didn't date, never had the time or found a man who interested her enough to pull her from her work.

Yet Chase had done exactly that for one hour. He'd gotten her to leave the office and he'd put very little effort into doing so.

But he'd smiled, he'd been adorable in that over-bearing sort of way and he'd offered to donate to Tomorrow's Leaders. Albeit, the donation came at a price. Well, she couldn't be bought. She would just continue to work on other contributions where her social life didn't have to come into play.

Damn that man for making her read too much into him. He wasn't after her, per se. He wanted a position that she could help him with…if she wanted to do such a thing. Which she did not.

Becoming CEO would be up to Josh. Her personal feelings weren't the deciding factor.

"Are you going home any time soon?"

Haley glanced up from her computer screen, which she'd been staring at blankly for the past ten minutes, and spotted Josh.

"In a bit," she told him with a smile.

Josh's dirty-blond hair looked as if he'd been raking his fingers through it over the course of the day. He'd already shed his suit jacket, which he had draped over one arm. He'd loosened his tie and she figured the stress of finding a replacement was getting to him. This was certainly not a decision to be taken lightly.

"I can't believe you're leaving," she added. "It's

not even six o'clock yet. You usually have a few more hours in you."

Josh's smile widened. "Sophie made me promise to take off early. She's surprising me with dinner and some other plans she's keeping to herself."

Haley loved that Josh and Sophie had found each other. The two were so in love and Josh had definitely turned into a totally different man because of her. Not so long ago, the stress and CEO position had really been getting to Josh, so much so he would bark orders at her or just be frustrated and act almost as if he didn't want her here.

During those times she cleverly did not point out the fact she'd been here even longer than he had, knew the inner workings as much as he did. When she'd been in college, Haley had actually worked for Vernon Lowell as an intern. Her loyalty to this company was the reason she stayed while almost every other employee bailed when Josh took over. She helped him rebuild Black Crescent.

Recently, Sophie had softened something in Josh, and now Haley almost hated to see him go. He was like the brother she never had. Well, she had a brother, but there was no solid relationship there. Haley was honestly closer with her work family than her actual biological family.

"I hope you have a good night," she told him. "Sounds like fun."

"Speaking of fun, what made you get out for lunch earlier?" he asked, a wry grin on his face as if he knew some dirty little secret.

"Sorry to disappoint." She turned in her chair to face him fully. "It was just a business lunch with an acquaintance."

A really over-the-top-sexy acquaintance who had charmed her into submission.

Not that Haley would tell Josh exactly whom she'd had lunch with, especially since Chase had already had an interview with Josh. Added to that, several weeks ago Sophie had caught Haley and Chase flirting.

Sophie had intervened, asking Haley if everything was okay. Thankfully, Josh knew nothing of this harmless encounter. Haley didn't want to be seen as flirting or dining with a potential prospect for the highest position at Black Crescent. Haley had never slept with a coworker or her boss and she sure as hell didn't intend to start now.

And she hadn't been lying when she'd told Sophie she could handle Chase. She could...until he'd shown up with that absurd gift that ultimately landed her in his car and at his personal table at one of her favorite restaurants.

She'd have to be more vigilant when it came to that sly mogul. She'd also have to get serious about that research so she could uncover more about the man who wanted to become her boss. She needed more hours in the day to get everything done, but this little bit of work couldn't be shared. She didn't want anyone to know her special project on the side. This was totally personal.

"Well, take the night off," Josh told her, pulling

her back to the moment. "You've been working too much."

Haley laughed. "Never thought I'd hear you say that. We're both such workaholics."

"I just have a different outlook on life now." Josh shrugged with a wide grin. "I need to get going. Have a good night," he told her before he headed down the hall.

Considering she and Josh were usually the last two to ever leave the building, she had to assume she was alone. Haley pulled up her favorite playlist on her computer and set the music to a higher volume to help distract her from the wayward thoughts regarding a certain billionaire competing for her attention.

As she searched through her emails and hummed along to the songs, Haley was pretty proud of herself for making her way through the bulk of the latest résumés before sending them on to Allison Randall, who would narrow the list even more. Josh wanted only the top three for interviews. With Ryan out, and Chase and Matt already interviewed, that meant they were getting close.

Her cell chimed and she did a quick glance, then stilled. She didn't recognize the number, but with having a charity, she couldn't ignore calls just assuming the other end was a telemarketer.

She paused her music and grabbed her phone.

"Hello?"

"Miss Shaw."

That low, familiar voice shouldn't send shivers through her, but here she was trying to tamp them down.

Haley eased back in her seat and pulled in a deep breath. "Mr. Hargrove. I won't insult you by asking how you got my personal number."

His rich laughter slid through the phone and did nothing to help those shivers she was trying to ignore. No man had ever had such an effect on her before. Dates were one thing, kisses were another. Those could lead to shivers... But a voice through the phone? Never.

"I assume you're still at work," he said.

"I am."

"Do you ever leave that office?" he asked.

Haley came to her feet and circled her desk. She crossed to her small refrigerator she kept in the corner and grabbed a bottle of water. She wasn't about to remind him that she did indeed leave the office when she was coerced by a sexy, charming lunch date.

No, not a date. She'd better be more careful where those thoughts wandered. Sexual fantasies were one thing, and something she couldn't avoid, but thinking in terms of dates and an actual relationship could get her into more trouble than she was ready for.

"I take quite a bit of pride in my work," she informed him. "Besides, I'm rather busy trying to fill some very big shoes."

"Yes, the CEO position. What evening do you think you could take some free time for yourself?"

"All to myself?" she countered, taking the bottle

back to her desk. "Or are you asking for my time to be spent with you?"

"Beautiful and smart. I like that."

Haley wasn't about to address the *beautiful* comment. Allure oozed off him and words were so easy to string together for someone like Chase. A man with power and money was likely used to getting what he wanted and just assumed all women found him irresistible.

Damn it, she couldn't deny she fell into that category. But what else could she do when sexy was his default mode?

"So what is it exactly that you're trying to ask, Mr. Hargrove?"

She took a seat and crossed her legs, leaning back in her chair and trying to maintain her composure.

"I have Broadway tickets for Wednesday night," he informed her. "I'd like you to join me."

Haley stilled. Broadway tickets? Like…a date? Hadn't she just finished her mental lecture on not dating this guy?

Lunch during business hours was one thing, but a play with a man trying to become her boss was an entirely different matter.

"I'm not sure that's a good idea."

"I assumed you'd say as much," he retorted with another low chuckle. "What would make you feel better? If we called this a date or if we called this a business meeting?"

She pursed her lips and considered her options.

"What would make me feel better is honesty. You called me, so what context did you call me in?"

"A date."

His swift, confident reply had her heart beating faster, her nerves kicking into high gear. Did he really want to ask her out? Could he really be chasing her as a woman and not for the part of her that was a stepping-stone to the most prominent position at Black Crescent?

"And I'm the only woman you could think of to ask?"

"You're the only woman I *wanted* to ask."

Oh, why did he have all the answers, and why was she allowing this fascination to pull her in more and more?

Because she was curious. She couldn't ignore her attraction any more than she could stop the sun from setting. Besides, it was just a play. They couldn't exactly get too carried away in a very public place... right?

"Fine."

"Fine?" he asked, then chuckled. "Well, don't get overly excited about it."

"Mr. Hargrove, if you want someone excited and falling all over herself at the idea of a date with you, then you've asked the wrong woman."

That rich laughter filled the phone and she gripped it tight. Her heart beat even faster and her stomach flopped at the prospect of being out with Chase.

"Oh, I've asked the right woman," he corrected.

"And you're going to need to call me Chase since we're dating."

"We're not dating," she corrected.

"Not until Wednesday. I'll see you then, Haley."

He hung up, leaving her speechless and wondering what the hell she'd just agreed to.

Four

"Are you sure this is what you want to do, sir?"

Chase watched through his window as the city streets went by. He paid his driver to drive, not to dole out unsolicited advice. Granted, Al had been Chase's driver for over ten years and he often gave advice…which Chase normally valued.

He didn't want to hear it now. Maybe Chase was making a mistake, but he wanted Haley and that had nothing to do with the revenge or the job and everything to do with the fact that she intrigued him. He couldn't explain why this woman was the one whom he wanted to spend time with, the one he ultimately wanted in his bed.

But he wouldn't ignore what he wanted…not the

job and not the woman. There was no reason he couldn't have both.

"I'm positive," Chase replied.

"I'm not sure getting cozy with Haley Shaw is the best move at this time. She's innocent in all of this."

Al knew everything. He knew the backstory of Chase's father going to prison due to the money trail left by Vernon Lowell, and Al was aware that Chase refused to rest until the Lowell family was brought down…even if that meant seeking justice via Vernon's children.

But he was right in the fact that Haley was an innocent. Granted, she'd stuck through the scandal and Vernon's skipping town and then the transition when Josh took over. She had to know everything that went down, but she was ever the loyal employee…and Chase's best option for finding any nugget of inside information he needed to plan his attack.

"She's the in that I have," Chase stated, turning to catch Al's judgmental reflection in the rearview mirror.

There was one secret Al didn't know. There was no way in hell Chase would ever mention that what started out as harmless flirting and using his charms had turned into a full-on attraction that Chase couldn't fight.

He hadn't expected to find her conservative, stuffy exterior so damn sexy. Those slim dresses that hit just past her knee combined with simple nude heels gave him fantasies that he was best to keep to himself.

"I can't talk you out of this, can I?" Al asked as he pulled in front of Haley's house.

Chase smiled. "Just wait here. We'll be back."

Al's sigh of disapproval didn't escape Chase, but he didn't need approval. While he respected Al as much more than a driver, Chase also had to live his own life and make his own decisions…and mistakes.

Taking Haley to a Broadway play wasn't a mistake, though. Bedding her? Well, that might be a mistake, but he wouldn't turn down the opportunity. He certainly hadn't gone into this thinking of seduction, but he also wasn't taking it off the table.

No man in his right mind could ignore the natural, simplistic beauty that Haley offered. The fact that she didn't fall all over herself and almost posed as an unexpected challenge was a hell of a turn-on. Combined with her loyalty to her job… He admired a woman who remained focused.

Still, he had no clue what made her remain so faithful to the Lowell family and Black Crescent. Haley had been with them since college, from everything he'd learned about her. Why the hell would she stay during the scandal when Vernon literally ruined people's lives? How did she justify such actions?

No matter what her reasoning was, that wasn't his problem. He needed to get some scoop from her, anything that would help him in getting ahead and solidifying his revenge.

His cell chimed in his pocket, but he ignored it. Nothing was more important than taking Haley out tonight. Maybe by getting outside the office, after business hours, she would relax and let loose. And perhaps she'd be easier to uncover.

Chase knocked on her door and within minutes Haley stepped out. It took every ounce of Chase's willpower to keep his mouth from dropping.

If he thought she was sexy in those little conventional dresses at the office, that was nothing compared with this sleeveless black jumpsuit with a plunging neckline. She wore a pair of strappy black sandals showing off her red polished toes… He hadn't expected the red.

With her blond hair curled and red glossy lips, Haley looked completely different from every other time he'd seen her.

And she'd just changed the dynamics of this little game. He didn't know she'd be bringing her arsenal of sex appeal into battle, but he was more than ready to tussle with her. Haley wasn't stupid or naive. She'd dressed like this on purpose with every intention of throwing him off his game.

Well, maybe it would be her who was thrown off. She agreed to this date, so he obviously had some hold over her if she couldn't turn him down. Chase had to make sure he kept the upper hand here or he'd wind up losing sight of everything he'd set out to gain.

Chase composed himself and took a step forward to greet her.

"You look sexy as hell," he murmured when he got closer.

Haley smiled. "It's not often I go on a date, so I wanted to be a little extra tonight."

"I appreciate it."

Haley's eyes leveled his as those red lips curved into a killer smile. "Oh, I did this for me. I love a feeling of empowerment... Don't you?"

She sashayed past him. Chase shook his head as he followed those swaying hips down the front steps.

What in the hell had he gotten himself into? The woman was purposely antagonizing him and clearly loving every second of the torture.

Chase might not know what he'd gotten himself into or how this would ultimately play out, but he knew this task of schmoozing Haley was not going to be boring.

The real question was...just who was seducing whom here?

Haley had no idea how Chase got tickets so last-minute to the most popular show on Broadway, but she didn't care. Their seats were the best, the show was spectacular and now they were walking down the busy city street in Manhattan.

Lights twinkled from each and every building, the warm late-summer air washed over her and people bustled about. She loved this city, especially in the summer. It wasn't often she got away from work to enjoy a social life out on the town. Once the new CEO was in position, she really should take more time for herself and get back into the swing of nightlife and a good time. She was still young, she still had memories to make.

"You up for a drink?" he asked.

"I have to be at work early in the morning," she told him.

He slid his hand into hers as if that were the most normal next step into this evening. Everything about this night felt like a real date. He hadn't brought up work, which was both surprising and refreshing.

"One drink," he promised. "I know the perfect place."

No doubt he knew the perfect place, a place where he took all his ladies. She didn't want to fall in that same line of the women he had a pattern with. She wasn't one of his usual dates and she didn't want to think of this as anything more than what it was…a game.

While she wasn't quite sure his angle or why he was going to such lengths to charm her, she had to keep her guard up. Having a bit of fun in the process wouldn't hurt anything. A little flirting, sexual banter, maybe even a fling… But anything that happened would be on her terms and because she wanted it to progress. Chase couldn't, and wouldn't, have a hold over her.

Yeah, right. Just keep telling yourself that.

"One drink," she replied. "But only because I'm out of Pinot at home."

And there went that rich laughter again. That pure male, all rough-and-low laughter she'd come to associate with him. The weeks of flirting and harmless banter had somehow led them to this night, and she wasn't sorry she'd said yes. Quite the opposite. Haley was well aware of what this was and what it wasn't.

Chase wasn't out for some exclusivity or a relationship. He wasn't out for even a fling. He wanted to get that top slot and he was really going all out to win her affection.

"I'll have to make a note to get you a box of Pinot," he told her. "I know a wonderful distributor. They can be at your door first thing in the morning."

Haley glanced his way as he assisted her toward the next block. "I think that's a bit of overkill, don't you? I mean, what would I do with an entire box?"

"Throw a dinner party," he suggested. "Or maybe go smaller and invite someone over to help you drink it. Glasses optional. I think other, more intimate ways could be the theme."

He threw her a glance that had her head spinning and visions forming. Late nights with a glass of wine on the balcony off her bedroom before moving into her oversize master and having the pale liquor poured all over her while Chase's tongue traveled the same path—

"How many students are you going to fund this fall?"

His question caught her off guard and had her mind spinning in another direction. "Excuse me?"

"With your charity," he added, guiding her across another busy intersection as if he hadn't just put a naughty thought in her head. "How many teens were you able to fund?"

"Oh, um, eighteen. I'm hoping we can squeeze a couple more out of the applicants that came through."

"Do you get much else done besides looking at résumés and applications?" he asked. "Between the charity and Black Crescent, I mean."

Haley hadn't thought about her work in that manner, but she actually didn't get much else done.

With a shrug, she smiled. "I love what I do. Both jobs. I wouldn't have it any other way."

"You're clearly giving your time to everyone around you. Is that why you don't date much?"

He gestured toward a doorway with a large black-and-gold awning. Thankfully, they were here and she didn't have to dive into the boring whys of her social life. Couldn't someone just enjoy her work? Why did she have to defend her lifestyle to someone who didn't even know her?

In no time, she and Chase were escorted up the stairs and into a private room with their own bartender. But of course they were. Why would he take a seat at the bar with common folk when money talked and he could have privacy?

Haley took a seat at an intimate, curved booth. Chase slid in beside her, but he didn't crowd her. They placed their drink orders and were left alone. Haley couldn't ignore the tingle of arousal that coursed through her. The way Chase had looked at her all night, the simple way he took her hand—she might be a helpless romantic, but those were the little things that got to her.

The sexy man in the suit didn't hurt, either. There

was something to be said about a well-dressed man who knew how to fill out a tailor-made jacket.

"We could have sat down in the bar," she told him.

Chase flashed her a smile and eased his arm along the back of the bench. "We could have, but then I wouldn't be able to hear you. If you want good music, though, downstairs is the place to be. I happen to know the owner."

"Are you the owner?" she asked.

Chase laughed. "No, but we went to college together."

"Harvard? Yale? I can't remember what Ivy League school you indicated on your résumé."

He shook his head and leveled that dark stare her way. "Hardly Ivy League. I went to Ithaca on a football scholarship and I studied business. I was smart in school, but nothing an Ivy League school would've looked twice at. My family couldn't have afforded for me to go anywhere without my scholarship, so I'm just thankful I was athletic."

Interesting. That was a whole side of him she didn't know. A man who came from meager beginnings to make a name for himself and become a billionaire mogul was quite impressive. Maybe he wasn't the egotistical man she'd first believed. There was nothing wrong with an ego, but now that she knew he warranted that sense of pride, she could appreciate him so much more.

The bartender delivered their drinks and promptly left them. Haley took a sip of her Pinot and toyed with the stem of her crystal glass.

"I went to community college," she found herself saying before she could stop herself. "I have zero athletic ability. My only hobbies are singing off-key in the shower or making spreadsheets in my sleep."

Chase's chuckle seemed so genuine, not like he was purposely trying to appease her or keep her attention solely on him.

"I'm sure you have talents," he stated. "You don't have to be athletic."

"I played softball once." She lifted her glass and took another sip. "It was a short-lived career. I was eight and I did cartwheels around the bases instead of running them during warm-ups."

Chase's lips twitched as if he was holding back his laugh. "And did you end up taking gymnastics?"

"No. My parents couldn't afford lessons." She glanced to her glass and slid her thumb up the delicate stem. "I didn't always see eye to eye with them about most things anyway."

"Are you close now?"

Haley shook her head. "We still don't have the same vision."

"They have to be proud of your work," he replied, shifting to face her better. "You've become quite successful."

Haley smiled and pulled in a breath. "To them, I'm a secretary. Nothing near as exciting as a doctor or lawyer like they wanted my brother to be."

"And is your brother a doctor or lawyer?"

Haley shook her head again. "No. They paid for him to go to a fancy college and he ended up flunking out. Too much partying, but that's none of my business."

"How can they not be proud of all the work you've done?" he asked. "You've been with Black Crescent for so long, you're irreplaceable."

Haley bit the inside of her cheek to keep from laughing. She always felt like she was invaluable, too, but that was just her battered ego. She liked to think that they couldn't live without her, but if she left, someone would replace her and the company would keep running.

"You really do know how to get on someone's good side," she informed him. "Flattery doesn't always get you to the top."

"No, but my impeccable résumé will." He flashed that killer grin once again and took a sip of his bourbon. "Everyone knows you're the backbone of that operation. Who knows what would've happened all those years ago during that scandal if you hadn't stayed on."

"I was just an intern back then."

"Who was far more knowledgeable than most," he retorted. "When Josh stepped into the role of CEO, I guarantee you were the one who had to get him going and made him look good to the general public."

Haley shrugged. She didn't need accolades or credit for her work. She truly enjoyed helping others, and just because Josh's father had been a liar and a cheat didn't mean Josh or his brothers were the same.

Many people in the town didn't feel that way,

though. Some still blamed Josh for Vernon's actions. The brothers had all been held under a microscope when their father split, but Josh was the one who had truly stuck, trying to salvage the family name and business.

"So what's your angle here?" she asked Chase, smiling when he quirked a brow. "You want the CEO position so bad that you're willing to fake date me? Or is there something else you're after?"

His eyes darkened as they dropped to her lips. She realized her open-ended question held too many possible answers the moment the words had slipped out.

"Oh, there are several things I want, Haley."

You can bet they center on that promised shipment of wine.

She'd put herself in this position. She'd wanted to know what it would be like to go out with someone like Chase, knowing she had the upper hand because he needed her.

But now? Well, she wasn't so sure her control hadn't slipped. If she wasn't careful, she'd wind up in bed with the man, and just her luck, he'd also become her boss.

Haley leaned in closer and murmured, "Sex isn't on the table."

"No?"

He kept that dark gaze on her. Part of her wanted to back away, come to the realization that Chase wasn't in all this for her. But the other part wanted to ignore those waving red flags and see what would happen if she just leaned in a little. Would he close that distance between them and put his lips where his eyes had been? Would she let him?

Yes, she would. She wanted to know what those lips would feel like. She wanted to feel his hands glide over her bare body. Would that fantasy ever become reality?

"I'm aware I'm not actually your type," she informed him, picking up her glass and draining it. "But I'm going to figure out your angle. I can't believe you're going through all of this just to land a position at Black Crescent."

He eased over in the bench, his arm sliding even farther behind her back as he leaned in closer to her face. Those eyes once again dropped to her lips and she couldn't stop that knee-jerk reaction of licking them.

Anticipation soared through her. Was this when he'd kiss her? Was this when she'd welcome that much-awaited touch?

"Maybe I'm trying to land you," he murmured against her lips.

Haley couldn't suppress the shivers and couldn't deny the flirting and fun and games had taken a new direction, and she wasn't sure which way she was supposed to go.

Five

"Are you with me?"

Haley blinked away the daydream and stared up at her boss. Josh stood in front of her desk, one hand in his pocket, the other holding a résumé.

"I'm sorry. What?"

His brows drew in. "Is everything okay? You seem off this morning."

Maybe that's because she was left hanging for that kiss last night on her date/nondate with Chase. Maybe because the man was driving her out of her ever-loving mind as she tried to anticipate his next move. Or maybe she should remove herself from this crazy ride she'd gotten on and save her own sanity.

"Yes, I'm fine," she assured him with a smile.

Haley came to her feet and straightened her pencil dress. "You were saying?"

Josh stared at her another minute before glancing down to the paper in his hand. "I was saying that I'd like to set up a second interview with Matt Velez. Remember I told you I talked to him outside of the office? I'd like to bring him in again."

Haley was well aware of Matt's résumé. Along with Allison, they'd vetted each and every one that had come through. Haley wasn't sure Matt was the perfect applicant for the job of CEO, but she was also slowly getting swayed by her hormones and not her common sense.

She had an obligation to the company to help secure a solid future, which also meant her job and many others. She couldn't let Chase and his methodical plans to woo her hinder her decisions.

"I'll get that interview set up right away," she assured Josh. "Do you prefer Monday morning after your conference call?"

"That's fine. I know it's short notice, but see if Allison can fly in for it. And like the other ones, I want you in there with me," he told her. "It's only fair that you have a say over who you'll be working closely with. After all, you're the one who will be with our new CEO the most."

Haley nodded, pleased that he was taking her feelings into consideration. But if she had to weigh in on whom she wanted to spend most of her days and evenings with here at the office, her answer certainly wasn't Matt.

A commanding man with dark brown eyes and light brown messy hair came into mind. The man with broad shoulders, perfectly tailored suits and heavy-lidded eyes who made her think only of rustled sheets and sleepless nights.

"Haley?"

"I'll get it scheduled," she told him, forcing herself back to the moment and her duties. "No problem."

"Is there anything you want to tell me?" he asked, brows drawn in.

Josh cared about each of his employees. Haley had come to think of him as a friend, someone she could trust and rely on. But there was no way she could confess what was truly going on. He wouldn't understand and he likely wouldn't like that she'd been technically dating one of the applicants.

Haley reached for the résumé and laid the paper on her desk. "I'm just a little distracted, but nothing that will affect my job."

Well, that was somewhat of a lie considering she spent a good portion of her time fantasizing when she should be focusing on the next phase of Black Crescent.

Josh sighed and slid his hands into his pockets. "You know you can talk to me," he told her.

"Just a date I had the other night," she confessed. "I'm trying to tell myself he's not the guy for me, but it's getting more difficult because I'm developing feelings I really shouldn't have."

Josh's intense stare quickly turned amused as a wide grin spread across his face. "I didn't think Sophie was for me, either, but look how that turned out. I didn't realize you were dating anyone."

Neither did she, and she wasn't quite sure what to call all of this she and Chase were doing. He was toying with her. He had to be. But she was human with very real feelings and she couldn't stop her attraction. She had to believe he was attracted; either that or he was a damn good actor.

Still, that didn't mean she could let her guard down. Chase wasn't gullible and he wasn't stupid. He was meticulous and no doubt had a well-laid plan. She just had to make sure she stayed one step ahead of him.

"Well, we only had one date," she explained to Josh. "I've just been so wrapped up in work and Tomorrow's Leaders, I haven't had much of a social life lately. I'm sure I'm making a big deal out of nothing."

"Don't discount your feelings," he warned. "You're allowed to have a social life and you're also allowed to leave before it gets dark outside, you know."

Haley laughed. "I'm aware, but I feel guilty when there's so much to be done to get ready for the transition of the CEO."

"You stood by this company when the shit hit the fan with my dad. I have no doubt whatsoever that you will make the next transition smooth, and anyone who takes my place will be thankful to have you."

She wasn't one who thrived on compliments; that's not why she did her job. But she wasn't going to ignore Josh's praise by blowing off his kind words.

"I appreciate that," she told him. "I'll get this interview set up for Monday."

"Great." He started to turn away but stopped and met her gaze once again. "Whoever this guy is, he's damn lucky to have you."

Haley smiled and simply nodded her silent appreciation.

How did she explain that she went on a date with an applicant? Or the fact that, while there was most definitely sexual tension, she wasn't fully convinced that he had the truest of intentions.

The next morning, Haley took a seat at her desk and opened a new tab on her computer. She didn't necessarily have the time to devote to extra work right now, but she needed to dig deeper into Chase Hargrove.

Instead of fantasizing about him, she had to find out who he really was. Haley wanted to know more behind the man, more about his motives for seeking out not only the CEO position, but also for being so aggressive in pursuing her.

She went to one site, then another, falling down the rabbit hole of this world-renowned investment mogul. He had a home in Cannes for which he'd paid over twenty million dollars, and Haley found herself basking in the view for just a moment before moving on.

She couldn't even imagine owning a home like that or even having the time to get away for a luxury vacation. Clearly Chase had made some damn good investments and took care of his clients or he wouldn't be able to afford such extravagance.

And knowing a sliver of his background and that he came from meager beginnings made this revelation all the more impressive.

The further back she went into his world, the more she realized he was much more than what was on his résumé.

He also hadn't been born Chase Hargrove. When the hell had he changed his name, and why? There had to be a story there because from what she could tell, his parents were still married, so the name change didn't make much sense.

Maybe digging into his parents was the way to go. Were they all estranged? He hadn't mentioned any such thing during their dinner the other night.

Yet more secrets she wanted to uncover.

When her cell chimed on her desk, Haley jumped. She glanced to see Chase's name lighting up the screen. She thought about letting him go to voice mail, but she couldn't deny the man and she wondered if that would ultimately be her downfall.

She liked to tell herself she wasn't saying no to him simply because she wanted to learn more… But in reality she wasn't saying no because she was selfish and wanted more. She just wished she knew where her curiosity would end up taking her and how far she'd let this game play out.

Pushing away from her computer, Haley turned to grab her phone.

"Good morning," she answered.

Chase's familiar chuckle slid through the line. "Nope, it's now noon."

She glanced to her computer screen and he was right. Obviously she'd fallen down the rabbit hole of Chase's life. Not that she would ever admit any such thing to him.

"You caught me," she replied. "It's been quite the morning."

Like finding out he wasn't exactly who he said he was. She wondered why, but that was something she'd definitely be finding out. If she flat out asked him, would he tell her the truth?

"Are you free tonight?" he asked.

"Depends on what you had in mind."

Another date? Did she want to keep getting tangled with a man who obviously had ulterior motives?

Yes, she did. She was intrigued, she was charmed... She was turned on. She simply couldn't turn off such strong emotions. Chase was a powerful man in more ways than one.

"I'll take that to mean you're free."

His low, gravelly voice did crazy things to her hormones. Things she hadn't felt in far too long, which made them impossible to ignore.

Why couldn't she get a grip with this guy? Why couldn't she just deny him and move on?

Because he'd left her wondering what those lips would feel like against hers. He'd left her wondering if he wanted her just as much as she wanted him. There was really only one way to find out.

"I can pick you up at your place at six if you're up for a surprise," he added.

She leaned back in her seat and stared at her screen, seeing the evidence in black-and-white that he wasn't on the up-and-up. But she never backed down from a challenge—hence why she was still at Black Crescent even after all of the scandal and their tarnished reputation. She'd stuck by Josh's side during the most difficult time when it would have been all too easy to pack up and leave like everyone else did.

So, Haley wasn't about to shy away from Chase. Didn't everyone have a few skeletons in their closet?

"I'll be ready," she told him. "But can I ask what I should be ready for? Are we skydiving or watching a movie? I need to dress accordingly."

Once again he laughed, and she hated how such a simple act could produce so many emotions. The arousal, the excitement, the thrill of the chase—though she still wasn't sure who was chasing whom.

"And what would you wear for skydiving?" he asked.

"Probably a blindfold because I'd be terrified," she joked.

"Bring that blindfold," he stated. "I'm sure we can find a better use for it."

The instant erotic image filled her mind and she knew without a doubt that he was crossing the line of flirting, and she didn't mind one bit. She was human, she was a woman with basic needs. Why should she deny having a little harmless fun?

Oh, right. Because he could end up being her boss at one point and she knew he was lying about something.

All of that still didn't squash her desires or turn off her attraction. The blindfold comment left her more than intrigued about what might or might not turn him on. She wouldn't mind digging into his fetishes.

"I'll be ready at six," she informed him. "Sans blindfold."

"Fine by me. I have a few you can borrow. See you then."

He hung up, leaving her wondering if he was serious or joking about that blindfold collection. Every part of her had a feeling he was quite serious, and that only aroused her even more.

How had they gone from harmless flirting to discussing veiled sexual games? Chase was a smooth one since she didn't have a clue how to answer that question. It was those smooth ones who could get a girl into trouble...but oh, the best kind.

Haley sighed and put her phone back on her desk, turning her focus back to the computer and back to the hunt to find the real Chase. She wondered why he changed his last name. What made him want to take on another? Surely he didn't have a falling-out with his parents. Or maybe he did. That was certainly something she could easily find.

She didn't have too much time to keep devoting to Chase today, but she wasn't done digging. Perhaps on their date he might divulge a little more and she could slowly uncover what type of man he truly was…other than sexy as hell and too charming for his own good.

He never did tell her exactly what they were doing or how she should dress. Still, surprises were fun. She didn't remember the last time someone surprised her with anything…save for the slew of flowers and pastries that came through from would-be applicants.

Pushing aside thoughts of Chase and any other distractions, Haley turned her attention to the latest résumés Allison had vetted. There was still a position to be filled and Haley wanted the absolute best possible candidate, considering she truly loved this company and she'd have to be working with that said individual day in and day out.

Part of her couldn't help but imagine Chase in that role. What would he be like as a boss? Could they even have a standard working relationship?

Granted, they hadn't actually crossed any lines physically, but mentally… Hell, she'd crossed them all several times. If they ended up in bed, how could they turn back and go to boss/assistant?

An instant image of him sweeping off his desk and laying her down filled her mind. She couldn't just ignore the need she had or the possibilities that rolled through her.

Chase Hargrove, or whatever his last name used to be, wasn't in the CEO position just yet, so that still made him free game. If he was going to come on to her like he wanted her, Haley was going to show him just how much she wanted him. There was no code of ethics that said she couldn't have a social life with an applicant.

If he was playing some sort of game with her, then she'd make him regret it. But what if there was no game? What if he actually wanted her and wanted to be CEO of Black Crescent Hedge Fund? There was no reason he couldn't want both, right?

And if that was the case, she had a feeling Chase Hargrove might just become a permanent fixture in her life...in one way or another.

Six

Haley sank deeper into the corner of her sectional sofa and curled her feet beneath her. Like most companies with summer hours, Black Crescent had short Fridays. After Chase's call, she finished a few things then packed up and headed home for the afternoon.

With the much-needed extra time, she planned to work on finalizing submissions for Tomorrow's Leaders, but she had already finished going through the list and she still had a few hours before Chase was due to pick her up for her date.

And she'd spent her time wisely, considering she uncovered more about him than she ever thought possible.

Haley stared at the computer screen, utterly stunned at the evidence she'd found. Her questions about Chase's motives were answered, but she didn't like what she'd uncovered and was almost sorry she'd been digging.

Chase's father, Dale Groveman, had done business years ago with Vernon Lowell. When everything with Vernon and Black Crescent exploded, apparently Dale took some of the fall and landed in prison.

According to everything Haley had found, that was about the time Chase's mother moved into a low-income apartment from their ritzy home out in the country. Then she was hospitalized shortly after at a mental health facility, but those records were sealed tight. Haley could only imagine the poor woman had a nervous breakdown considering there had been no prior medical issues.

They had lost everything and no doubt Chase was out for revenge. Her heart hurt for his family and so many others who had been affected by Vernon's actions. But was Chase using her? Was he interested in her on a personal level or only interested in using her as leverage in his plan to possibly destroy the company she'd loved for so long?

Haley closed her laptop, not wanting to see any more. She'd learned enough to have her mind shooting in all directions. There was a yawning ache deep in the pit of her stomach, one that she feared wouldn't be fixed anytime soon. She'd allowed herself to get swept up in this web. While she wanted to curse herself for being naive, she also had that sliver of hope that Chase wasn't only taking advantage of her. He seemed genuinely interested... Didn't he? Was he that focused on revenge that he'd turned into a hell of a good actor?

Had Chase targeted her specifically because he thought she would be easy access to get into Black Crescent? Did he like her as a woman at all or was everything an act?

Too many questions to try to decipher answers on her own. Only time would tell because she couldn't exactly go to him and flat out ask. She needed to play this smart and be cautious.

While the hurt continued to slide deep into her, this was nothing new to Haley. People had underestimated her for as long as she could remember. Her parents didn't think she was good enough or smart enough like her brother, which was why they'd invested all of their money into his schooling and not hers.

When she'd started as an intern at Black Crescent Hedge Fund, she'd been seen only as a young blonde with a curvy figure, so what could she possibly know?

Well, look at her now. She'd been around the longest and was the right-hand woman to the CEO. She was damn proud of herself for all she'd accomplished. True, she could go somewhere else with her credentials, but she loved this company and they had always given her the time she needed to work on her own charity.

Her mind circled back to Chase. She still didn't know why he'd changed his last name or what his plans were exactly, but she wasn't about to just let him do anything he wanted or try to harm this company in any way.

Turning the tables wouldn't be easy, but she was up for the challenge. First thing would be to get ready for this date and use every weapon in her arsenal. A killer outfit, sexy heels... She didn't mind making him suffer a little because she would maintain control of this situation now that she had a better handle on his motives.

If only she knew his exact plan...

Haley sat her computer on the coffee table and headed toward her en suite. A relaxing bubble bath would help calm her because she had a feeling she was getting ready to dive into a hell of a storm.

"That was the most amazing thing ever."

Haley's excitement seemed to radiate off her. Her smile widened, her eyes lit up and she seemed completely relaxed...just how he wanted her.

Of course, he was anything but relaxed since he'd picked her up and she'd come out wearing another sexy-as-hell jumpsuit. This one had a halter top, leaving her back exposed and taunting him with all that pale, creamy skin. The pants had slits that went high up onto her thigh, and the material had separated when she'd sat in the seat next to him in the theater. It had been all he could do not to toy with that high V over her leg and see just how far she was willing to let him go.

He'd started this charade months ago with harmless flirting, but he'd had no idea just how much being with Haley Shaw would affect him as a man.

When he'd first set out to destroy the Lowells, he honestly had no idea he'd come in contact with anyone as intriguing, as sexy or as challenging as Haley. Under other circumstances, he'd date her, seduce her the proper way and not have these damn guilty feelings getting in the way of his goals.

Damn it. He wanted Haley and it had nothing to do with the job or his revenge plot. She intrigued him, she aroused him and she flat out got under his skin in ways he'd never allowed another woman.

Chase slid his hand into hers as he led her back to his car. He'd given Al the night off, as he wanted total privacy with Haley.

"All I did was take you to see a movie," he told her.

She jerked her attention to his. "That wasn't just any movie," she reminded him. "That was an early premiere of the biggest blockbuster that will hit cinemas this year. I don't know how you managed the private showing, but that movie had been on my list since all the hype around it last year."

"I'm glad you enjoyed it. The producer is actually a friend of mine, so I had a strong connection."

As they reached his car, Chase maneuvered her toward it, expertly spinning her until her back was pressed against the door. He leaned in, one hand on either side of her shoulders.

Haley's eyes widened, then dropped to his mouth.

Arousal slammed into him, but he kept control over his emotions.

"Are you going to kiss me now?" she asked, her lips quirking into a slight grin as if she were daring him.

"It's time, don't you think?"

"Past time."

Chase leaned in closer, surprised and utterly turned on even more when her hands came up to frame his face as she pulled him down to meet her lips. She opened for him, threading her fingers through his hair, taking the kiss like she'd been starving for his touch.

He understood that all-consuming need. Since seeing her in her office on day one in her conservative dress up until now with her inner vixen coming out for their date, Chase was hanging on by a very thin thread.

Damn the job and his revenge. He wanted Haley with a fierceness that he'd never known. Why her? Why now? He was supposed to be focused on the plan he'd set into motion years ago. He'd waited for the perfect opening into Black Crescent and here it was…only this sexy distraction stood in his way and he had no clue where she fit in. Oh, wait. She didn't. There was no plan for a hot fling with the sexy assistant.

Chase trailed his fingertips over her bare arms, eliciting a shiver from her that racked into his own body. He'd thought he could control this kiss, but he wasn't so sure now.

How did one woman have so much power over him? How could she make him forget his goals, his well-thought-out plans of revenge and redemption?

Because she was sexy as hell, she was loyal to a fault—a trait he could understand and appreciate—and she challenged him in ways no woman ever had.

Haley laced her fingers through his hair and shifted, aligning their bodies in a way that left no doubt how turned on he was.

Chase reached down to her hips, gripping them in his hands, and held her still. He wanted her, but out here in a parking lot was certainly not the place. He'd planned on only a quick kiss, something to take the sexual edge off, but all he'd done was fan the proverbial flames.

Chase forced himself to ease away. Haley's lids slowly opened as she focused her attention on him.

"That was intense," she murmured. "And long overdue."

Chase agreed on both counts, but wasn't about to say anything. He needed to maintain his head about him, to focus, but Haley was charming, more so than he'd originally noticed. She had a heart of gold with her charity—one he'd looked up and thoroughly investigated.

He didn't want her getting caught up in the middle of his anger and retaliation. Chase wanted to go after Vernon himself, but since the old bastard was still MIA fifteen years later, Josh Lowell was next in line. There were other sons, but Josh was the one who had taken over Daddy's reins.

"Are you ready for the next phase of the date?" he asked.

Haley's brows rose. "Was that kiss a stepping-stone?"

Chase laughed, unable to ignore the way her brazen, bold attitude turned him on even more. At any other point in his life, he would love to see just where this fiery spirit led him, but he had to stay on track.

"Actually, we have reservations and we're going to be late if we don't get moving."

Haley slid her hands to his shoulders. "And would being late be such a bad thing?"

Honestly? He was ready to forget dinner and these reservations altogether. There was nothing he wanted more than to yank the silky tie around her neck and see that black material float down over her breasts. He wanted her alone, with no distractions, no outside forces giving him reasons they shouldn't be intimate.

If they'd met under different circumstances, he would've already had her in his bed. But he'd deceived her from the start and because he'd respected her as a woman, he'd taken this slower than he'd ever taken a seduction.

There was going to come a breaking point, though, and he had a feeling that moment would be sooner rather than later.

"Being late wouldn't be a bad thing," he finally replied. "But when I have you, it won't be quick and it won't be from making out in a parking lot."

He didn't miss the way her eyes widened at the term *when*. That's right. There was no more second-guessing where this was going because they both wanted it, and he wasn't going to ignore that sexual pull or deny either of them any longer.

"Awfully sure of yourself," she told him with a slight grin.

"Or maybe I'm sure of you," he countered as he slid his lips over hers before releasing her. "You're the type of woman who goes after what she wants. Am I right?"

Her eyes grazed over him, an emotion he couldn't quite identify coming over her.

"You have no idea how right you are," she replied.

As he helped her into the car, Chase couldn't help but wonder where he'd started to lose control. But if he didn't regain a hold over this situation, he was going to find himself lost and swept into Haley's world…where he had absolutely no business going.

Seven

"This view is ridiculously breathtaking."

Haley stared out at the skyline of Manhattan from their corner table on the third floor of The Pavilion. The setting sun cast a breathtaking orange and dark pink glow across the horizon. There was something so intimate about sharing a cozy dinner in a posh restaurant while the day came to an end.

Haley had been here only one other time for the wedding of a college friend, but that had been it and she'd always wanted to dine here with a romantic date.

She wasn't sure this fell into the romantic category, but her date fantasies were most definitely fulfilled—sexy man, sunset, dinner and wine.

"I couldn't agree more."

Haley turned her attention back to Chase and noted he wasn't looking at the skyline at all, but directly at her with a hunger in his eyes she recognized all too well.

She shouldn't fall for those perfect one-liners, but she couldn't help herself. He was damn good at this game. The kiss had left her wanting so much more, even though she knew she shouldn't.

Haley had no idea where he was going with his plans. She knew his motivation, but she had to keep on her toes or someone would end up getting hurt.

She pulled in a deep breath and leaned forward, resting her arms on the table. She had to know more about his motives, about the man who was even more mysterious than she'd first thought.

"Tell me why you want to be CEO of Black Crescent Hedge Fund."

To his credit, he didn't look surprised, but he did give a crooked smile and leveled her gaze. That lethal combo was what had landed her here to begin with. She couldn't turn down his charming words and his devilish looks.

So she was human. So what? She didn't know another woman who would turn down the advances of Chase Hargrove.

"Are we starting the second round of interviews already?" he asked.

Haley shrugged. "I'm just your date trying to get to know you better."

He kept his stare on hers as he leaned back in his seat. "Over the years, I've traveled and started up many investment companies. I know what it takes to make a successful company run smoothly, and Black Crescent is in my hometown. I love the people here and want to ultimately settle down."

Settle down? She hadn't expected that part. A man like Chase Hargrove seemed more the jet-setting, panty-dropping type than the wife, kids and minivan guy.

"So you're sliding into a family-man role, as well?"

He lifted a shoulder and grinned. "Someday. Family is very important to me and nobody would be happier about this than my mother, who reminds me often that she has no grandchildren."

So they weren't estranged. That helped her put another piece of the puzzle together. And he'd just handed her the perfect segue into her line of questioning, though her thoughts tumbled over one another because she had an instant visual of Chase in the role of a father and he just became even sexier.

"So, no siblings?" she asked, reaching for her glass of wine. "Were you terribly spoiled?"

She tried to remain calm, but her insides were a bundle of nerves. Between the growing attraction and tension and all of the unknowns surrounding Chase and his plot, Haley wasn't sure which emotion would overtake her first. This was all new territory for her, but she had to remain loyal to Black Crescent and Josh. They were like her family and she wanted to keep them protected at all costs—even if that meant sacrificing her own happiness.

But when Chase had kissed her, she'd gotten lost. Having his lips and hands on her had made her forget that she even needed to uncover his truths to begin with.

"Not much," he explained. "My mother had a large family, but she was unable to have any more children after me, and I definitely pulled my weight around the house. Maybe that's why I want a family. I want a houseful of children and a wife."

"Someday," she reminded him with a smile.

"Exactly. I'm in no rush."

And it was silly of her to instantly have thoughts pop into her head of being that said wife. She wasn't ready for marriage. She barely had time to do her laundry, let alone feed into a committed, long-term relationship. And children? She really loved her career, so she hadn't thought much about having a family.

Considering her background, she wouldn't even know what to do with a family of her own. Could she even be affectionate? Could she be supportive and loving? As much as she'd like to say yes, she honestly didn't know. There wasn't much to fall back on by way of role models in her past.

"So are you close to your parents?" she asked, toying with the stem of her wineglass.

Dinner had been served and removed long ago, yet they still remained chatting and drinking. Haley was in no hurry to see this night end. She rather enjoyed the company of a sexy, mysterious man.

"Very close," he replied. "My mother was ill for

a while years ago and my father wasn't able to care for her during that time. It was a difficult period for all of us, but I think we are stronger as a unit now than ever before."

Obviously that was the time she'd uncovered when they'd moved into a smaller place and his father went to prison. But she still wasn't 100 percent sure how his mother had been sick, though Haley had her suspicions.

"Is your mother okay now?" Haley asked, sincerely wanting to know.

Chase blew out a sigh and sat forward. "She's amazing. We all bounced back. Not much can keep us down."

"Determination is a big component of running a company," she told him.

He smiled and reached across the table to slide his hand over hers. "Determination is all I have these days."

The way he locked his eyes on hers and delivered such a statement with such conviction, Haley didn't know if they were talking business or not anymore.

"Care to carry this conversation back to my place?" he asked.

Those bold eyes continued to captivate her and she found herself nodding before she could fully think of why this was not a good idea.

"Why should I do that?" she asked. "You could end up being my boss if you have your way about this."

He leaned farther across the table, lifting her hand slightly and lacing his fingers with hers.

"I saw the sunset with you and now I want to see the sunrise."

Her heart tumbled and something clicked into place…something she hadn't known was missing. It wasn't just the sultry words; it was the fact she wanted this man. She wanted him from the moment he'd stopped into the office the very first time. She wanted him when he'd flirted with her over a bundle of silly highlighters. And she wanted him because she recognized determination and that was one very strong common thread they shared.

Maybe they wanted totally different things out of life and maybe he was trying to take down the company she loved so much. But this was just one night. Sex had nothing to do with the job and she was entitled to a social life, right?

For once she was putting her career aside for a night. Tomorrow, she would go back to being on the hunt for the secrets and motives Chase kept hidden. Who knows, maybe she would uncover something at his house. Maybe he'd slip and tell her a nugget of information that she could use to solve this mystery.

Haley wasn't giving up on finding out what he had planned, but she also wasn't giving up on this attraction. The sexual pull was too strong, too overwhelming.

She squeezed his hand and smiled. "I'd love to see that sunrise with you."

* * *

Chase hadn't planned on inviting Haley back to his place, but seeing her in that cast of the sunset, looking like she'd never seen anything more beautiful, had really given him a punch of lust to the gut.

Knowing she'd come from such a humble background and knowing how determined and loyal she was only made her that much more attractive. As crazy as it sounded, she was turning into someone he wanted to spend time with, someone he wanted to *be* with, and his newfound emotions had nothing to do with Black Crescent.

He knew he wanted her. That had never been a secret. But he also didn't want her hurt in the end. Nothing would make him give up his revenge against the Lowells. Absolutely nothing.

All he could do at this point in the game was make sure Haley was out of the direct line of fire. When he ultimately took down the company, he would make sure she had a very well-paid, well-positioned place within one of his own companies. He respected her, trusted her, and he couldn't blame her for anything that took place regarding the scandal that Vernon Lowell had orchestrated.

Chase pulled into the drive of his three-story home on the cliffs overlooking the river. He pushed aside all thoughts of Vernon. The old rogue man had been in the forefront of his mind and the main component of this revenge plot for years, but tonight, the only person Chase wanted occupying his mind, and his bed, was the beauty beside him.

Finally, he'd be able to peel her out of her clothes, just like he'd wanted to since he first saw her. He loved how she was conservative by day, but a little sultry, a little more of a vixen, at night.

The perfect woman…if he was looking for such a thing.

Chase pulled into the garage and closed the door behind him. He killed the engine, then turned to face Haley. Only the glow from the overhead garage light illuminated the car, but that was more than enough to see the desire in her eyes and the way her tongue darted out to moisten her bottom lip.

"You're sure about this?" he asked, not wanting to force her into anything she wasn't ready for.

Without a word, Haley leaned over the console and curled her hand around the back of his neck, pulling him toward her as she covered his mouth with hers.

Within the confined space, Chase didn't have the room to touch her like he wanted, like he'd been craving for weeks. He did maneuver one hand up to stroke the side of her face, then he trailed his fingertips down the column of her throat and into the deep V of her halter top.

She trembled beneath his touch and his arousal slammed into him. He wanted out of this car to where he had the freedom to do what he wanted to the woman he craved more than anything else.

At this moment, he craved her more than any revenge…and that was a hell of a dangerous game to play with himself.

Chase eased back and smoothed her hair from her face. Her warm breath washed over him. Her taste on his lips only urged him to hurry this process into the house.

He exited the car and went around to help her out, but by the time he circled the vehicle, she was out, staring at him like he was her every walking fantasy. The feeling was quite mutual, especially with her lips swollen from his. He couldn't wait to explore her passion further, to see her come undone at his touch.

Haley slid her hand into his and he led her into the house. The dim lights turned on as he made his way through to the sunken living area with an entire wall of windows. The sun had all but set and the twinkling lights across the river reflected off the blackened water.

"Your home is gorgeous," she stated, sounding almost surprised and impressed.

Chase didn't know why her approval made his chest puff with pride. Perhaps because his family had lost everything, including their pride, at the hands of the company Haley was so damn loyal to.

Refusing to ever be vulnerable like his parents, Chase clawed his way to the top. When his father had gone to prison and his mother had a nervous breakdown, their bank accounts had been wiped out and their home had been repossessed. Chase had vowed in that dire moment to never, ever be dependent on anyone ever again. He vowed to never let anyone have that much control over his life because everything could be taken away in a single second.

"This view is what sold me on the place," he told her as he gestured toward the impressive set of windows.

Haley stepped down into the living room and crossed to the glass wall. The reflection gave him the opportunity to see her both from the front and the back, offering him the best view of this remarkably sexy woman.

She stood there a moment, taking in the sights before she glanced over her shoulder.

"Do you bring many women here to seduce them?"

Chase couldn't help but smile at her bold question. "I'm not so sure I'm the one doing the seducing here."

Her brow quirked as her eyes gave him the once-over. "Nice dodge of the question, but I'll take your answer as a compliment."

She would. Haley liked retaining power just as much as he did. She was a dominant woman, likely underestimated in her position at Black Crescent. Did they realize what a dynamic powerhouse they had in their possession? Because Chase had been with her only a few times and he could see that she deserved to be in a higher position, definitely higher pay. He had no clue what her financial status was, but she deserved more. Having someone like Haley on his team would be invaluable.

And he fully intended to have her on his team... and in his bed.

Two totally different scenarios, yes, but he wanted her in any way he could have her. Now he just had to figure out how the hell to make sure she didn't hate him when all of this was over, but even more than that, he had to find a way to make sure she wasn't hurt. That was the last thing he wanted in the end.

"You're staring."

Her statement pulled him back and he realized she was still looking at him over her shoulder.

"Maybe I like having you here and I just wanted to mentally capture the moment."

Haley turned fully to face him, crossing her arms over her chest and pursing her lips. "Do you practice those charming lines in the mirror each morning or are you that smooth by default?"

Unable to keep the distance another minute, Chase moved forward and closed the gap between them.

"Nothing to practice," he countered, reaching up to stroke the back of his hand along her jawline. "I see you and something just pulls me. I can't explain it."

Something came over her eyes, something other than desire. Guilt? Worry? He had a heavy dose of both himself, but those emotions had no place here. Not tonight.

"I can't explain it, either," she replied. "But I know what I want and I don't care about the rest of the outside forces right now."

Another way they were so alike. They both shared a passion for each other and they hadn't even removed their clothing yet. He couldn't wait to get her in his bed, to bring out that fire in her and have his fantasies fulfilled.

"Nothing is more attractive than a woman who

knows what she wants." He reached around to toy with the ends of the tie on her jumpsuit. "Except maybe this outfit. Did you wear this to drive me crazy?"

"Perhaps. How did I do?"

He gave the tie a yank, sending the material floating down away from her breasts. Now, fully bare from the torso up, Haley merely stood before him with her eyes locked on his, clearly confident in her radiant beauty and sexuality.

"Damn good," he stated before he covered her mouth with his own.

Eight

Haley wrapped her arms around Chase's neck and arched her body into his. Was this really happening? Was she letting it?

Yes, and oh, hell yes.

Work didn't matter now. The CEO position didn't matter now. Those alarm bells going off in her head telling her why this was going to be a terrible idea in the long run didn't matter, either.

All that mattered was that she and Chase were both adults. Both very consenting adults who were going after what they wanted. She'd come here knowing full well what was going to happen. The promise of seeing that sunrise from his bed had been impossible to turn down.

But it was the anticipation of all the thrilling

things between now and that sunrise that had her more than ready and willing to come home with Chase.

"I've wanted you here for weeks," he muttered against her lips. "I want to take my time, but I need you too bad."

The feeling was quite mutual. She didn't care if he moved fast or slow, she just wanted to get this going before the ache inside her became too overwhelming.

Chase's hands roamed up her bare back as he eased away and stared into her eyes, then that heavy-lidded gaze traveled down to her exposed chest.

The way he looked at her made her feel sexy, like she was the most beautiful woman he'd ever seen.

With a boldness she felt only with him, Haley reached for the buttons on his shirt and slid each one through the slot...one by one. He kept his eyes on hers as she revealed tanned skin and a dark smattering of chest hair. She parted his shirt and yanked it from his pants.

In a flurry of hands and an occasional laugh when they fumbled, they had their clothes off and flung all around in a matter of moments.

Haley's heart beat so fast. She wasn't an innocent by any means, but there was something about Chase that made her want to remember this, that made her feel like something about this moment was special.

But it couldn't be. No. They were both playing a game of cat and mouse and she had no idea which position she was in...or maybe they kept trading off.

Either way, this night was only about physical because there could be nothing more between them.

"If you're scowling, then I'm doing something wrong."

His words brought her back and she smiled.

"You're doing everything right," she told him, looping her arms around her neck. "And I'm assuming these windows are one-way?"

Chase nipped at her lips, then her chin, and traveled down the column of her neck. "Privacy is imperative to me."

He released her for just a moment before grabbing his pants and pulling out protection. In no time, Chase had himself covered, and he turned back to her with a hunger in his eyes that had her entire body heating up even more.

When he hoisted her up and plastered her back against the glass, Haley shivered at the very idea that anyone could see them. Though she knew they couldn't, just the thrill of having Chase so out of control had her anticipation building even more.

"Tell me if you don't like anything," he murmured against her lips.

Haley locked her ankles behind his back and laced her fingers around his neck. "I won't like it if you keep talking."

He offered her a naughty grin as he joined their bodies. In an instant, everything around them vanished. Haley had been waiting for this moment, this man.

One hand gripped her hip and the other cleverly

traveled over her bare skin. He touched her, kissed her, consumed her. Every part of this was so perfect.

Haley arched her body against his as Chase's lips landed on the swell of her breast. Between the expert jerk of his hips and those hands and lips, Haley let out a moan she could no longer suppress. She was done hiding her feelings, done ignoring what she wanted. For tonight, she would be herself.

She might not trust Chase with his business motives, but she wholeheartedly trusted him intimately…because he wanted the same thing from this that she did. A good time and no strings.

His fingertips tightened on her hip as he pumped faster, his warm breath washing over her heated skin. Haley couldn't hold back her climax another second. The pleasure spiraled through her as her knees pressed into his sides. Chase captured her lips as his own body jerked and stilled.

She clung to him until her tremors ceased, and even then she wasn't ready to let go. She wasn't ready to face reality or harsh truths. She wanted to be selfish just a bit longer.

Chase eventually eased back, smoothing her hair away from her face as he stared down into her eyes. There was something she couldn't quite put her finger on, something almost remorseful in his gaze.

"Regrets already?" she asked, only half joking.

The muscle in Chase's jaw clenched as he shook his head. "I don't do regrets."

Well, that was good to know. She'd hate to think she was considered a mistake.

He slowly helped her get steady on her feet and Haley had a sudden sense of insecurity. She stood before him completely naked after having frenzied sex against a window.

What was the protocol now? Did she make a joke to take out some of the tension? Did she just get dressed like this was no big deal?

But this was a big deal. An extremely epic deal because she didn't do one-night stands. She didn't do flings. She sure as hell never slept with someone who could become her boss.

He wasn't her boss yet, though.

"Regrets?" he asked, mimicking her earlier question.

Haley threw him a glance as she went to gather her clothing. "No regrets, just trying to figure out what to say."

"You don't have to say anything," he told her, clearly comfortable with his state of undress...as he should be. "There are no rules here, Haley. We're adults."

Yes, but there should be rules. Shouldn't there?

"I should go."

Haley quickly dressed. She figured staying wasn't smart since this was just a fling.

As she adjusted the tie on her jumpsuit, Chase's hand settled on the small of her back. Stilling beneath his touch, Haley threw him a glance over her shoulder.

"Don't get lost in that head of yours," he told her with a smile. "Despite what you might think of me, I don't do this type of thing, either."

"And what thing is that?" she countered. "Flings? Sleeping with someone to get ahead in a job?"

As soon as the words were out of her mouth, she regretted them. She was being bitchy because she was confused and flustered. She still felt the tingling effects of their encounter and she was trying to sort all of this out, which was damn hard considering she still felt his touch.

"I'm sorry," she told him, turning to face him fully. "That was uncalled for."

Chase pushed her hair over her shoulders before framing her face and stepping to her. "Nothing to apologize for. But let's get one thing straight right now. When I land CEO, it won't be because we slept together. I wanted you. I want the job. The two have nothing to do with each other."

The confidence he exuded was so sexy. Everything about him was sexy, alluring, mesmerizing. Maybe that was why she was so confused about her feelings. Because she didn't do flings, she could easily see herself getting more wrapped up in this man, and that definitely would be a bad idea.

Chase slid his lips over hers. "Stay," he murmured. "No expectations. Just…stay."

As if she could refuse this man anything.

Haley wanted to stay, so she'd just have to figure out all the other stuff later.

After pouring Haley a glass of wine, Chase stepped out onto his balcony and crossed to the outdoor sitting area.

"This view never gets old," he said, handing her the glass. "It's always so peaceful and the perfect way to unwind after a long day."

She took the glass and curled her feet beneath her on the sofa. "I'd be tempted to sleep out here," she stated with a smile. "I'd definitely settle out here in my downtime with a good book."

Chase took a seat beside her, extending his arm along the back of the sofa as he shifted to face her.

"Downtime," he repeated with a chuckle. "Is that something you have?"

Haley sipped her wine and shrugged. "Lately? No. Josh pushes me to leave when he does or even take a day off, but there's just too much to be done."

Ah, yes. Josh. Let's talk about him.

"So your boss isn't demanding?" Chase asked. "All of this work is self-imposed?"

"Maybe a little of both," she corrected. "I demand enough of myself and take pride in my position. Josh and I used to really rub each other the wrong way when the transition was taking place and here and there over the years. He sees me as a little sister, and brothers and sisters argue."

Just like Chase thought…a bastard like his father. Haley was brilliant and anyone who couldn't identify that was a damn fool.

"It took a couple of years but he now sees me as an equal." Haley laughed and took another sip of her wine. "Actually, he's come to see that I'm invaluable in my position and he's been asking my opinion on the new hire. He's a great guy and I'm happy for him for going after his dreams instead of staying out of duty. That's a fine line to hold on to. Love or loyalty."

Love. Chase wouldn't know about that, but loyalty…hell, yes. He was going through all of this out of loyalty to his family. To seek justice and secure redemption.

"You will be invaluable to me when I take over," he told her.

Her smile widened. "You're so sure this is going to happen for you."

"Because it is," he assured her. "I wouldn't have started if I thought I would fail."

"Do you fail at anything?" she asked.

He thought to when he couldn't save his family, when his father went to prison and his mother had a nervous breakdown.

"Only one time. I vowed to never let myself get that vulnerable again."

Haley finished her wine and set the glass on the table before settling back into the sofa. Her head dropped back against his arm, her eyes meeting his.

"What makes you want this job so bad?" she asked. "You're successful already. You don't need the boost in your finances or ego…or maybe you do. I really don't know much about you."

Yet she'd slept with him and hadn't gone home. That just proved she was more invested in whatever was happening between them than he'd ever anticipated.

And maybe so was he. While he wasn't looking for any type of relationship, he couldn't ignore that he wanted her here, that he enjoyed her company even outside the bedroom. She challenged him, made him smile during a time when he'd been so hell-bent on revenge. She was refreshing at a time when he didn't know happiness or distractions were even possible.

"Finances aren't an issue," he agreed carefully. "I'm always looking for ways to grow and better myself. Black Crescent is the perfect next step in my life."

"Because of that whole family thing," she reminded him with a smile. "And what happens if you don't get the position?"

Chase couldn't help but laugh. "You're not a great motivational speaker, you know."

Haley's smile tugged at him… Everything about her seemed to pull him little by little closer to her world. It wasn't her world he'd set out to infiltrate, yet here he was spending more and more time with her and slowly being pulled away from his ultimate goal.

"Listen, I'm not the final decision-maker," she explained as she leaned closer. "I also shouldn't even be discussing this position outside of work. Not only is it unprofessional, it is disrespectful to Josh."

Yes, Josh. The golden boy. Well, Chase had been doing some digging on Josh. It was best to find out any hidden secrets and dirty details when taking down an opponent. Besides the whole replacement aspect he was working on, Chase also heard rumors that Josh had fathered another woman's baby…not his fiancée's.

Granted, Josh wasn't the one who had destroyed Chase's family, but the guy had swooped in and taken over his crooked father's company. There had to be some semblance of Vernon Lowell in the son who was so take-charge. Chase hadn't wasted his time digging into the other brothers' pasts, though it would be impossible to ignore the rumors that surrounded Oliver and his heavy addiction.

Chase leaned closer to Haley and rested his hand on her upper thigh. "You're invaluable to your company and I don't want you discussing anything you're not comfortable with."

Haley settled her hand over his and smiled. "It's not my company. If you ask my parents, I'm just an assistant. I'm pretty sure they think I sharpen pencils and make coffee all day."

More than once she'd mentioned her parents and their lack of respect for not only her, but also her critical role at Black Crescent.

"Have you ever told them your worth to the company?" he asked. Forget the fact she should be invaluable to her own parents as a remarkable daughter.

Haley let out a humorless laugh. "It's really not worth the fight. I struggled for good grades in school. I had to work my butt off for Bs and Cs. So they naturally dismissed me from growing up to be successful."

"Naturally?" he questioned, trying to tamp down his rage. "That's not natural parenting, Haley. Some kids work harder than others and some just have an easier time. That doesn't mean you can't be successful."

"Yes, well, I'm used to it and actually over it." She eased closer and slid her hand around his neck. "Let's not talk about them anymore."

That desire flashed back into her eyes, and if it was a distraction she needed, then so be it. He didn't mind being used by Haley to keep her mind off unpleasant things. Besides, he shouldn't want to get that personal with her anyway, right?

Yet he couldn't help himself.

Tonight he would take what he wanted, in return keeping Haley's thoughts solely on him. Tomorrow he would go back to trying to pry deeper into the company via her mind.

The end was in sight, and he was too close to having it all to turn back now.

Nine

"No, Mom. I'm fine."

Chase assured his mother once again. He couldn't be angry at her for consistently asking. The woman was worried about her son taking on the family that nearly destroyed them.

He clutched his cell and turned away from his desk to face the large picture window.

"I promise, I'm careful," he assured her as he glanced out onto the river.

The sun shone high in the sky and Haley had gone home after breakfast…which he'd served in bed. Last night had been a turning point, though he still wasn't quite sure which direction he was actually pointing to at the moment.

"I can't help but be concerned," she told him. "I hope you aren't making a mistake."

"Life doesn't come with guarantees, but I didn't set out to lose," he stated. "I know what I'm doing with Black Crescent."

With Haley, though, not so much. Oh, they'd had a hell of a good time last night, but he had no idea where this would go. If they'd gotten together under much different circumstances, Chase wouldn't mind seeing where this could lead. Considering he wasn't being completely honest with her, and that he wanted to bring down her beloved boss, Chase knew this fling could only be temporary at best.

"Promise that you'll check in so I don't worry."

Chase smiled. "I promise. There's nothing for you to worry about."

Once he finished the call, Chase held his cell at his side and pulled in a deep breath. While he always loved talking to his mother, he'd been waiting on his private detective to call this morning. He had been doing some deeper digging into Josh Lowell's past and Chase needed as much information as he could get if he was ultimately going to slide into that CEO position.

Haley was proving to continually be the ever-loyal employee and was not letting much slip. His plan had been to spend more time with her, to get her to somehow unknowingly let slide tidbits of information about the company, but she was still so close-lipped. If anything, she only sang Josh's praises and the company's as a whole. She'd been there during the fallout, so there was no way she wasn't fully aware of every dirty deed that went down. Not everything was public and it was those insider details he needed to uncover.

His cell vibrated in his hand. Chase glanced to the screen and saw the call he'd been waiting on. Maybe now he would get that ammunition he needed to secure his spot at Black Crescent and take down the Lowells once and for all.

Matteo Velez sat across from her desk and waited for his interview time. Haley watched as he went from checking his phone to glancing around the room. He seemed distracted, like something more important occupied his thoughts.

More important than an interview for the CEO position? That seemed quite off and extremely unprofessional.

Did he even want to be here?

The handsome businessman would certainly be a sexy replacement for her current boss, but Haley still had her sights set on another mogul.

While Matt may be a head-turner with that dark suit and his intense stare, he wasn't the one who had her questioning her sanity and getting lost in thought during working hours.

No, that privilege belonged to the mysterious Chase Hargrove.

Josh stepped from his office and caught Haley's

eyes, pulling her from her thoughts and back to the moment and the interview.

"Matt," Josh stated, turning his attention to the latest applicant. "I hope I didn't keep you waiting."

Coming to his feet, Matt shook his head and buttoned his suit jacket. "No problem at all. I'm thankful I managed a second interview."

"You deserve it," Josh corrected. "With a résumé like the one you have, you are already high up on the list."

Matt nodded. Haley found it odd that he didn't smile or seem thrilled at the prospect of being the next CEO. What was going on with this guy?

"My assistant, Haley, will again be sitting in on the interview," Josh said, gesturing to her. "She's been with Black Crescent the longest and she will be your greatest asset to the company."

Matt flashed her a grin. "The right-hand woman," he stated. "There's always one major player in any company who remains behind the scenes and works the long hours."

Haley laughed. "I'd say the long hours are a toss-up between Josh and me, but yes. I do love my job and whoever takes over this position will be working closely with me."

"Let's step into my office. Allison couldn't be here in person, but I have her on conference call."

Josh gestured to the open door behind him and let Haley step in first. She wasn't so sure that Matt had the truest of intentions. He didn't seem overly thrilled to be here, which could always be just nerves or anticipation. He could be a man who just held his emotions close to his chest.

He could also have ulterior motives like Chase. And if that was the case, then Haley had more work cut out for her. She'd never considered the applicants might have past issues with Josh's father or the family in general. It was fifteen years ago. Did people even hold grudges that long?

That was certainly something she needed to take into account. If she came up with too many red flags, she'd have to meet with Josh and express her concerns. Vernon had certainly destroyed quite a few families so it wasn't beyond the realm of possibility for those kids to now want revenge.

Haley settled into her seat and listened as Josh and Allison conducted the interview. Every now and then she interjected and asked her own questions, impressed by Matt's answers.

Maybe Matt should be in the running, but part of her wondered how she would feel if the position went to Chase…and how she would feel if it didn't.

The time was drawing near when a decision would be made and she would have to adjust no matter what the outcome.

All the more reason for her to follow up with that investigator she'd contacted Saturday afternoon about digging into Chase's past and the past of his parents.

There was more to the story than what she'd uncovered on her own and she wouldn't rest until she discovered the full truth of the man she was falling for.

* * *

"So you're telling me you finished your schooling in half the time?"

Just when he thought she couldn't get any more amazing, Haley threw out another fact from her past.

"I buckled down and wanted to be done," she told him as she propped her feet on his lap. "I still lived at home and working as an intern gave me enough to save so the second I graduated, I had enough to get my first apartment and a cheap car."

No wonder she was so loyal. Black Crescent and Vernon Lowell had given her a break and taken a chance. Likely they had been her haven when she wanted and needed to be appreciated and probably loved in a way she hadn't been before.

Ironic that's what she'd found in a company run by a scoundrel, but Vernon did different things for different people apparently. Or maybe Josh had taken on the new intern. Chase didn't know the dynamics there, and he'd be jealous if he wasn't sure Josh thought of Haley as a sister.

Chase slid his hand over Haley's delicate ankles. He'd coerced her into coming for dinner, where he'd prepared everything himself. He'd given his chef the night off again so he and Haley could have complete privacy.

Even Al had been given the night off from any duties. The less his well-meaning father figure/driver/shoulder to lean on knew the better.

"Where did you learn to cook like that?" she asked, resting her head against the back of the sofa

and offering him a lazy smile. "I know they don't
teach you how to whip potatoes on the football field."

"No. No, they don't," he laughed in agreement.
"My mother is an amazing cook and she taught me a
few things. Others I've learned on my own through
trial and error. I do have a chef for various events
and when I have company, but I wanted tonight to
just be about us."

Her eyes held his, her smile slowly fading away.
"Is there an *us*?"

"Whatever is happening here constitutes as an
us." His hand slid higher on her leg, but he kept his
eyes locked on hers. "Let's not look any further than
this."

"*This* as in sex?"

Her bold question had him smiling as his thumb
grazed over the curve of her knee. "We're both too
married to our careers to worry about anything else
right now."

Her legs shifted as she nestled deeper into the
sofa, her eyes drawing heavier in that sexy, bedroom-
glare type of way—the way that did absolutely nothing to hide the hunger and the desire she possessed.

The idea of her sharing that passion with another
man set off a wave of jealousy he hadn't experienced
with another woman. Part of him wondered if he'd
just gotten in too deep with her, if their relatable
backgrounds and drive for business made her seem
like the perfect woman.

"People like us?" she repeated. "You told me you
wanted a family."

"I do," he affirmed, his hand now splayed across her thigh. "But right now, I have other goals in mind."

Her gaze dropped to his mouth, then back up to his eyes. "We're not talking about the CEO position anymore."

"We're not talking anymore at all."

He inched up her body, his hands taking the hem of her little sundress higher, as well. He wasn't ready to talk, wasn't ready to look into all the messed-up emotions rolling through his mind.

Part of him wanted to know what would have happened had he met Haley under different circumstances. Part of him wanted to know what his mother would have thought of Haley. No doubt they would've gotten along…if Chase had let such a meeting take place.

But that was all a ridiculous line of thinking and a dangerous path to take at this stage in the game.

Haley arched against him, letting out a soft moan as her lids fluttered closed. That reaction was exactly what he wanted. Having her beneath him, ready to join together in the most primal, intimate way, was more than he'd ever thought when he'd first met her. He might not know what the hell he was doing in the long run with her, but he wasn't looking at anything beyond tonight. He couldn't even think about that or the guilt would overcome him.

Chase gripped her hips and jerked her beneath him even more as he settled between her legs. Her eyes shot up to his as a wicked smile spread across her face.

When she opened her mouth, Chase covered it with his own. He really didn't want to talk now and he was afraid of what she'd say. Communicating through their bodies seemed the safest way…at least for now.

Without words, Chase slid her panties down her legs, quickly rid himself of his pants, found protection and settled exactly where he wanted to be. And, if her moans and soft cries were any indicators, this was exactly where she wanted him to be.

Resting his elbows on either side of her head, Chase smoothed her hair from her face and made sure to keep his focus solely on her as he joined their bodies. Haley's ankles came around to lock behind his back, urging him deeper.

When her eyes connected with his, Chase stilled. There was some underlying emotion staring back at him, one he couldn't afford to dig into and one that would likely scare the hell out of him.

Closing his eyes might be the coward's way out, but there was no other option…not now.

Haley threaded her fingers through his hair, tugging ever so slightly. Chase rose up, gripping her hips as he went. Looking down at her with her hair a mess over his sofa, her dress bunched around her waist and her breathing coming out in short bursts had him quickening the pace.

There was something so addicting about this woman and until he found out how to break this cycle, he was damn well going to hang on for the ride.

"Chase."

The whispered word that slipped through her lips as her body tightened all around him had Chase reaching his own peak. Pleasure tore through him, his fingertips dug into her hips and Chase let himself go. Haley continued to whisper his name over and over. He found himself wrapped in her arms and legs, and he wondered how he'd been looming over her and was now being cradled by her warmth, her...

No. Not her love. Love didn't belong here and he sure as hell didn't want it.

As he lay half on, half off her heated body, Chase knew reality would hit sooner rather than later. At some point, he would have to complete his revenge and keep Haley out of the path of destruction in the process.

Ten

Haley stepped inside her front door and immediately slipped out of her heels. She'd been running around all day and had barely even sat at her desk. Between the ongoing interviews with Josh and CEO prospects and running to Tomorrow's Leaders to greet the newest recipients, Haley's feet were killing her.

She'd also missed lunch and the time had well passed any normal dinner schedule. Perhaps she should just pop open a bottle of Pinot and relax in a hot bubble bath. She definitely hadn't taken enough personal time lately with all the spare time she'd been spending with Chase.

Not that she was at all sorry. Her feelings for him were growing each time they were together. Granted, intimacy had a tendency to force people together at least in an emotional manner. Haley didn't do flings and she didn't take sex lightly. If she hadn't had some deeper pull toward Chase, she never would have slept with him.

She hadn't seen him since she'd left his house the other night after he'd blown her mind on his living room couch. They'd texted, but they'd both been busy with work… At least she assumed that's what he'd been busy with.

Haley bent to retrieve her shoes as she made her way toward her master suite. The next thing to go after the shoes was always the bra. She was so done with this day. While she'd accomplished quite a bit, she had run out of steam.

Her cell chimed in the purse she still had over her shoulder. With a groan, she stepped into her room and tossed her purse onto her bed before digging out her phone.

Marcus's name lit up her screen. With a sigh, she swiped the screen and made her way into her adjoining bath.

"I just left you," she said in lieu of a hello. "Is something wrong?"

"Not at all," Marcus replied. "In fact, everything is rather amazing. We had an anonymous donor just give enough to cover all of the textbooks for each of the new recipients starting college in the fall. The amount also covers anything else they may need as far as laptops, notebooks and individual class fees.

There's also a buffer amount for anything that may have been overlooked."

Stunned, Haley turned and sank down onto the edge of her bed. "Who paid for all of that?"

"The money came in electronically with a detailed note of what to purchase for the incoming students," Marcus explained. "There was also a message stating that there would be more donations at the beginning of each quarter for new classes. But honestly, that padded amount that's left would more than cover an entire year. I don't know who this guy is, but he's certainly invested in Tomorrow's Leaders. I mean, I'm glad, but I wish we knew who to thank properly."

Yeah, she did, too, but she also had a good idea who would suddenly be invested in her beloved charity. Not that she would divulge that information to anyone, not even her right-hand man.

"Well, let's just be thankful," she replied. "It's not like we haven't had anonymous donors before. We just typically don't have such specific notes."

"I know you would've seen the email, but I wanted to give you a heads-up," Marcus told her. "Go about your evening. I'm sure you were about ready to dive into a much-needed bottle of wine."

Haley laughed as she turned the knobs on her large soaker tub. She grabbed a bottle on the edge and dumped a hefty dose of lavender bubble bath in.

"You know me so well."

"I know you don't take enough time for yourself, so go enjoy. I'm sure I'll talk to you tomorrow."

"Thanks, Marcus. Good night."

She disconnected the call and stripped out of her clothes. After grabbing her kimono off the back of the bathroom door, she headed to the kitchen to get that glass of wine while her tub filled with hot, bubbly water.

Chase and his wily ways had her smiling. He thought he was sneaky—or perhaps he didn't. Maybe he'd fully intended for her to figure out who had deposited such a large sum.

Oh, sure, someone else could've left that deposit with a detailed email, but she didn't think so. He'd been impressed with her charity and had been eager to help.

Moments later, Haley padded back through her house and into her bathroom. The suds filled the white bathtub and the aroma instantly relaxed her. She set her stemless glass on the edge and slid the knot from her tie. The kimono landed on the floor as Haley stepped into the warm water.

She sank down, letting the bubbles consume her. Her glass and cell sat beside her, but she closed her eyes and dropped her head against her bath pillow. For just a moment, she wanted to lie here and do absolutely nothing.

Okay, maybe she wanted to think about Chase and those damn gestures that made her like him even more. Maybe she wanted to reach out to him and call him out on it. If nothing else, she did want to tell him thank you. She didn't have to make a big deal about thanking him and she didn't plan on embarrassing him, but she did want him to know how much she appreciated what he'd done.

Her cell vibrated again and she peeked out of one eye to the screen. Emails. Always emails.

Another vibration had her screen lighting up with a text from the PI she had digging a little deeper into Chase's parents.

Her curiosity got the best of her and she reached with her dry hand and swiped the screen. The text told her she might want to check her emails ASAP.

Urgency had her tapping on the email icon and opening the message. Haley wanted to take in the entire email at once, so her eyes scanned over all the bullet points before she went back and read each word at a slower pace. Her heart clenched at the information revealed, the ache in the pit of her stomach gnawing as she read very plausible motivations for Chase's urgent desire to take over Black Crescent Hedge Fund.

His father had been incarcerated after a paper trail from the company and Vernon forced the police to take action. She'd known Chase's father had also been part of the embezzling, but she hadn't been sure as to what extent. According to the email, he had been a minor player in the game, but Vernon's well-laid trail led straight to Dale's door.

She read on, finding that his mother was institutionalized after she'd had a nervous breakdown, just like Haley had originally thought. Their family home had been foreclosed after his father went to prison and then his mother had fallen ill. Once his mother was hospitalized, Chase was left alone. No wonder that football scholarship had been so important. That's all he'd had left—his sport and his education.

Is that why he wanted to help her organization so much? To give kids a chance when they wouldn't otherwise have one?

She also read where he'd changed his name right after his mother had been sent for psychiatric help. He'd legally done so and the patterns from then on showed a timeline in black-and-white of Chase working toward revenge on Black Crescent and the Lowell family.

Haley swallowed as a burning sensation pricked her eyes and the back of her throat. He'd been angry for years, so angry he'd changed his major from education to business and graduated in record time... something he'd failed to mention when they'd been discussing her accomplishments.

Setting her phone back on the edge of the bathtub, Haley grabbed her wine. Sipping was out. Gulping was necessary now.

Clearly he'd been planning on trying to infiltrate Black Crescent. Had he been waiting for the CEO position to open up? There was no way he would've known that Josh wanted out because initially Josh had planned to stay. Granted, being a business mogul hadn't been Josh's first choice. He did put his family first and had done everything to rebuild the family name.

Yet now that he'd fallen in love with Sophie and

the two were planning a life together, Josh decided to pursue art, his true passion. Haley couldn't blame him. After all, he'd put his life on hold when his brothers didn't want to step up...or in Oliver's case of addiction, he couldn't step up.

Haley knew Oliver was doing better, had put that hellish time behind him, but he still wasn't up to taking over a corporation the magnitude of Black Crescent.

Finishing off her wine, Haley settled back against the cushy pillow and let all of this information roll through her mind. As much as she wanted to confront Chase and find the answers to her questions— mainly wanting to know if she'd been part of the plan all along—Haley knew she had to be patient and take her time here. There was too much at stake... namely her heart, but also the integrity and future of the company.

If Chase ended up as CEO, what would he do to the place that Haley basically called home? What would happen to all the employees who were loyal to Josh? Not to mention the elite customers they dealt with. Wouldn't taking down Black Crescent just be déjà vu of what happened years ago with Vernon?

Haley didn't like lies, betrayal or deceit. She prided herself on honesty and transparency, but she also prided herself on her strength and ability to withstand the toughest of situations.

There was only one way to find out what Chase's true motives were, and she was going to have to go against everything she valued and held dear.

Haley was going to have to turn a blind eye to her honesty and set a trap for Chase…all the while pretending everything between them was perfectly fine. In truth, the dynamics had completely changed. Her emotional involvement had already surpassed anything she'd expected or even wanted.

While she had no clue what would happen next or how her plan would play out, Haley was certain of one thing… Someone was going to get hurt.

Eleven

Chase wasn't at all surprised that Haley reciprocated the dinner idea and invited him to her place. There was something stirring between them, something that had nothing to do with his revenge plot or his career.

He genuinely liked her, wanted to spend more time with her. That caring side of her had him wondering how she could ever have stayed loyal to a company run by such a bastard. For someone so loving and giving of herself to others, she'd started working at a young age for the exact opposite type of personality.

On the positive side of things, Vernon had left before he could corrupt Haley. Chase hated to think what that man would've done to someone as innocent and generous as Haley.

With a firm hold on the raspberry torte he'd made, Chase rang Haley's doorbell and stepped back to wait.

Seconds later, the door swung wide, revealing a stunning hostess. Her hair tumbled over her shoulders and the little red dress she wore left absolutely nothing to the imagination, stopping high on her thigh and with a deep V in the front. The woman was already driving him crazy…and from the naughty smile, she knew exactly what game she was playing.

Damn his hormones and her for making him live in a constant state of arousal and need.

"Perfect timing," she told him. "I just took the dishes out of the oven."

Her eyes darted to the dish in his hands, then back up to his face.

"Did you throw the box away and put your dessert in that fancy dish just for me?"

Chase scoffed. "A box? I'll have you know I made this with my own two hands. I didn't buy it and I didn't even have my chef make it."

Haley's brows rose as she stepped back and gestured for him to come inside. "Why don't you tell me how you know how to make such a decadent-looking dessert over dinner."

She turned from the door and sashayed back into her home. Chase's gaze instantly fell to those swaying hips as he followed her, closing the door at his back.

The spacious open concept offered him an even bigger glimpse into her life. Simplistic furniture in pale grays in contrast against dark flooring but pops of colors in greenery from plants and bright throw pillows really pulled in both sides of Haley. The career woman in Haley always had a polished, conservative look. But that inner vixen and good-time girl came out to play once business hours were over.

The more he uncovered about this woman, the more he wished like hell they could have met under very different circumstances.

Haley busied herself scooping dinner onto plates and then she poured two glasses of red wine. She hummed a soft tune he didn't recognize but that he instantly found relaxing.

"My mother always hummed." The thought hit him and just tumbled out before he could stop himself. Interestingly enough, he found that he wanted to share more about his past with her. "When I was younger, she would always hum 'You Are My Sunshine.' Cooking dinner, folding laundry, that was just her song."

Haley stared across the long kitchen island and offered one of her sweet smiles. "You don't talk much about your parents. That's a beautiful memory."

His parents meant everything to him and while they certainly had their difficult times—some had seemed so bleak and dire—they always had each other. He and his mom and dad never lacked love or loyalty.

That was the entire reason he was here today. That path he'd started years ago led him to Haley. Guilt grew more and more each day. What started out as rage and anger had turned to desire and passion.

"Everything okay?"

Haley's concerned question pulled Chase back to the moment. He nodded and grinned.

"Fine," he assured her. "What can I do to help?"

She continued to stare, her brows drawn in worry. Chase didn't want to get into the mess going on inside his mind, and even his heart. While he did a damn good job of keeping his heart protected, that didn't mean he was a complete bastard. He cared for Haley, there was no denying that, but he also still had a job to do…literally.

He hadn't come this far in his life, in his plans, to get sidelined by hormones and an innocent woman who had him questioning everything.

When she continued to stare, Chase came around the island and picked up the plates. "Where to?"

He waited, hoping she wouldn't pry any deeper into his past. There was nothing more he could reveal without giving away who he truly was and what he was doing centering himself into her life.

"Let's go out on the balcony," she finally stated. "It's such a nice night."

She led the way through the living room and out onto the spacious balcony overlooking a sloped backyard with a small pond and fountain. Such a simple space, but so perfect for Haley. She had a beautiful home in an upscale part of town and she didn't have to tell him that everything she had, she'd worked her ass off for. No one had helped her, least of all her family. All of her accomplishments were only because this woman had drive and determination and wouldn't let anyone stand in her way.

And that right there was so damn sexy, he couldn't even deny that she was quite possibly the most perfect woman he'd ever met.

Too bad she could never be his.

"Oh, do you care to go into the dining area and grab the napkin holder from the table?" she asked. "I'll go get the utensils."

"Sure."

Chase stepped back into her house and passed through the living area to the small dining room. Spread across the table were papers, which caught his attention with the Black Crescent Hedge Fund logo on several documents. The napkin holder was nowhere to be seen on the table, but the highlighters he'd brought her were lying in a bundle on the side.

As much as he wanted to glance through those papers, he couldn't. A month ago, if given this opportunity, he'd sure as hell have taken advantage, but now... Well, everything had changed.

"Damn it," he muttered as he turned to glance around the room.

The sideboard had a decorative napkin holder full of napkins. Chase grabbed it and started to head out, but not before one last longing glance at the papers. Josh's signature was scrawled across the bottom of a few documents, but Chase ignored his curiosity.

Now wasn't the time to betray Haley's trust. He vowed to himself not to let her get hurt. He would do everything he could to prevent Haley from getting caught in the middle of this twisted web.

Walking away from those papers was the most difficult thing he'd done in a while. Maybe they wouldn't have shed any light on his master plan, but there was a possibility they would have.

What should he have done, though? Stood there sorting through the piles, or perhaps pulled out his cell and started snapping pics so he could look over them in his private time? And do all of that while Haley waited for him on the balcony for a romantic dinner? Only a complete jerk would do such a thing.

When he stepped back out onto the balcony, he saw that Haley had lit two small candles and had arranged a colorful bundle of flowers in a simple glass vase between their plates. She held her arms out, gesturing toward the table.

"Ta-da."

Chase laughed. "Is that why you had me step away?"

She shrugged and pulled the chair out for him. "I just wanted to do something nice. I mean, it's no bouquet of highlighters or homemade raspberry torte, but..."

Chase couldn't remember the last time someone did something for him. Not something that didn't have to do with business or using him to get ahead. Haley had no reason to use him, no reason to play him. No, in all of this he was the one using, and that damn weight kept mounting on his shoulders... Soon the heaviness would become too much to bear.

This sweet gesture of dinner and a romantic ambiance put a vise around his heart and he'd done so well in keeping his heart out of this equation so far.

Chase set the napkins on the table and turned to face her. That punch of lust he always experienced when he looked at her now layered with something else…something deeper, more meaningful, but definitely something he couldn't label.

Honestly, he didn't want to put a label on any of this because that would hint dangerously close to a relationship.

But physical, that was something he could grasp and control. It was an emotion, a reaction he knew.

Reaching for her, Chase curled his fingers around that dip in her waist and pulled her closer.

"This is all amazing," he told her, leaning in. "The dinner, the atmosphere, sexy dress. You didn't have to do all of this for me."

Her smile widened as she looped her arms around his neck. "Maybe I did it for us. Maybe I like spending time with you and I wanted to look nice even though we're staying in."

Hell yes they were staying in. There was no way he was taking her out because he wasn't sure how long he'd be able to control himself. Peeling her out of that dress had just jumped to the top of his priority list…even above those papers in the other room.

"Staying in is the best idea I've heard all day." He nipped at her lips, holding her hips flush against his own. "Did you wear this dress to drive me out of my mind?"

She tipped back, laughter dancing in her eyes. "Is it working?"

"You're lucky we've made it this long with our clothes still intact."

Haley framed his face and laid a quick kiss on his lips. "Dinner first. Then we can discuss dessert options."

She stepped from his hold and gestured to the chair she'd pulled out for him. "Sit and eat before it gets cold."

Reluctantly, he took a seat. "If this is some sort of foreplay, you're winning."

She reached for a napkin and snapped it open, then laid it in her lap. "I never lose," she promised with a leveled gaze.

As if he needed another reason to find her even more irresistible. But he needed to focus. Those papers and her sweetness layered with a heavy dose of sex appeal had really thrown him. He wasn't about to mention the papers, though. Likely she'd brought work home, and that certainly didn't surprise him.

Haley picked up her fork and speared a piece of beef. "So, tell me all about how you came to make amazing-looking desserts."

"Oh, they don't just look amazing, they taste incredible."

"Just add humble to your list of attributes."

Chase took a bite of what tasted like homemade noodles. "Humble has no space in my life. Confidence and risks have taken me everywhere I need to be."

"Please, no work talk," she begged. "I already had to bring home some forms to sort out and I just want one evening of doing absolutely nothing."

Chase set his fork down and reached across the small round table. "I'm glad you're taking some time for yourself."

"With you."

Chase raised his brows. "Is there someone else?"

"Oh, yes," she laughed. "I've been seeing all of the CEO applicants on the side. You know, just so I can see who I'm most compatible with."

He couldn't help but smile. A snarky comeback was another quality he appreciated.

"I deserved that," he told her. "When was the last time you dated before me?"

"Are we dating?" she asked.

The idea didn't bother him. What bothered him was the fact all of this was temporary. There was no long term here, even if he had the time to start feeding into a serious relationship.

"I'm exclusively sleeping with you and we've been out," he countered. "What do you want to call that?"

Haley pursed her lips as she reached for her wine. Swirling the contents, she leaned back in her chair and kept her focus on him.

"I'm not sure," she finally answered. "I like seeing you, I like sleeping with you and I don't want to do that with anyone else right now."

Right now. Did that mean she also thought this was temporary? Because the only reason he wasn't pursuing more was because he knew she would never forgive him for going after her beloved company.

So what was her reasoning for thinking this wouldn't grow into more?

And why the hell was he offended?

"So, about that torte," she went on. "Care to tell me how you came to that and are there any more hidden secrets you want to share?"

Hidden secrets? She wasn't ready to hear those, though he knew they would come out eventually. With the position he currently was in, he just had to make sure she didn't hate him and understood his reasoning for his actions once this was all said and done.

Twelve

Haley rolled over, her hand reaching for Chase, only to find the spot not only empty but also cold.

Confused, she sat up in bed and glanced around the darkened room. A sliver from the hallway light filtered in.

After dinner, she and Chase had enjoyed more wine and a brief chat on the balcony. It didn't take long for them to move inside for some much needed privacy. They barely made it to the living room before their clothes were shed. Once that frenzied sex had taken place, Chase had carried her in the most romantic way possible to the bedroom, where they'd taken their time exploring each other.

So where was he now? She'd fallen asleep in his

arms, nestled right against all of his strength and warmth.

The papers. Damn it. She'd left those out as part of her initial trap or plan or whatever the hell game she was playing in an attempt to test Chase's loyalty. She'd actually forgotten all about them once they'd started dinner. Of course, she'd sent him into the dining room to find her scattered mess. She'd purposely left the napkins in there, needing to get his curiosity pumping.

The papers she'd left out were actually private, but nothing that would harm the company. They did hold information that only she knew; not even Josh was aware of some of the contents. So if anything was leaked, there would be only one source.

Guilt curled low in her belly as she pushed the sheet aside. Swinging her legs over the side of the bed, she sat for just a moment and wondered what she should do now. She didn't like playing games, but she had to know where Chase really stood. Did he indeed want the CEO position or did he just want to destroy the company from within?

Did he want to destroy her in the process? Had she been part of his plan all along?

Fear spiraled through her, layering with the guilt and the worry. If he wasn't playing her, then she hated how she'd tried to set a trap. But she had to protect not only herself, but also Black Crescent and everyone in their employ.

Haley came to her feet and grabbed her kimono from the antique trunk at the end of her bed. After sliding into it and securing the tie, she padded out into the hall. The decorative clock on the wall showed just after five in the morning. Considering this was a Sunday and not a typical workday, she'd like to have slept in a little longer in the arms of the man she was falling for.

Falling for and possibly being deceived by.

Mercy, this was starting to become a serious mess.

Haley stepped into the open living area where she saw Chase in the kitchen, standing over her coffeepot.

Wearing a dark suit certainly made Chase Hargrove drop-dead sexy, but having him in her kitchen wearing nothing but black boxer briefs and a mop of bedhead was a whole new side of sex appeal.

Haley couldn't examine too deeply just how having Chase in her home made her feel. Inviting a man into her personal space wasn't something she did, but she'd needed to set the trap.

Ugh. Even those words floating through her mind made her nauseated. But thinking he was using her, that he might have gone into her dining area and leaked information about Black Crescent, made her feel even worse.

She shuffled her feet across the wood floor, causing Chase to turn. He offered her a crooked grin and raked a hand down his chest.

"Did I wake you?" he asked.

Haley shook her head. "I rolled over and you were gone."

"I'm an early riser."

Or maybe he wanted to catch her while she was asleep and rifle through her things? How long had he been alone in her home? Had he taken photos of the documents and already called his assistant or his family? Were his parents backing him?

She had way too many questions about the man standing practically naked in her kitchen.

Chase turned back to her coffee maker and sighed. He tapped a button, tapped another and shrugged.

"I was trying to figure out how to make coffee in this damn pot of yours, but there's only so far my degrees can take me."

Haley laughed, making her way around the bar island separating the living area from the kitchen. She stepped in beside him and glanced to the water, then the mess of coffee grounds he'd made on her counter.

"Well, it certainly helps to get the grounds into the filter," she stated. "Why don't you go have a seat and I'll do the coffee?"

He threw a heavy-lidded glance over his shoulder. "Is it because I've made a mess? I was going to clean that up, you know."

Haley patted his cheek. "I'm sure you were, but I can't stand chaos and this is already making my eye twitch."

Chase nodded and took a step to the side. "At least show me how to use this damn thing for next time."

Haley stilled, her attention going from the messy counter to the messy relationship.

"Next time?" she asked. "How often do you plan on staying over?"

Chase reached out and gave a slight tug on the tie of her kimono. "As often as you'll let me."

In a perfect world and under much different circumstances, she'd want nothing more than to have this man in her bed each night. She could think of no other way she'd like to fall asleep.

Unfortunately, she was almost positive she couldn't trust him and she had convinced herself that he was playing her…which meant she needed to stay at least one step ahead of him until she uncovered the real truth.

An uncomfortable heaviness settled deep within her. She needed space. She couldn't stand here next to him, both of them wearing very little, with all of these emotions. There was too much to consider, too much to worry about and contemplate.

With a smile, Haley faced him. "Let me handle the coffee. Go back to bed and I'll meet you there."

He leaned in, covered her mouth with his and caught her so off guard she had to grip his bare shoulders to keep upright. He released her just as quickly and took a step back.

Haley reached for the edge of the counter to maintain her balance as Chase headed back toward the bedroom. She waited until he disappeared down the hallway and into the master suite.

Blowing out a breath she hadn't realized she'd been holding, Haley closed her eyes and gathered herself. After she cleaned up the coffee grounds and got the brew going, she glanced toward the hallway once more before going to the dining area.

The light from the kitchen illuminated into the space and onto the table. The papers were exactly how she'd had them. Not one had been moved, and even though they looked like a mess, she knew in what order they had been placed.

Was he not using her? He'd had the perfect opportunity to look over these documents and she was pretty positive he hadn't done a thing.

The sound of the coffeepot coming to the end of the cycle pulled her away from the table. Her plan worked, or didn't work, depending on how she wanted to look at things. He knew these pieces were here, so if he'd truly been out to sabotage her or the company, wouldn't he have moved them around to read them or snap pictures?

What if he was in this only for her?

But then if that was the case, what happened if he was hired and became her boss? Then what would people think? The staff knew Haley had sat in on the interviews. Would they think she'd chosen him because he slept with her?

Haley tried to push aside all the questions as she made her way back to the coffee. Chase waited on her in her room, and now that she knew his intentions might be real and honest, she couldn't wait to spend the morning with him and maybe see where all of this could lead.

"I have some more information."

Chase steered his SUV through the streets of

downtown and listened as his personal investigator gave the details Chase had been waiting on.

"The information wasn't easy to come by and it's certainly going to cost you."

Chase rolled his eyes. The guy was the best in the business, but his ego seriously grated on Chase's last nerve. He wasn't in the mood for games. He just wanted the scoop he was paying for.

"What did you find?" Chase demanded as he came to a stoplight.

"The doctor that delivered the love child that is rumored to belong to Josh might have been a bit shady and untrustworthy...as was the mother of the child."

"How shady are we talking?"

"The doctor or the mother?"

Chase gripped the wheel and prayed for patience. "I want to know everything you found."

"Well, the doctor had been known to falsify a few birth certificates in his day," the investigator replied. "Hundreds if not thousands, in fact. He also manually changed DNA results once they were processed for a nice sum from his desperate clients. He practiced for over thirty years before he was caught and he's now incarcerated."

Interesting. The shady doctor working for a shady family. How quaint.

"The results also mention that the father could be Josh or his twin brother, Jake."

Well, at least that was something.

"And the more I dug into Josh's past, the more I found he's actually an upstanding guy. Nothing at all like his father. The guy seems to just want out of the family business, and I can hardly blame him. It has to be hell having the black cloud of Vernon Lowell hanging over your head your entire life."

"Send me over everything you found," Chase told him. "I need to see a few things for myself. I've already sent your payment, plus an extra bonus since you worked so hard."

Stroking that overinflated ego kept his investigator loyal and quiet. Those were two main qualities Chase demanded.

He disconnected the call with a tap to the screen on his dashboard. Instantly, music filled the vehicle and he cranked the metal up. He needed to think and when things were silent was when he nearly went out of his mind.

The light changed and Chase turned to take the familiar route leading to his parents' home—though his mind was still back on spending the weekend with Haley and those damn papers.

There was no way all of that was coincidence. He firmly believed she'd left those there for him to find. For one thing, the woman was neat as a pin and everything had a place. No way in hell would she leave papers spread about like that and not in tidy little stacks.

For another thing, she wouldn't leave out confidential work knowing someone outside the company was coming over. She was much more professional and much smarter than that.

Which meant she knew he had a plan. She might

not know exactly what his plan was, seeing as how his path had changed a few times, but she knew he wasn't on the up-and-up.

So now what? Did he keep playing this game? Damn it, he hated calling any of this a game. His revenge wasn't a game. His feelings for Haley weren't a game.

But he was too far in to all of this to pull back now. There had to be a way to get the company and the woman. And if Joshua Lowell was truly a stand-up guy, then Chase had to rethink that angle, as well. Josh wanted out, so clearly he wasn't like his old man.

As Chase turned into his parents' subdivision, his mind was already formulating ideas on how, if at all, he could meet up with Josh outside the office. Maybe Chase could tell Josh what he'd found and that would gain Chase more leverage over the competition.

Maybe there was a way to salvage all of this… the revenge and the uncertain relationship he was in.

Thirteen

The warm embrace of his mother always settled his mood for at least that moment. That same familiar body lotion she so loved still took him back to when he was a child and she'd hug him and tell him everything would be alright.

Now he was the one making sure everything would be alright.

Chase eased back. "Is Dad here?"

His mother shook her head. "He's out golfing with some buddies today. I'm so glad you could come by."

She reached around him to close the door, then turned. "Let's go into the living room. Do you want a drink or anything? I just made some cranberry muffins."

"No, I'm fine."

Chase followed his mother into the living room. He'd purchased this place for his mother once she'd finished her care and while his father was still in prison. The neighborhood was nice and quiet and the spacious home was all on one floor because he wanted easy access to things for his mother.

She took a seat on the sofa and Chase sank into the leather wingback chair across from her. She looked nice today, refreshed with a yellow top and white jeans. She'd pulled her dark hair back into that signature twist she always did.

"You look nice, Mom."

She laughed and narrowed her gaze. "You always said that when you wanted something from me."

Chase shrugged. "That might be true, but there's nothing I need. Can't a son compliment his mother?"

"Hey, at my age, I'll take all the compliments I can get," she laughed.

"I hardly think fifty-eight is old."

She reached over and patted his cheek. "I'm fifty-nine, which you well know, but thanks for that extra boost of confidence."

Chase eased back in the seat and rested his arm on the side. "So, what did you need to see me about?"

"You know I love to visit with you," she told him. "And I hadn't seen you for a few days."

Maybe because he'd been a little preoccupied by the only woman who could ever distract him from his goals and reality.

"Now who's the one who wants something?" he

countered. "You texted me to come over and I don't think it was so you could sit and stare at me."

She crossed her legs and lifted one slender shoulder. "Fine. I did want to talk to you not over the phone or text. I want to know what's going on with this revenge you're hell-bent on seeking and I want to know who the woman is who has been keeping all of your time lately."

His once feeble, meek mother had blossomed into a bold woman since her treatment. While he was damn proud of her for overcoming her demons, part of him was terrified. She was still his mother, she still deserved respect and the truth… He just didn't know how much to reveal at this delicate stage.

"I have been seeing a woman named Haley Shaw," he told her.

"And how does she tie in to this whole thing?"

Chase wasn't about to play dumb or insult her intelligence, so he answered honestly.

"She's Josh Lowell's personal assistant."

His mother swore under her breath before letting out a deep sigh. "Don't pull an innocent into this mess, Chase. She couldn't possibly know what happened years ago."

"Actually, she was hired by Vernon while she was still in college," he informed her. "But, I will agree that she is innocent. I started out just flirting, hoping to gain some inside information from her."

"And how has that worked for you?"

That knowing stare she held him with had all of that guilt he'd tried to suppress coming to the surface. He'd never wanted Haley to get so involved in his plot, but he couldn't stop the roller coaster he'd put her on, either.

"Oh no."

Chase pulled his attention back to his mother at her statement.

"What?" he asked.

"You're falling for her."

Shaking his head, Chase shifted in his seat. "I'm not falling for her. We're spending time together, we've gone out. She's an amazing woman. Career oriented and loyal, so that's something I can appreciate."

"You're falling for her," she repeated. "Or maybe you're already in love."

"I have no time or room in my life for love right now," he scoffed.

"Most people aren't looking for it when it happens, son, but you're in deeper than you think. Or maybe you're lying to yourself, I don't know, but if you can't face the truth then someone is going to get hurt."

Like he hadn't already thought of that? Like he wasn't sick thinking of the prospect of Haley getting caught in the crossfire?

Or worse…that she'd hate him forever. Once all of this was over, would she understand where he'd been coming from? Would she believe his feelings for her were real?

Oh, hell. They were real. Now what? Oh, this might not be love like his mother suggested, but there was definitely something more than just sex.

When all of this was over, and he was the CEO of Black Crescent, was there even a chance Haley would listen to him?

"Looks like you have some decisions to make."

His mother's soft tone had Chase easing back in the chair and closing his eyes. These weren't the decisions he wanted to make. He hadn't lied when he'd said he had no time for this, but he was going to have to make time and dig deep to find out where Haley stood. Was she more important than this vendetta or would he have to push her aside to continue his decade-old plan?

"I'd say the interviewing process is about to come to an end. If Ryan Hathaway had taken the job offer, this would've been over weeks ago."

Haley glanced across the large metal and glass desk to Josh. He leaned back in his black leather office chair and seemed quite content this morning. Not typical behavior for a Monday morning, but she was having a great start to her own week. She and Chase had spent the past two days together. They'd made love—could she even use that word at this stage?—and they'd gone to the local coffee shop for mimosas and waffles yesterday morning. They'd watched old movies and shared more details about what made up their personalities. Who knew the man had a secret crazy sock collection?

"Have you decided who you want to take your place?" she asked, crossing her legs and trying not to show her hand or hold her breath.

"I've narrowed it down to three I'd like to talk to again." Josh laced his fingers together and rested his forearms on his desk as he leaned forward. "But I need to talk with you before we move forward with anything else."

She didn't like the tone of his voice or the way he was staring at her like he knew her dirty little secret. Did he know?

So what if he did. Chase wasn't her dirty secret. He was the man she was seriously falling for.

"I've heard a rumor about you and one of the applicants. Chase Hargrove."

Haley inwardly rolled her eyes. Rumor? More like gossip mill. While she truly loved Black Crescent, she also knew this place was like any other office building and one little spark of news always escalated quicker than anything else.

"And what exactly did you hear?"

Because she guaranteed it wasn't near as juicy as what was truly happening, but that was certainly something she'd keep to herself.

Josh glanced down to his hands and blew out a sigh. "Listen, you know you're more than my assistant," he started. "I'm definitely on your side here."

Irritated, she sat up straighter in her seat. "I wasn't aware there were sides."

"There aren't," he amended. "Just listen. I'm not talking to you as your boss, not yet. Right now I want to talk to you as a friend. I've heard you were out with Chase Hargrove. Actually, I heard you were quite cozy while out, which makes me believe there

was nothing involving Black Crescent going on between you two."

"I have been out with Chase a few times, yes. He's
not an employee."

"No, but he is being interviewed and some might
see that as a compromise on your part."

Haley relaxed her shoulders, settling deeper into
the seat. She knew Josh wasn't her enemy. Her enemy
was all of those negative thoughts inside her mind
telling her that she should never have let things go
this far, so long as Chase was a contender for the
CEO position.

"You should know that Chase is in the top three
to take my place," Josh went on. "Would you continue seeing him or do you think you should take a
step back?"

Haley wasn't sure what to do. This company literally meant everything to her and Josh was like
family. She would continue her loyalty to him and
to Black Crescent Hedge Fund…but did that mean
she had to put aside her emotions? Did that mean she
had to put aside the one personal relationship she'd
sought out in years?

"I would never tell you who you can and can't
see," Josh went on. "I'm not in any position to tell
you what to do. That's all on you. My concern comes
from the friend standpoint and I don't want you hurt."

Well, that made two of them. But if Chase hadn't
touched those papers, then surely he wasn't using
her…right?

"I want to make sure he isn't trying to get close

to you in order to land this position," Josh added. "You're one of the most intelligent people I know, so I'm well aware that you wouldn't purposely let yourself be used. If you tell me you're positive he's on the up-and-up, then I'll believe you."

Haley offered a smile that she hoped was convincing enough for Josh to drop this matter for now. "Chase and I enjoy each other's company. We rarely talk work. In fact, we tend to discuss Tomorrow's Leaders. He's made some generous contributions and…"

The contributions. Damn it. Was he using her? Had she been so foolish, so blindsided by charm and sex appeal that she'd completely fallen for the oldest trick?

"Be careful, Haley."

Josh's concerned tone pulled her from her thoughts. She wasn't about to voice her own opinions or worries here. That was something she needed to sort out on her own.

"I'm careful," she stated as she came to her feet and smoothed down her burgundy pencil dress. "Was there anything else?"

"Should I call him for another interview or would you rather I not?" Josh asked, also standing. "I mean it when I say I want you comfortable with the person who steps into this role."

Not every boss would take that stance. Most people would only choose the person who was most qualified to be in such a leadership position, and no doubt Josh kept all of that in mind, but he also worried about her, which made her sorry he was going to be leaving. She'd been with him so long, she wouldn't know how to come in each and every day and not see his face.

"Are you tearing up?"

Haley blinked, cursing at the burning sensation in the back of her throat. "Shut up."

Josh laughed as he came around his desk and pulled her into his embrace. "If it helps, I'm going to miss you, too. But I promise to stop in. You won't be completely rid of me."

Haley wrapped her arms around him and smiled against his chest. "I'll let you take me to lunch so I can tell you all about the new CEO and we can talk freely."

"I look forward to it." Josh leaned back and stared down at her. "Especially if that person is Chase Hargrove."

Haley didn't say anything. What could she say? Maybe falling so fast, so hard with Chase had been a mistake, considering their positions. Maybe taking a step back for the time being was the wise move to make. Then once the new CEO was decided, whether him or another, then she could revisit a relationship and see where they stood.

But for now, and for the short foreseeable future, she needed to focus on the job and help Black Crescent cross over into a new chapter.

Fourteen

Haley had texted Chase that she needed to speak with him and that she was leaving work around five. Considering that that time was early for her, he had to believe whatever she wanted to discuss was serious.

After their weekend together, he thought they were progressing into something more. But he also had to come to the very real conclusion that she knew that his intentions weren't completely honorable.

None of this should surprise him, though. Haley was a smart woman. She didn't get to where she was by being played for a fool.

Granted there were people, like her disrespecting parents, who saw her only as an assistant. Chase knew full well the value of a loyal, well-trained assistant. They were just as vital in the daily goings-on within the company as the CEO. Just because their faces were behind the scenes didn't make assistants any less esteemed.

Chase pulled into the drive of Haley's cottage home and killed the engine. He wished like hell he knew what he was walking into. How could he formulate a game plan when he didn't have a clue about his opponent?

He cringed at his initial thoughts. This whole ordeal wasn't a game and Haley wasn't an opponent. She'd turned into so much more. At first he'd definitely been using her, but that was just harmless office flirtation. It wasn't until he uncovered her kind heart, her giving nature, the passion within that he realized he was in over his head.

But by then everything had escalated and there was no way he could back out.

There was also no way he could remain in his car mulling over all the ways his detailed plan spiraled out of control. He had to face Haley, but he would say nothing until he knew why she'd called him here. He knew all of this would come out eventually, but he'd hoped his secrets would expose themselves as he took over the company that destroyed his family. Not just his family, but also the lives of several other families in Falling Brook.

Chase stepped from his SUV and readied himself for whatever lay ahead of him. No matter what, he wasn't about to lose everything he'd worked so damn hard for...and that included Haley.

Before he could knock, the door swung wide and she stood before him still wearing her work clothes. Another one of those little dresses that seemed conservative but that drove him absolutely out of his mind. Her hair was down and over one shoulder and her feet were bare.

But that smile was missing. That smile she always greeted him with, that smile that always made him want to scoop her up and escape somewhere, just the two of them, and ignore the rest of the world... that smile that always managed to kick his guilt up another notch.

"Thanks for coming by." She gestured for him to step inside. "I hope you weren't busy."

"Never too busy for you," he assured her.

She closed the door behind him and started toward the open living area. He'd just left here only yesterday, yet the atmosphere seemed so different now. What exactly did she know or did she *think* she knew?

When she didn't take a seat, he knew nothing good was about to happen.

"What's going on, Haley?"

She licked her lips but leveled his gaze. "I've been lying to you."

Well, that was a bold statement to just jump right into and not one he was expecting at all. She was lying to him? There was so much irony in that statement.

"And how have you been lying to me?" he asked.

Haley took a deep breath. "I thought you might

not have the purest of intentions when it came to Black Crescent or to me. When you first came in, there was the flirting that I dismissed, but then things progressed."

He waited, listening to her reveal her truth all while he held his darkness deep inside. The guilt gnawed at him, more than he'd ever felt before, but he had to let her continue. He had to let her get this out into the open and off her chest... Then he could see how to proceed and what, if anything, he should reveal.

"Because I'm so protective of Black Crescent and Josh, I did a little digging around on you," she went on. "The attraction and the job became two totally different things and I did struggle with the separation of the two."

That guilt he had suddenly became layered with anger. She had been investigating him? From the beginning?

He had no right to be angry... But damn it, he was.

"Then I uncovered that you had changed your last name," she told him. Her eyes held his as her brows drew in. "I'm not completely certain why you did that, but I have some ideas. There is also the fact that while other applicants sent me flowers and cupcakes, you sent me highlighters and took me out to expensive plays and dinners."

"And those are all strikes against me?" he asked, still irked that she'd had him investigated.

"I couldn't be sure if they were strikes or gold

stars," she told him. "I wanted to think someone like you could be attracted to someone like me."

What the hell did that mean? He didn't get a chance to ask before she went on.

"Once you really started showing more interest, I couldn't help but wonder if it was me you were after or the CEO title."

Chase gritted his teeth and crossed his arms over his chest as he continued to listen. She had been second-guessing everything from the start. She had wondered his intentions from the very beginning and yet she still went out with him… She still slept with him.

"I decided to lay a paper trail to see where your loyalties laid."

That got his attention more than anything.

"You what?" he demanded.

"I'm so sorry," she told him, taking a step closer. "I had to know if you wanted to be with me or if you were really just out for the job."

Fury filled him and he hated himself for so many reasons, but namely for being played from the beginning. He was the one who was supposed to gather all of the information. He was the one who was supposed to make sure his game plan was flawless. But he'd been too occupied with the end result to realize that he'd veered off course of his well-laid plan.

"I know now that you didn't try to deceive me and I just… I had to tell you." She pursed her lips, her gaze continuing to hold his. "I didn't want anything between us because I think there's more here than either of us wanted."

Chase said nothing. What could he say? He was still processing the bomb she'd just dropped. Here he thought he was coming over because she had uncovered his secret, but she had turned the tables and everything he'd known thus far had all been a lie.

She'd questioned him from the beginning, but she'd never outright just asked him. So much sneaking, so many hidden thoughts that were damning to their relationship.

And he was just as guilty, he totally understood that, but he never expected this behavior from Haley. She'd been the bright spot in all of this, she'd been the distraction he'd needed, she'd been the one comfort he'd had because she provided something positive and perfect.

"You deceived me," he accused as the hurt continued to roll through him.

"I did." Haley took another step toward him, then another. "In my defense, I didn't know you well and I had to put my job and the company before any feelings I was developing."

He should've realized that from the beginning. One of the main things that had turned him on about her was that steely businesswoman she seemed to be.

Damn it, he had no right to be angry, but he couldn't help himself. Maybe he was angrier with himself for not seeing what was going on and for letting this happen... Because he had started all of this.

No, Lowell had started this colossal mess when

he'd chosen to interfere with the lives of Black Crescent's clients and then dole out part of the blame before fleeing and leaving everyone else to take the fall.

As Haley stood within reaching distance, Chase realized he wasn't the only bad guy. Here he'd been having guilty feelings, wondering how he could protect her from the fallout when he should have just kept his focus straightforward on his goal and not gotten sidetracked by sex. He never should've tried to incorporate flirting into the mix; that was such a rookie business mistake.

"Say something," she pleaded. "I'm sorry I didn't believe you. I'm sorry I went behind your back, but I'm telling you now hoping we can move on."

But they couldn't move on. While all of this newfound information from Haley threw him for a complete loop, Chase still couldn't give up on his goal.

Which meant he had to give her up. She'd come clean on her actions so they could move forward, but she had no clue that he was still lying. His anger right now stemmed from shock. He never would have guessed she would be playing him right alongside his own game…which just proved how remarkable she truly was.

Damn it, he wished he would've met Haley under much different circumstances. They would have been a dynamic duo had they teamed up together.

Chase took a step back. Haley's eyes widened as a shroud of sorrow filled her stare.

"I understand your reasoning for what you did," he began, but held his hands out when she started to step forward. "I don't think we should move forward with a relationship."

Haley stared a brief moment before she visibly composed herself. Crossing her arms, widening her stance and tipping her chin up were all indicators she was ready for a fight. But he'd been emotionally knocked for a loop and didn't have the energy right now. He needed to get out of here, to regroup. If that made him a coward, then so be it.

"You're that quick to throw away your feelings?" she asked. "Because I kept secrets to protect my job and my boss? I didn't know you in the beginning, Chase. If the roles were reversed, you would've done the same exact thing."

The roles weren't reversed and he'd done more digging and scoping out the competition than she knew.

"I came clean when I realized I had feelings for you," she went on. "Maybe you don't feel the same, though. Maybe you don't need me anymore now that you had such a great interview and Josh is considering having you in again to talk."

Another shocking revelation, but at the same time, Chase wasn't surprised. He was damn qualified for the position...a position that he still wanted and was starting to realize was all he had left.

Circling around to his ultimate goal was where he needed to land. Even though there seemed to be a vise around his heart, he had to remember the reason he'd started all of this to begin with. To seek justice for his family and all of those who didn't have the means to fight back. He had to make this right, and getting wrapped up in an even bigger web of lies with Haley was not the way.

"We both knew this was risky," he told her. "You stated more than once that I could become your boss and then where would we be? It's better to end things now, Haley."

He thought for sure he saw her chin quiver, but her eyes were dry and narrow. She pulled in a deep breath and nodded.

"Fine. I won't beg you to listen to my side and I sure as hell won't ask you to give me another chance. I'm not sorry for the why of all of this, but I am sorry if I hurt you. I would have thought you of all people would understand my justified actions."

Oh, he understood. Which was why he was getting back on track with his plan and putting any unwanted emotions aside.

Haley took a step forward, but she walked around him and went to the front door. He heard the click, but other than that there was complete and utter silence.

Of all the scenarios he imagined of how this would come to blows, Haley opening up about her secrets was sure as hell not one of them. And to add another tally mark to his coward column, he simply couldn't tell her he'd been lying from the start.

That guilt he'd had layered in a messy, sloppy manner with a dose of wounded pride.

Chase turned to face her, but she merely stood there with the door open and stared straight ahead to the wall. He took in her stoic profile and honestly didn't blame her for being angry. Hell, he was plenty angry with himself right now.

At least she was out of the equation for the most part if he could keep her aside. And in keeping her out of the way, he could regain his momentum and control over this takeover and revenge.

Without a word, and without stopping to look at her one last time, Chase made his way to the door and left. He'd barely stepped over the threshold when the door closed ever so softly at his back, but it was that definite click of the lock that was like a slap of reality to the face.

And he had nobody to blame but himself. He also had some serious decisions to make.

Fifteen

Chase loosened his tie and crossed his study to the bar in the corner. Drinking was never the answer, but considering he didn't have the answers, he didn't see how a drink would hurt.

He'd attempted a few online conference calls, but he didn't even care about business today. He'd dodged calls from investors, letting them go to voice mail.

For the past twenty-four hours since he'd walked out of Haley's house, he'd been in a foul mood. Trying to be a professional at this point was beyond even his realm of possibility.

He was still trying to figure out what the hell happened and how he'd missed any clues that Haley didn't believe him.

Chase poured two fingers of scotch and tipped the tumbler back. Slamming the glass back down, he was just about to pour another round when his cell vibrated in his pocket.

He pulled the phone out and glanced at the screen, fully intending to see a work associate, but his father's name popped up.

He might shirk his work for right now, but he'd never purposely ignore his parents.

Chase swiped the screen and answered. "Hey, Dad."

"I hope this isn't a bad time."

Chase stared down into the empty glass. "Perfect timing. What's up?"

"I won't keep you," his father went on. "Your mother said you were here the other day and we've been talking. I need to tell you that it's time to move on."

Chase gripped his phone and stepped away from the bar. He paced the study and ended up at the window behind his desk. The sun had started to set, giving a warm, orange glow across the horizon. The view should be calming, and would be at any other given time, but not today.

"Move on from what?" he asked, knowing exactly what his father was about to lecture him on.

"You're not a fool, Chase. Let this vendetta go," his dad pleaded. "I did my time and Vernon Lowell's sons aren't to blame. They are nothing like their old man. I was guilty of assisting in various acts and you're not mad at me."

Oh, he'd been plenty angry with his father when all of this went down. Chase had been pissed at his dad for putting their entire family's future in jeopardy. But this was the man who had provided and worked hard for their family, so forgiving him was much easier to do for Chase.

"I want that company," Chase stated. "There's no better poetic justice than for me to take over the place that ruined my family."

His father's deep sigh resounded through the phone. "Son, we aren't ruined. We had setbacks, we had a curveball thrown at us, but look us now. Your mother is healthy, and I'm living my life and not dwelling on the past. Let it go. Let it all go."

Chase ground his teeth, listening as his father made sense with each and every word. That didn't mean Chase had to like it. He wanted to get revenge, he wanted to make things right for his family and complete this circle once and for all.

"You need to focus on something else," his father went on. "Or *someone* else."

Of course his parents had discussed Haley, and while Chase would love nothing more than to focus on Haley, she had deceived him…and he had deceived her. What future could they base a relationship off with that kind of start?

And when she found out, she would hate him anyway. Because his deceit was far worse than what she had done. Now that he'd had a little more time to process things, that was the crux of his anger. He couldn't be too upset with her for only looking out for the only type of family she'd truly had. Isn't that what he was doing? Just looking out for family?

He admired the hell out of her because she didn't have to tell him a damn thing…yet she had. She'd been honest and up-front, which was a far cry above where he stood. So if he was going to look down in judgment to anyone, it would have to be himself.

"I know you don't want to hear any of this because you've been determined for so long," his father went on. "But I thought you should at least understand my side. I've moved on and I swear, once you do, you'll find peace and happiness that no revenge could ever bring you. Seeking your own justice will not change the past. Don't let this eat at you any longer."

Chase dropped his head between his shoulders and closed his eyes. The thoughts swirled around in his mind. A raging storm that continued to pound him over and over.

Could he find peace if he let all of this drop? Could he move on with his life?

For the first time in years, a sprig of hope popped up that had nothing to do with Vernon Lowell or Black Crescent Hedge Fund.

"Haley?"

Blinking away from her computer screen, Haley looked up to see Josh standing at her desk. "Yes?"

"I've said your name three times."

"Really?" she asked. "I didn't hear you."

His dark brows drew in. "I was standing right

here and you've been staring at a blank screen for several minutes."

Busted. She'd never been one to daydream at work or get caught in a zombie state.

Haley pushed back and turned her chair to fully face Josh, who still stared down at her like a worried parent.

"Maybe I just need more coffee," she joked.

Unfortunately, Josh knew her too well and wasn't buying her lame attempt to dodge his concern.

"What's going on?" he asked. "You've not been yourself for two days now."

Two days. That was when Chase had walked out of her home after he'd broken things off with her. She'd told him only a portion of what she'd done, what she'd found. She wanted to give him the chance to come clean himself, to tell her anything he wanted to get off his chest.

But he'd ended their relationship using some ridiculous reasoning and he hadn't acted like he was even bothered by letting her go. Perhaps their relationship had been growing on only one side.

"There's no issue if you end up hiring Chase Hargrove. He and I won't be seeing each other in a personal capacity anymore."

Josh glanced over his shoulder to the bustling staff around them. He leaned forward and lowered his voice.

"Are you alright?" Josh asked. "Because I was coming out to tell you he's on his way in."

"Wait." She sat up straighter in her seat. "He's

coming here? I don't have him down for an appointment or another interview."

She immediately turned back to her computer and pulled up the schedule, knowing full well Chase's name was nowhere to be found.

"He contacted me directly," Josh stated.

Haley refocused her attention back on her boss.

"That's another reason I came out here," Josh went on. "I figured something was up with the way you've been acting and the fact that he called my direct line, bypassing you completely."

Bypassing her, yeah, that sounded about right with his attitude last she'd seen him.

She couldn't deny that knowing he was on his way sent an unhealthy dose of panic through her. She wasn't ready to face him just yet. She hadn't quite found her emotional footing since he'd ended things.

"Do you want to talk about it?" Josh asked.

Haley smiled. She truly appreciated the way he cared for her, the way he wanted to help that had nothing to do with their working relationship.

"That's sweet of you to offer, but I'm fine," she assured him. "I mean, I'm hurt and angry, but I'll be okay."

The words slid out easily, but she knew actually living up to the promising statement would be much more difficult. And as much as she wanted to get up and head to the break room or anyplace else in this office to avoid seeing Chase again, she would sit right here, hold her head high, and put on the biggest damn smile.

No way would she let him know that inside she had been completely crushed to pieces. How silly was that? How foolish and naive to fall for someone in such a short time? She shouldn't have let herself get so swept away by charming words and a sexy smile, not to mention the way he filled out those damn suits.

And without the suit? That was even more impressive.

"I won't call you a liar, but you're not okay," Josh told her. "Chase should be here in about ten minutes if you want to step away from your desk."

Haley laughed. "You know me better than that."

Josh leaned back and smiled. "Yeah, I do. You're one of the toughest people I know, and for what it's worth, he's a fool."

"Yes, he is," she agreed. "But don't let the personal issues affect what's best for Black Crescent."

"You want me to beat him up for you?" Josh joked.

"Maybe if we were in third grade on the playground I'd take you up on that, but no. I'm going to sit here with a smile and act like nothing happened."

"I expect nothing less."

Josh turned toward his office, but glanced back over his shoulder. "Feel free to make him wait when he gets here. I wouldn't blame you if you want to be a little petty and spiteful."

Haley laughed again. "We'll see how nice I'm feeling once I see how he treats me."

Josh nodded and headed back into his office. Haley turned back to her blank computer screen and blew out a breath. There was no way she could start a new project and get anything of worth done in the next ten minutes. All she could think of was the moment when Chase would step through the doorway.

Being strong was the only way she would get through this. Her life didn't revolve around Chase or their fling…though what they'd shared had been so much more. He'd cared for her, she knew he did.

But she wasn't going to beg. She had too much going on in her life and she deserved someone who would be there for her as her equal supporter, not someone who required her to ask for the love she desired.

Ugh. Love. Did she love him? After such a short time?

Yes. She did. She loved the guy who took such interest in her charity, who spoke of his own struggles with education and trying to make a better life. She loved how he was witty, charming, commanding and attentive.

Haley closed her eyes and took a deep breath. She was going to have to shove all of those thoughts aside to get through this impromptu meeting. She wondered what Chase needed to discuss with Josh that was of such urgency, but Josh would tell her after Chase left.

She just had to remain calm and plaster that smile on her face to remind him of what he could have had and what he let go.

Sixteen

"I'm withdrawing my name from the list for the CEO position."

Chase stood in front of Josh's desk, wanting to do this in person instead of over the phone or email. Or maybe he'd just wanted to be a masochist and see Haley because two days without her had been too damn long.

"You found something else?" Josh asked as he leaned back in his leather chair.

"No, but at this point in my life, I feel it's best I continue with my global travels and work with startup investors. Black Crescent is a wonderful company, you should take all of the credit for that, but someone else should take over."

Josh's brows dipped in for a split second. "Does

this have anything to do with Haley or are you strictly talking from a business standpoint?"

Of course Haley would talk to Josh. They were close, as most coworkers were. When people spent over forty hours a week together, they tended to share everything and lean on each other for some sort of support. Haley considered Josh like her family, so her confiding in him was no surprise. Chase just wondered exactly how much she'd shared.

"Both," Chase answered honestly. "This is the right decision for all of us, trust me."

Though he had to admit, especially to himself, Haley had changed everything in him. His personality, his hatred toward this family, his outlook on the future.

Coming in here and letting go of this vendetta wasn't something he ever would have considered had his father not told him it was time to move on. After all, if his dad could let go, then Chase figured he could, too.

And with Haley in mind, Chase knew it was time to move on with a more positive mindset.

"If this is what you want, then I respect your decision." Josh pushed back in his chair and came to his feet. "But I'm going to offer some unsolicited, extremely unprofessional advice."

Chase nodded. "I assumed you would."

"I don't know the dynamics of what is going on or not going on between you and Haley, but I will say this. You will never find anyone more loyal to have in your corner."

"I'm well aware of how loyal she is," Chase stated.

So loyal she'd gone behind his back and dug up who knew what. But then she'd confessed once her feelings grew deeper…which was more than he could say for himself. He was still stunned at her honesty, but at the same time he was impressed that she'd exposed her secrets.

Everything about Haley touched something deep inside him, something he'd always kept hidden. That little nugget of emotion he didn't want anyone to tap into because he didn't have time for such things… not while he was so hell-bent on revenge.

But his father had said to let it go, and there was one more thing he could do to take things a step further to let all of this hatred go.

Chase slid his hands into his pockets and pulled in a breath. "I need to give you some advice as well and I'm completely overstepping my boundaries here."

Josh jerked slightly. "What's that?"

"It's no secret, the rumors of you having a secret baby."

Josh's jaw clenched, but he said nothing. Yeah, Chase was definitely walking a fine line, but this was pertinent information for Josh to have.

"I have some connections," Chase went on. "The hows and whys aren't important here. What you need to know is the doctor involved in all of this is shady as hell. He's been known to change DNA results for a nice fee."

Josh's lips thinned. "Is that right?"

"There's also a chance your brother Jake is the father," Chase said. "I thought you should know. Do what you want with the information, but if you look deeper into the doctor, that's where you'll find your answers."

Josh blinked, not showing much emotion. "Why did you dig into my past? What's in this for you?"

Chase had resigned from the potential position and he had given up some valid information, but he had hoped to avoid this part. Moving on, though, would consist of coming clean and telling the truth.

"I'm Dale Groveman's son," Chase replied. "My father used to work for yours and ended up going to prison for fraud."

Josh's eyes widened as he circled his desk. "Are you serious? What the hell were you doing trying to get a job here?"

He stopped, his eyes narrowing as he clearly mentally answered his own question. "You wanted to take over this company for what? To run it into the ground? Destroy it?"

Chase shrugged. "Honestly, I wanted to just prove that I could take it over. I wanted some type of justice, knowing that I was now in charge of the company that nearly tore my family apart."

Josh crossed his arms over his chest, his dark eyes zeroing in on Chase. "What made you change your mind?"

Haley.

"Everything changed since I first sent my résumé," Chase said honestly. "I've learned there's more to life than revenge."

Josh nodded. "There is and it's amazing how a woman can change your entire outlook on life, isn't it?"

Chase wasn't discussing his personal relationship with Haley. He'd come for what he intended and now he was done. There were other places he needed to be, other projects he should be focusing on. Because moving on wasn't just something he was doing regarding Black Crescent. He had to move on from everything that held him here…including Haley.

He'd lied to her, deceived her in ways that were unforgivable. Now that he'd cleared his conscience, he could go.

Ignoring the question, Chase pulled in a deep breath.

"I have the doctor's name who worked on the DNA and the facility he used," Chase stated, circling back to the paternity issue. "I can forward you all of my findings to do with as you wish."

As he took a step back, then another, Chase said, "I can let myself out, and good luck with filling the position and everything else."

Chase had just turned to face the door when Josh's words stopped him.

"Don't be fooled by her smile and strength. She's not like any other woman you'll ever meet, and she's able to handle more than you think."

Chase didn't acknowledge the words, but he completely understood what Josh was saying. Haley would hurt deeply because she loved so deeply. She cared with her whole heart and poured herself into those around her.

Including him.

That guilt he'd been carrying around for weeks seemed to amplify even more since he'd walked out of Haley's home. Chase reached for the knob and opened the door, stepping into Haley's work space.

She didn't even look up from her computer. Her hands flew across the keyboard as she continued right on working. Of course, she knew he was beside her, so she either didn't care or she was purposely ignoring him because of everything. Likely both. He deserved nothing less.

He approached her desk, willing her to look at him, but she never did. Chase stopped beside her desk, noticing a small bouquet of daisies in a vase on the corner. This was a far cry from all of the arrangements she'd had only a few weeks ago.

"Take care of yourself, Haley."

Chase continued toward the elevator without looking back to see if she even glanced up from her screen. He wanted her to have a good life, a great career and a lucrative charity. He'd already contacted his assistant to have more money sent next month, as Chase would be long gone from Falling Brook.

She was rather impressed with herself for getting a good bit of her work done for the day. She was trying to compile an informative welcome package to the new CEO...whoever that turned out to be. She wanted them to have a nice, smooth, easy transition.

Having Chase here made her wonder what was going on, but he'd left hours ago and Josh still hadn't said a word about the meeting.

And it was driving her crazy.

She checked her emails for Tomorrow's Leaders and replied to the ones that couldn't wait. Haley was about to shut down her computer when a message came across the screen for her to come into Josh's office.

Oh, now he wanted to talk after keeping her waiting for so long?

Haley pushed her chair back and moved toward Josh's closed door. Without knocking, she let herself in and found him standing at the window.

"Close the door behind you."

Haley did as directed and slowly crossed the office. "Are you finally going to tell me what that closed door meeting was all about with Chase?"

Josh turned and laughed. "I can't believe you didn't barge in here the minute he was gone and demand answers."

"I'm practicing self-control. How did I do?"

"Remarkably well." Josh smiled and took a seat on his windowsill. "I wanted to wait until the end of the day to talk. I had a few things to get done."

Haley stopped at his desk and crossed her arms. "So what did he want?"

"To withdraw his name from the running for the position of CEO."

"What?" Haley gasped. "He doesn't want the job? But why?"

"He said everything for him had changed," Josh explained. "He said he also had been seeking revenge because his father used to work for mine and his father ended up taking some of the backlash and ended up in prison."

Haley merely nodded.

"You knew?"

"I had him investigated," she told Josh. "I wanted to know more about him for myself, but I also wanted to know why he seemed so persistent. I knew there was more to him than just another billionaire mogul."

Every part of her was shocked that Chase had told Josh everything. He hadn't told her all of his history, but he'd come and revealed himself to Josh.

A good part of her couldn't deny the hurt that hit her hard from that revelation, but another part of her was rather impressed with Chase for owning up to his sins and secrets.

"I don't need to know what went on with the two of you," Josh said, then held up his hands. "I don't want to know. But I think he's a good guy. Despite the past issues with our fathers, neither one of us is holding grudges anymore."

Haley wasn't sure what to think, what to feel. It had taken everything in her not to turn and look at Chase as he'd left the office earlier. When he'd told her to take care, she'd bitten the inside of her cheek to keep from responding.

"I'm not sure what you want me to do with this information," Haley finally replied. "I mean, he's not going to be working here and we broke things off. You're singing his praises like that's something I need to take with me."

Josh shrugged and shifted in the windowsill to rest easily on one hip. "What you do is up to you," he told her. "I'm just saying, it might be smart of you to reconsider just letting him go. The man obviously loves you."

"Loves me?" Haley asked, shaking her head. "No, he doesn't. He's never said that, never even hinted such a thing."

"Because men have no clue how to express their feelings," he defended. "We're a little dumb in that area, so cut us some slack."

Haley couldn't help but smile, knowing how hard Josh and Sophie had fought to get together. There was something about people falling in love and finding happiness that made them want to play Cupid with others. That was fine. She was thrilled Josh had found his happily-ever-after and, who knew, maybe one day she would, too.

But she truly didn't believe it would be with Chase. No matter that she couldn't just turn off her switch to these feelings for him, if he didn't want to be with her, then things just weren't meant to be.

"I can see thoughts swirling around in your head."

Josh's words pulled her from those thoughts.

"My mind is always working," she told him. "You know that."

"I know that you're probably thinking more about a man and less about work."

"So what if I am?" she countered with a shrug.

"I'll be fine, though. My personal issues won't affect my job."

"I never thought they would, Haley." Josh came to his feet and crossed to her, placing his hands on her shoulders and staring down into her eyes. "Listen to me. If you want to be with Chase, then go. Don't just sit back and let life pass you by."

Haley took in his advice, wondering if she should go to Chase or just let him go. She didn't want to beg, but was going after what you wanted begging?

No. There was no reason she couldn't fight for what she wanted. She wanted to know what Josh saw that she missed.

Did Chase love her? Well, she didn't know, but she was about to go find out.

Seventeen

Chase laid the stack of dress shirts in the garment bag and hooked the hangers through the top opening. Once they were all in, he zipped up the bag and placed it aside on his bed with his other belongings from the closet.

Turning a full circle around his room, he figured he'd gotten almost everything packed from here and the adjoining bathroom. He didn't have many possessions he just had to take with him. The furniture was of no use and didn't hold sentimental value. So long as he got his personal items, he would be just fine. He could lease this place, rent it, sell it—hell, he really didn't care. His time was up and there was nothing holding him here now. His parents were used to him traveling for business, coming and going as

he chose, and he visited them often enough or sometimes flew them to where he was if he knew he'd be
gone for a lengthy time setting up new companies.

Once Chase left Falling Brook, he planned on
going to his condo in Florida. A little sunshine and
beach time would do him good. Maybe that would
clear his mind, who knew. He doubted seeing bi-
kini-clad women would wipe his mind of the one
he let get away.

Now there was only one thing left to do.

Leaving the old life behind without the black
cloud hanging over his head was the only way to
push forward. He needed closure and he needed to
clear the air with Haley.

The alarm on his front door sounded through the
house and Chase pulled his cell from his pocket to
access the camera from the front porch.

Haley. Her black-and-white image appeared and
his heart instantly clenched at the sight. He wanted
to run to the door at the same time as he wanted to
ignore her presence. If he hadn't lied to her in such
a severe way, he wouldn't be such a coward. All of
this guilt and pain had been brought on by him and
there was nobody else to blame.

When she'd told him what she'd done by investigating him, he'd been shocked, but all of his anger
hadn't been toward her… She'd just been an easy target at the time. No, everything that had gone wrong
between them was all on him, and someone so loving and caring and giving as Haley deserved so much
better.

How could one person pull out so many emotions, such a mixture of feelings?

He glanced to the screen again, noting her appearance. She still had on her work clothes, her hair left down but tucked behind one ear. Haley glanced toward the camera as if she knew he was looking at her at that precise moment.

His stomach knotted with nerves as his heartbeat kicked up. He shouldn't be surprised she was here after the bomb he'd dropped on Josh. No doubt Josh told Haley everything that went on in the office. He'd planned to see her before he left. A final piece of closure. But he'd been putting it off as long as possible because he was a coward. Now she was here and this was his last chance to make things right.

Chase tapped the button to let her in and he heard the front door open, then close. She was in his home once again and he had to remain calm. As much as he wanted to go to her and beg for forgiveness, he wasn't about to do that. First, he wasn't sure what all she knew, and second, maybe she wasn't here about that. Maybe she wanted him back.

Chase cursed under his breath. Hell no she wouldn't want him back, not if Josh told her what Chase's initial intentions were with Black Crescent.

Maybe she'd come here to tell him off, to berate him for using her… He would deserve nothing less. There was nothing she could say to him that he hadn't already said to himself. He was a total bastard for the way he'd treated her, but damn it, he hadn't expected to get so involved… He hadn't expected his heart to get involved, either.

Realizing he couldn't hide in his master suite forever, Chase stepped from the room and headed down the hall. The moment he crossed into the living room, his eyes met Haley's.

She stood there gripping her handbag, and for the first time since he'd met her, she almost looked nervous. Interesting. If she was here to explode all over him about his actions, she certainly didn't look upset.

"I didn't expect to see you again," he told her honestly.

"I didn't expect to be here again."

As much as he wanted to close this distance between them, Chase remained still. She'd come here for a reason. He just needed to give her the time to process her thoughts and speak or come to him when she was ready.

"So what happened to bring you here?" Chase asked. "You talked to Josh, didn't you?"

Haley stared at him for another minute, then glanced around, her brows drawing in as she spotted one of his suitcases by the sofa.

"Traveling for business?" she asked.

"You could say that."

Her eyes shifted back to him. "You're leaving."

Chase nodded. "I'm done here."

"Because plans didn't go your way?" she asked, a little extra bite in her tone than what he was used to.

"Because I ruined one of the only relationships

I've ever cared about and there is no reason for me to stay."

She jerked, obviously surprised by his response. Silence settled heavy between them, but Chase remained still.

Haley took a step closer, then another. She sat her bag down on the sofa, then glanced around the room. Chase didn't know what was going through her mind, but he wished like hell she'd say the reason for her visit because he was going out of his mind with scenarios.

He was also going out of his mind staring at her and not touching her. That damn black dress hugged each of her curves and he knew full well what each one felt like beneath his touch.

"Your father went to prison for his part in Vernon's scams," she stated, clearly not in the form of a question. "Then your mother battled her own demons."

Haley turned to face him, her eyes holding him in place. "And that left you alone to work through your anger without the guidance and love of those who mattered most."

Chase didn't like how she'd summed up his past in one statement that was so damn accurate. Yes, he'd been hurt, but his revenge hadn't been about his own hatred for Vernon Lowell. Chase had wanted vengeance for tearing his family apart and making them put all the pieces back together.

"Josh told you."

Haley folded her arms over her chest. "I've known

for several days, actually. Before I told you that I'd had you investigated, I knew. When I came clean the other day about what I'd done, I was giving you a chance to do the same, but you chose not to. You either didn't trust me enough or you were just continuing to use me."

Wait… She'd known? She'd known about his parents, what had motivated him to start this charade, and she still hadn't told him?

Because she was giving him a chance to speak up in his defense and what had he done? He'd walked out on her. Could he be more of a jerk?

"But Josh didn't act like he already knew when I told him everything," Chase stated.

"That's because I never told him." Haley dropped her arms and sighed. "Don't you get anything? Of course I was going to protect my company had I thought for a minute you would seriously do some damage, but I didn't want to tell him. I'd developed feelings for you and didn't want to betray you."

Something clicked into place at her final statement. The woman who had always put Black Crescent above all else, who'd even stood by their side during the most scandalous time, had put him first. She'd chosen to be loyal to him, to keep his secrets, and he didn't trust her enough to tell her the truth.

Chase pulled in a breath and took a step toward her. "You covered for me."

"I wanted you to tell me the truth," she told him. "I'd hoped if I told you what I'd done, that you'd tell me. So, when you broke things off and said nothing else, I assumed you were only in this to use me for information."

"That's not how it went down."

He took another step, and another, until he'd closed the gap between them. He was close enough to touch her, but Chase clenched his fists at his sides.

"You surprised me when you told me what you'd done," he stated. "I never thought you would have done something like that, but now I realize you were protecting Black Crescent and yourself."

"We do what we can to protect those we love." She offered a sad smile, one that broke his heart. "Before I go, I want to know if you ever had feelings for me, or was all of this just a game to you? Were you only after—"

Chase gripped her face and covered her mouth with his. He couldn't stand not touching her another second. He also couldn't listen to her doubt what they had anymore. Everything they'd shared was real. Everything he felt for her was real.

Now he wanted to show her.

Haley gripped his wrists and opened for him, her passion pouring out of her, and Chase wanted nothing more than to strip her out of this dress and show her exactly how much he'd missed her…how much he needed her.

He eased back slightly, resting his forehead against hers.

"Everything we shared had nothing to do with my plan," he told her. "I started flirting with you thinking I'd get information to use later, but then I lost myself. The flirting turned into a need I couldn't explain and before I knew it, I'd fallen in love with you."

Haley jerked back, her eyes wide. "You love me?"

He hadn't meant to just let that slip out, but yes. He loved her and it felt damn good to have those words out in the open.

The punch to the shoulder was quite unexpected and shocking. She struck before he even saw her move.

"What was that for?" he asked, shrugging his shoulder.

"For putting me through hell, you jerk!" she fired back. "Not only did you deceive me from the beginning, you didn't come clean when I gave you the chance, and now you say you love me? So, what, you were just going to leave town and take those feelings with you?"

"What was I supposed to do?" he countered, staring into her fiery eyes. "I'd screwed up. You deserve someone who's going to be honest and open with you. Someone who's devoted to you, who puts you above all else."

She stepped away from him, propping her hands on her hips. "And you can't be that man? Here all this time I thought there was nothing you couldn't do."

So now she was getting back at him by attacking his pride. That was fine, he deserved her frustration and anger…maybe not the punch, but he'd let that slide. He'd been a complete jerk to her from day one, yet here she stood.

Which likely meant only one thing.

"You love me."

Her brows drew in. "What?"

"You love me," he repeated, reaching for her once again. "I know you do or you wouldn't be here. You wouldn't be so hurt over what I did if you didn't care."

He gripped her hips and pulled her flush against his body.

"And you wouldn't have kept my secret from Josh if you hated me."

Her lips thinned, but she said nothing.

"No denying the truth now?" he asked with a smile.

"I hate you for making me love you."

Chase laughed, knowing he'd won. "That makes no sense, but you're even sexier when you're angry."

Her hands flattened against his chest as her bright eyes held his. She was so damn pretty she stole his breath. And she was his. There was no way he was letting her go again. She'd come here to fight for them, which just proved she was the one for him. He wanted a woman who wouldn't back down. He wanted a woman who understood his mind, his heart. He'd found her.

"You're not moving," she told him. "You're staying in Falling Brook."

Chase smiled. "Yes, ma'am."

She slid her arms up over his shoulders and around to the back of his neck, her fingers threading through his hair. "You're also going to marry me. That family you wanted? I want one, too...with you."

The excitement and anticipation pumped through Chase. He gripped her backside and lifted her body against his.

"Did you just propose?" he asked.

"If that's what you want to call it." She slid her lips over his ever so slightly. "More like I just laid out your life plan."

Chase nipped at her lips as he turned to head toward his bedroom. "Go right ahead and plan my life, so long as you're in every aspect."

She slid her mouth over his, silently answering him. The moment Chase stepped back into his room, he eased Haley down to her feet and went to make quick work on that zipper going up her back.

He peeled that dress off her body, watching as it slid down and puddled at her feet. She kicked it aside, leaving her only in her matching lacy bra and thong and her black heels.

"You're going to be the death of me," he murmured as he reached for her once again.

She laughed as she skirted out of his touch. "Not so fast," she told him. "You have on too many clothes and I don't like the look of this bed with so many bags on it."

He turned, remembering he'd been in the midst of packing when she'd come by. Chase took about two seconds to clear the garment bags off, discarding them onto the floor without a care. There was only one thing he cared about right now and she was standing before him with a desire in her eyes that he wanted to dive into.

Chase kept his gaze on Haley's as he jerked the shirt from his pants and unbuttoned just enough to slide it up and over his head. The rest of his clothes and shoes flew off in quick succession, leaving him completely bare. And the way her heavy-lidded stare raked over his body, he wasn't sure how much longer he could hold back from tossing her onto that bed and showing her just how much he'd missed her over the past few days.

"Now who's wearing too many clothes?" he asked, reaching for her once more.

"Take them off of me," she commanded with a naughty grin.

A blond strand fell over her eye, giving her an even sexier look. How did he get so lucky to have her come back into his life?

Reaching around her back, Chase flicked the bra clasp. Haley watched him as he removed the straps from her shoulders and down her arms. He flung the garment over his shoulder before moving on to her panties.

He hooked his thumbs in the lacy straps over her hips and eased them down, dropping to his knees as he went. Her hands went to his shoulders and she balanced on one foot, then the other as he removed her thong.

Haley standing there in her heels, staring down at him, might have been the most striking, breathtaking view he'd ever seen.

He trailed his fingertips up her legs, over her knees, inside her thighs and straight to her core.

Haley took a wide step as she continued to hold on to his shoulders and watch.

The second he eased one finger inside her, Haley's lids fluttered down as a moan escaped her. Chase held on to her hip with one hand while pleasuring her with the other. In no time, her hips pumped against his hand and Chase couldn't tear his eyes away from the erotic sight.

Haley's nails bit into his bare shoulders as she tossed her head back and cried out her release. Chase waited until her body stopped trembling before easing away and coming to his feet. He wrapped his arms around her and lifted her to carry her over to the bed.

"Tell me again," she muttered as he laid her down. "Tell me you love me."

Chase came over her, resting his elbows beside her head as he grazed his lips across hers. "I love you, Haley. Forever."

Eighteen

"I'm not sure I'm ready for this," Haley stated. "This is quite a step in our relationship."

Chase laughed as he pulled in front of a small cottage and killed the engine. He turned to face her, taking her hands in his.

"It's just my parents, Haley. You're not going before a firing squad."

Nerves danced all through her belly. It had been over a week since she'd gone to Chase's house and told him how she felt. It had been the best eleven days of her life, staying with him, talking of plans for their future.

But parents? What did she know about parent relationships? Hers were nonexistent and Chase knew that. Yet here they were, ready for Sunday afternoon lunch.

"You proposed to me," Chase reminded her. "Did you think you wouldn't meet my parents at some point?"

She glanced down to their adjoining hands and shrugged. "I hadn't thought that far yet. I just knew I wanted to spend my life with you."

He smiled and squeezed her hands. "This is part of my life. My parents are going to love you just like I do."

Haley let out a sigh. Having him say he loved her never got old. She could face anything with him by her side…even parents.

"I'm not good with parents," she whispered. "I don't know how to act or who to be. Are they proper like using the right fork or do I just follow their lead?"

Chase leaned forward and kissed her before easing back. "Honey, this isn't an audition. They already love you because I do. Trust me on this. Just be yourself."

Haley pulled in a shaky breath and nodded. Chase stepped from the car and circled the hood to open her door. He extended his hand and Haley held it tight as they headed up the steps to the cozy front porch with a swaying swing.

Before they could knock, the front door flew open and his mother squealed with delight. His father came up behind her with a wide smile. Haley instantly felt some of the pressure ease off her shoulders.

His mom threw her arms around Chase's neck and kissed his cheek. "I'm so glad you guys are here."

Then she turned her attention to Haley and hugged

her, as well. Stunned, Haley returned the gesture and wrapped her arms around Chase's mother.

"You don't even know how excited I am to meet you," she stated, pulling back with a huge smile. "I hope you like chicken and potatoes. I also made a cheesecake with a raspberry glaze."

"Stop fussing," his father insisted. "You're worrying over everything."

Haley instantly found herself relating to this woman. Fussing and worrying over everything was pretty much her job. Haley already felt a kinship to Chase's mother and they hadn't even made it off the porch.

"Come on in," his father said and gestured. "Lunch is ready. I put everything out on the back patio. It's such a nice day."

Haley followed them through the home and outside to a darling eating area beneath a pergola draped with wisteria.

"Have a seat anywhere," his mother told them. "We aren't formal here."

That was good to know. Haley could tell this place was one of those homes where everyone felt welcome and invited. There was no pressure to be someone you weren't.

Such a far cry from how she'd grown up. No wonder Chase was so giving, so…perfect. He'd had a loving environment and loving support system behind him at all times. Even during the difficult days, he'd had his family.

"Chase tells me you run Tomorrow's Leaders," his

mom said as she took a seat across from Haley. "I've heard of that organization and I think it's absolutely wonderful how you're looking out for those kids."

Haley smiled. "I don't do much," she stated. "It's the donors who really make things happen."

"Don't sell yourself short," his mom replied. "If it weren't for you, the donors wouldn't know how to help. An education is so important and there are too many kids who can't afford schooling. Not everyone can get a scholarship."

"That's exactly right," Haley agreed.

The conversation flowed from the charity to Chase's next project, which he informed them was setting up a company in LA to start up their own investment firm. He'd already asked Haley to accompany him, but she wasn't sure if she should leave for vacation in the midst of the new CEO hunt.

Though she doubted Josh would care. Josh seemed to like Chase and Josh totally understood what being in love was like.

"So tell me what my son did to get the attention of someone as wonderful as you," his father said after they'd finished eating.

Haley set her glass of wine back on the table and laughed. "Honestly, it was a bundle of highlighters."

"Highlighters?" his dad asked. "Son, you can do better than that."

Chase laughed and came to his feet. "I completely agree."

He dug into his pocket and pulled out a box. Haley gasped as she stared up at him.

"I know you already asked me to marry you," Chase started. "But we haven't made things official."

He opened the box and went down on one knee. Haley stared at the classic emerald-cut diamond ring and tears filled her eyes.

"I wanted to get you something that suited you," he told her. "Something classy, elegant, flawless."

"It's beautiful," she murmured through her tears.

"I want to spend my life with you," he told her. "I want to help you with your charity, I want you to help me grow to be a better man. I want everything, but only with you."

He took the ring from the box and Haley held out her finger. He slid the diamond on and it fit absolutely perfectly. She didn't know how he knew her ring size, but she wasn't about to question it.

Chase came to his feet once again and pulled her up with him. He wrapped her in his arms and kissed her as his mother let out a squeal of delight once again.

"Welcome to the family," his father stated.

Haley turned to see his parents across the table. Both were beaming and Haley realized she was inheriting a family to call her own. Having a man by her side and a loving family was all she'd ever wanted.

Chase wrapped his arm around her waist and Haley realized that she could indeed have it all, and that some things in life were worth fighting for.

* * * * *

COMING SOON!

We really hope you enjoyed reading this book.
If you're looking for more romance, be sure to
head to the shops when new books are
available on

Thursday 6th August

MILLS & BOON

THE HEART OF ROMANCE

A ROMANCE FOR EVERY KIND OF READER

MODERN

Prepare to be swept off your feet by sophisticated, sexy and seductive heroes, in some of the world's most glamourous and romantic locations, where power and passion collide.
8 stories per month.

HISTORICAL

Escape with historical heroes from time gone by. Whether your passion is for wicked Regency Rakes, muscled Vikings or rugged Highlanders, awaken the romance of the past.
6 stories per month.

MEDICAL

Set your pulse racing with dedicated, delectable doctors in the high-pressure world of medicine, where emotions run high and passion, comfort and love are the best medicine.
6 stories per month.

Celebrate true love with tender stories of heartfelt romance, from the rush of falling in love to the joy a new baby can bring, and a focus on the emotional heart of a relationship.
8 stories per month.

Indulge in secrets and scandal, intense drama and plenty of sizzling hot action with powerful and passionate heroes who have it all: wealth, status, good looks…everything but the right woman.
6 stories per month.

HEROES

Experience all the excitement of a gripping thriller, with an intense romance at its heart. Resourceful, true-to-life women and strong, fearless men face danger and desire - a killer combination!
8 stories per month.

DARE

Sensual love stories featuring smart, sassy heroines you'd want as a best friend, and compelling intense heroes who are worthy of them.
4 stories per month.

To see which titles are coming soon, please visit

millsandboon.co.uk/nextmonth

JOIN US ON SOCIAL MEDIA!

Stay up to date with our latest releases, author news and gossip, special offers and discounts, and all the behind-the-scenes action from Mills & Boon...

 millsandboon

 millsandboonuk

 millsandboon

It might just be true love...

MILLS & BOON

HISTORICAL

Awaken the romance of the past

Escape with historical heroes from time gone by. Whether your passion is for wicked Regency Rakes, muscled Viking warriors or rugged Highlanders, indulge your fantasies and awaken the romance of the past.

MILLS & BOON
True Love
Romance from the Heart

Celebrate true love with tender stories of
heartfelt romance, from the rush of falling
in love to the joy a new baby can bring,
and a focus on the emotional
heart of a relationship.